Praise for Rich Zahradnik

DROP DEAD PUNK

"The New York City ....sis of 1975 provides the dramatic backdrop for Zahradnik's frenetic sequel to 2014's *Last Words*. When police officer Robert Dodd starts to chase a mugger in Greenwich Village, Dodd's partner, Samantha Callahan, is unable to keep up. By the time Callahan catches up, Dodd and the mugger, who turns out to be punk rocker Johnny Mort, are both lying dead in the street after an apparent exchange of gunfire. Coleridge Taylor, an investigative reporter for the New York *Messenger-Telegram*, begins probing the oddities of the crime. When the newspaper folds and leaves Taylor without a job, he stays on the case. As he learns more about Mort, Dodd, and Callahan, he becomes convinced the shooting was a setup, but it's unclear who may have been the target. Taylor, who lives for the big story, makes an appealingly single-minded hero."
—Publishers Weekly

LAST WORDS

Last Words was a finalist in ForeWord Magazine's 2014 Book of the Year Contest, a bronze IPPY Winner, and a finalist in the New Generation Indie Book Awards.

"The tenacity of the main character will resonate as he overcomes barriers and reclaims his former life.... A fast-paced, deeply entertaining and engrossing novel. *Last Words*

is the first book in a mystery series featuring the intrepid investigative reporter. Readers will be glad these aren't the last words from this talented author."
—Robin Farrell Edmunds, ForeWord Magazine

4 Stars: "Mr. Zahradnik did a great job portraying the color and culture of the time. If you want to read about a slice of New York history during the 1970s then you'd probably enjoy this mystery for that reason alone. It's fast paced and the dialogue is natural sounding and I felt true to that era. With so many books now set during modern times with its cell phones and all the new gadgetry that can help a sleuth solve the crime, I found this one a refreshing change and will look for more in this series."
—Long and Short Reviews

"The story has a lot of twists and turns, which kept this reader on the edge of my seat waiting to see where the next turn leads. It was an exciting story right up until the end, and what an ending! For everyone who likes mystery, this book is for you."
—Ann's Reading Corner

"*Last Words* (A Coleridge Taylor Mystery) is a wonderful novel by Rich Zahradnik. He gives readers great visuals of New York City in the 1970s: how the Vietnam War changed social and economic conditions in the United States… The story is captivating, and it is obvious from his writing that Rich Zahradnik is familiar with the setting he describes so well. Coleridge and Voichek are likeable, classic characters, and I enjoyed learning Voichek's hobo language. *Last Words* is not only entertaining, but also informative about a past era."
—Michelle Stanley for Readers' Favorite

"Set in the 1970s, it is a fun return to the past and good crime

fiction, you'll enjoy Last Words. Recommended."
—Vikki Walton, I love a Mystery

"Zahradnik develops characters of all types and sizes in this novel. He gives readers a real sense of New York in the 70s via his cast, and the way that they view things. Top this off with an amazingly well developed and very interesting main character and you have a winner. Zahradnik's knowledge of the life of a reporter really shines through here, bringing the story to life."
—Pure Jonel, Confessions of a Bibliophile

"I didn't realize how much I missed seedy gritty corrupt crime-ridden New York City of the 1970s till I read Zahradnik's debut thriller. Last Words captures the palms-out politicians, the bully cops, the not-so-hapless homeless, the back-stabbing reporters of a city on the brink. The pace speeds up; the whispers and clues and leads all come together for a big empty-the-revolver and fling-the-vodka bottle finale. Well worth the trip back in time."
—Richard Zacks, author of *Island of Vice* and *Pirate Hunter*

"*Last Words* sizzles like the fuse on a powder keg. Hero reporter Coleridge Taylor is gritty and unstoppable as he plumbs the mean streets of New York City during its darkest days."
—Paul D'Ambrosio, author of *Easy Squeezy*, winner of the Selden Ring investigation prize and a Pulitzer Prize gold medal finalist

"Rich Zahradnik is a superb craftsman. Like a painter, he adds layers of detail to a canvas he loves until he has created a picture that enthralls. *Last Words* has both beguiling landscape and revealing portraits and is a picture worth all its thousands of words: Rich in intrigue."
—Jeff Clark-Meads, author of *The Plowman* and *Tungol*

Drop Dead Punk

Drop Dead Punk

A Coleridge Taylor Mystery

RICH ZAHRADNIK

CAMEL
PRESS

Seattle, WA

Camel Press
PO Box 70515
Seattle, WA 98127

For more information go to: www.camelpress.com
www.richzahradnik.com

Cover design by Sabrina Sun

Drop Dead Punk
Copyright © 2015 by Rich Zahradnik

ISBN: 978-1-60381-209-2 (Trade Paper)
ISBN: 978-1-60381-210-8 (eBook)

Library of Congress Control Number: 2015939127

Printed in the United States of America

In memory of John Rehl, the great teacher.
Of English. Of language. Of writing.

———◆———

ACKNOWLEDGMENTS

———◆———

THIS NOVEL TAKES places during the one-month period in 1975 when New York City teetered on the brink of bankruptcy. Had it tumbled into financial ruin, the impact on the nation and the world could have been catastrophic. All this is going on as Taylor is pursuing his own crime story. I am in debt to three writers whose work helped me make the details of the city's financial crisis as accurate as possible. Their books are *The Year the Big Apple Went Bust* (1976) by Fred Ferretti, *The Man Who Saved New York: Hugh Carey and the Great Fiscal Crisis of 1975* (2010) by Seymour P. Lachman and Robert Polner, and *The Restless City: A Short History of New York from Colonial Times to the Present* (2006) by Joanne Reitano. Two articles were also quite useful: "Overview of New York City's Fiscal Crisis," by Roger Dunstan from the California Research Bureau, California State Library, and "Gotham's fiscal crisis: lessons unlearned," *The Public Interest,* No. 158 (Winter 2005), by E.J. McMahon and Fred Siegel. Finally, the classic *Serpico* (1973) by Peter Maas was my bible for understanding the culture of corruption in the New York Police Department during the early Seventies.

I must thank my editors Jennifer McCord and Catherine Treadgold for everything they've done to bring Taylor to life on the page again. Thanks also go to my agent, Dawn Dowdle of the Blue Ridge Literary Agency, who continues to provide great advice. Finally, thank you to my wife Sheri for all her support through my first year of being an honest-to-god, for-real writer.

1

———◆———

THE GREAT HEADLINES of other newspapers were always to be despised. Not today.

The three ancient copy editors were on their feet, with Copydesk Chief Milt Corman in the middle. Taylor stopped his walk through the newsroom to find out why. If someone had made a mistake, it must be a colossal one to get those fat asses out of their seats. He looked over Corman's shoulder. The copy chief held the *Daily News*. It was that day's edition, Oct. 30, 1975. The 144-point front-page headline screamed up from the page.

FORD TO CITY:
DROP DEAD

Corman rattled the paper violently. "That's a work of art. Tells the whole story in five words. He gave the city the finger yesterday."

Jack Miller, one of the other old farts, moved back to his seat. You could only expect him to stand for so long. He settled into his chair for another day of slashing copy. "What do you expect from our *unelected* president? Veepee to Nixon. Goddamned pardoned Robert E. Lee two months ago."

"Didn't pardon him. Gave him back his citizenship."

"Same thing. The barbarians are running the country and now they're at our gates. We're the biggest, most important city on the planet, and he's going to leave us hanging to get himself *actually* elected to the job."

Corman flipped open the paper to the Ford speech story across pages four and five. "Just listen to this bullshit. 'I am prepared to veto any bill that has as its purpose a Federal bailout of New York City to prevent a default.' He blathers on about using the uniform bankruptcy laws. On and on and on. How do you police the streets and pick up garbage under the *uniform* bankruptcy laws? A Federal judge trying to run the whole damn city? Chaos."

"Ford's from Grand Rapids." Miller shook his big round head. "He doesn't know from anything about this place. He's talking to all the flatlanders—a nation that hates us."

"Will you listen to this at the end? 'If we go on spending more than we have, providing more benefits and more services than we can pay for, then a day of reckoning will come to Washington and the whole country just as it has to New York City. When that day of reckoning comes, who will bail out the United States of America?' He'll kill this city to keep his job." Corman looked from the paper to Taylor. "You're the crime reporter. Why don't you go after this? Write the story about the man who murdered New York."

Taylor laughed. "You can't kill New York."

"Rome fell."

"Rome wasn't New York. You know this is the same political bullshit. Made up numbers and budget magic and threats from Washington. New York will still be here long after. It's a great headline, though. You guys should try writing 'em like that."

He left the horseshoe copy desk before they could protest that wasn't the style of the *New York Messenger-Telegram*. He knew all too well the three of them would kill to be headline writers at the *Daily News*. That paper wasn't perpetually on the verge of failing like the *MT*.

Taylor gave New York's financial crisis about thirty seconds more thought as he wound his way around the maze of the newsroom. To him, the crisis was background noise. The city had become a dark place since the Sixties decided to end early, round about 1968. Crime lurked in the darkness, and he covered crime. He was too busy with New York's growth industry to pay attention to the mayor's budget problems.

Heroin everywhere.

Corruption in the police department.

Buildings in the South Bronx torched by the block.

Those were the stories he went after, not failed bond sales and blabbering politicos. Problem was the damn financial story had pushed everything else off the *MT's* front page. Taylor hadn't had a decent story out there in three weeks. He needed the quick hit of a page one byline, needed it particularly bad this morning. The cops had called him at home last night. Not about a story this time. They'd arrested his father, reeling drunk in his underwear outside his apartment building. Taylor had been up until three a.m. dealing with that mess. A good story—a good story that actually got decent play—and a few beers after to celebrate. Now *that* would pick him up. For a day or two at least.

Make the calls. Someone's got to have something. Now that Ford's had his say, there must be room on page one.

He'd almost slipped past the city desk when Worth called out his name. Taylor tried to pretend he hadn't heard and kept going, but Worth raised his high-pitched voice and just about yelled. Taylor turned and went back to the pristine maple-topped desk of City Editor Bradford J. Worth, Jr.

"I've got an assignment for you."

That was *always* bad news. "Haven't made my calls yet."

"Doesn't matter. Need you down at City Hall."

Taylor brightened. *Crime at City Hall. A murder? That would be big.*

"What's the story?" He sounded enthusiastic. He shouldn't have.

"You're to go to the pressroom and wait for announcements. Glockman called in sick."

"C'mon, Worth. Not babysitting. You've got three other City Hall reporters." *Who've owned the front page for weeks.*

"They're all very busy pursuing *the* most important story in this city's history. Your job is to sit at our desk in the pressroom and wait for the mayor to issue a statement on Ford's speech. Or the deputy mayor. Or a sanitation worker. Or a cleaning lady. Anybody says anything, you phone it in. Rumor is they're working on using city pension funds."

Worth's phone rang, and he picked up. "Yeah, I'm sending Taylor down. No, he'll do for now." He set the receiver lightly on its hook. "You've been down in the dumps since your *friend* Laura left us. Was it her going or the fact she got a job at the *New York Times*? Because you'll never get there, not with the way you dodge the biggest stories."

"Hey, you and I are *both* still here."

Worth frowned. Ambition rose off the man like an odor as strong as the cologne he wore. He'd made city editor at thirty without ever working as a reporter. Everyone knew he wanted more, and to him, more meant the *New York Times*. He'd almost been as upset as Taylor when Laura Wheeler announced she had the gig, and Worth wasn't the one in love with Laura. He had been sure he was leaving next.

"Both here, but I'm the one doing his job. Now get to City Hall."

"You have to be able to find someone else." Exasperation through grit teeth. "Crime is big for this paper."

"I decide what's big." He picked up the phone, dialed an inside extension, and showed Taylor his back.

Sitting at City Hall waiting for a press release was the perfect way to ruin Taylor's day, something the city editor liked doing so much it had become a bad habit.

Taylor arrived at his own desk to find the other police reporters gone, probably making their rounds.

The desk that had been Laura's reminded him of her—of her dark brown eyes, her black hair, her beautiful face. She'd left an aching emptiness inside him. They'd lasted a month after she'd moved to the *New York Times,* and then she'd broken it off. She said she realized the only thing they had in common was the *MT.* She hadn't been mean about it. And she wasn't wrong. The paper had been their life during the day and their conversation at night. He wondered if it also had to do with his age, 34, and where he was—or wasn't—in life. He pushed his hand through his brown hair. He'd even found himself considering his thin, angular face, something he'd never done before. Was that it? Laura was beautiful. Taylor couldn't think of a word for what he was.

He recently heard she'd started dating a guy on the foreign staff, Derek something. He wondered how old Derek was. Late twenties and optimistic, he guessed, unbowed by life. From a good family too, probably. It was always going to end. So why did it hurt like this?

Truth was Taylor had been living with emptiness for years before he met her. Over that time, he'd gotten used to it, let the job fill his life. Only, having her and losing her made him understand how much he disliked this lonely hole inside.

Really should leave right away.

The black phone in front of him was too much temptation. Worth couldn't see Taylor from the city desk. He picked up the receiver, pushed the clear plastic button for an outside line, and dialed the number for Sidney Greene at 1 Police Plaza. Greene was perhaps the most discontented, dyspeptic minor civil servant Taylor had ever encountered. He leaked stories not to expose injustice or right a wrong, but to screw his bosses. He simply loved watching them deal with the chaos he created by tipping off Taylor.

"Anything up?"

"Oh, a real shit show. Officer down."

Taylor flipped open a notebook. Even in the midst of this dark age of drugs, muggings, and homicides, a police officer murdered was still a big story. A page one story. "Where and when?"

"Avenue B and East Eighth, just in from Tompkins Square Park."

"What happened?"

"That's all I can do for you. They're doing the headless chicken dance down here. You'll be ahead of the others if you get to the scene quick. Not by much, though."

Taylor left the newsroom for the Lower Eastside. He'd check for press releases at City Hall after visiting the scene of the cop's murder. Worthless would have his head if he missed even one minor announcement. Screw it. Taylor couldn't ignore a big story. A real story.

HE HUSTLED FROM the subway across the blocks to the crime scene. The day offered near perfect New York fall weather, with the air crisp and clear, tingling with energy. He unwrapped a stick of Teaberry gum and stuck it in his mouth. The temperature had dropped from yesterday's high of 70 and would only make it into the mid-fifties today. Jacket weather—Taylor's favorite. Not so hot he broke into a sweat on a good walk, and cool but not cold—he wasn't fighting the brutal winds of winter that blasted down the avenues. Easy weather put New Yorkers at ease. He could sense it as he walked. More smiles. Sidewalk trees even showed off muted reds and gold. Taylor knew it was nothing like the color upstate but it would do.

Taylor's press pass got him inside the cluster of patrol cars guarding the ambulance. A couple of fire engines had also rolled to the scene, which was a dilapidated brownstone with half its windows boarded and a huge hole in the roof. The place was a true Lower Eastside wreck in a neighborhood where hard luck meant you were doing pretty well for yourself.

Taylor climbed the cracked front steps. A "Condemned Building" sign was nailed to the open door. The first floor had few interior walls, only piles of rubble from when the roof had come down, bringing chunks of the next three floors with it. The smell of must mingled with the stink of garbage. Two uniformed and four plainclothes police stood around a uniformed body sprawled across a pile of plaster chunks and wood slats in the middle of what was once probably a living room. Off to the right in the front corner was a second body, guarded by no one.

Seeing an opportunity, Taylor moved closer to the body in the corner. The man, young and apparently startled by death, had taken one shot to the chest and one in the leg. Blood soaked a black T-shirt printed with big white letters Taylor couldn't read unless he adjusted the man's leather jacket, which was also covered in blood. The man's heart must have pumped his life's blood out in minutes. Faster maybe. His right hand was on his stomach and clutched a green leather purse with a gold chain strap. Taylor knew better than to touch anything. Instead, he leaned in and was met by the iron and musk odor of blood. The top of the man's hand was tattooed with a spiral pattern, an eye at its center. The fingers were inked with the bones of a skeleton, like an X-ray of what lay beneath the dead man's skin.

The face was young—twenties, probably early twenties—bony and pale, with a tattoo of a spider web that started below the shirt line and crept up his neck to his chin and right ear. His hair was short and spiky, in the punk style—as was his whole look. Many of them had recently moved into this neighborhood to be near the punk rock club CBGB and the other bars that were the heart of the punk rock scene. Many were squatters.

"Don't touch nothin'." A short chunky cop with a gold badge in his belt walked over.

"I'd never do that, Detective." Taylor rose from his crouch. "I'm very sorry about the loss of an officer."

"Yeah, thanks. And who the fuck are you?"

"Taylor with the *Messenger-Telegram*." Taylor tapped the laminated pass.

"The *Empty*, huh? Read it sometimes. At least you're not the fucking *Times*. I hate those pricks."

Five years since the *New York Times* interviewed Serpico and broke the story of massive corruption in the NYPD, and the paper was still on every cop's shit list. At the time, Taylor had gone crazy trying to follow the *Times'* scoops. He'd admired what the *Times* had done and hated being behind on such a big story. He didn't need to tell the detective that, though. It was fine with him if the man liked the *Messenger-Telegram*. Taylor himself liked cops, the honest kind at least. When he'd started at the paper, police reporters were almost cops themselves. Or adjuncts, at least. They helped the police, publicizing successes, ignoring failures, and drinking in the same places. Not anymore. Trust had been lost, and it wasn't going to be won back anytime soon.

"What happened?"

"This jamoke holds up a woman for her purse when she comes up from the subway at Astor Place. Officer Robert Dodd and his partner give chase. The mugger runs across St. Mark's Place, through the park and into this hole. They exchange shots. Both are killed. At least that's what we can figure so far."

"Dodd's partner?"

"Couldn't keep up. Poor Dodd was stuck with a meter maid. When little Samantha Callahan gets here, they're both dead. What's the point of having broads patrolling if they can't back you up?" Lights flashed across the detective's jowly face. He looked out the glassless window at the car pulling up. "Assistant chief. I've got to make sense of this for him."

Taylor jotted down the name on the detective's plate, *R. Trunk*. He dug out a business card and handed it to the detective. "Anything more comes up, call me. We take care of cops at the *MT*." Laying it on thick never hurt. "Dodd's a hero. His story should be told right."

"Yeah, we'll see. Your paper may not be awful. Doesn't mean I trust you. Now get out of here. We got work to do."

Trunk turned as another plainclothesman walked up. "Still haven't got the kid's gun."

"Well, find the fucking thing. Assistant chief's going to be on us like stink on shit."

That was odd. If Dodd took out the mugger, the man's gun would be right here somewhere. It couldn't have walked away on its own. Taylor put that detail in his notebook. Anything odd always went in the notebook. He walked a wide arc toward the door to get a quick view of the dead officer. Dodd was a complete mess. He had to have been shot in the face. Taylor couldn't make out the nose, the eyes, anything in the gore and blood. That meant he had to have shot the mugger first.

2

———◆———

TAYLOR SQUEEZED BETWEEN two patrol cars. At the other end of the street, the *Daily News's* Eastside radio car rolled up. The *News* had so much damn money, it ran cars with photographers around the boroughs twenty-four hours a day looking for good pictures. Last time the *MT* could afford anything like that was in the late Fifties, right when Taylor joined the paper. He walked quickly to the far sidewalk so the *News* guy wouldn't see him. He didn't want a competitor to know he'd gotten here first and been inside. He counted himself lucky for the two minutes he'd had in the building. With the assistant chief here, Taylor might end up being the only reporter to get that kind of look.

He stepped up on the curb. The Channel 7 truck arrived next.

Ladies and gentleman, children of all ages, the circus is about to begin.

About 20 feet farther from the scene, a female officer sat by herself on the stoop of another condemned building. She stared ahead, her face a mask. He approached. Her nameplate read *S. Callahan.*

"I'm very sorry about your partner."

Samantha Callahan looked up. Her gunmetal blue eyes seemed both sad and angry. "That's what everybody's saying. Sorry. They won't tell me what's going on. They look at me like I'm the guilty one." She shook her head. Taylor had watched male officers break down at the loss of a partner. Maybe Samantha Callahan didn't think that was an emotion she could afford.

The uniformed cops who weren't inside the derelict building stood at least 15 yards away to the left. No one was providing support or comfort to Callahan. Taylor wondered if they held the same views on female officers as Detective Trunk. There was a very good chance. Women had only been assigned to patrol in 1970. The ones he'd interviewed were bright, eager, and brave in more ways than was necessary to be a cop. They were going into a tough job knowing they weren't welcome. At all. Taylor liked that kind of guts.

A few hundred, maybe a thousand, rode in patrol cars now. That was out of a force north of 35,000.

"Trunk said there was a chase down St. Mark's Place."

"Who are you?"

"Taylor with the *Messenger-Telegram*."

"Shit." She put her head in her hands. "That's all I need. A reporter. This is awful."

"Maybe you need someone to tell your side of the story."

"Maybe, maybe not. But for Christ's sake, *not here*." She looked over at the nearest cops. "Leave me alone before you give 'em more reasons to put weight on me."

"My card will be on the back bumper of the blue Ford Falcon. Take it, fine. Don't take it, fine."

He left. The *not here* was all Taylor needed for an invitation. Her mouth had stayed a straight line, but her eyes had changed to something like pleading. He'd track down Samantha Callahan off duty and find out what was going on with her. He couldn't say there was anything wrong with this shooting—not yet. Just an oddness. So many good stories started out with something being a little bit odd.

ROOM 9, THE City Hall pressroom, held the still, stale air of the waiting room of a funeral parlor. Old men sat at old desks, waiting. Any moment might come the next drip of information in the Chinese water torture that was the city's never-ending financial crisis. Lucky for Taylor, he hadn't missed a thing. The Room 9 regulars went about their business, which meant doing not much of anything, and ignored him for the first half hour.

Finally, the old guy from the *New York Post* turned from his desk and looked over his second cup of tea at Taylor. "You're filling in for Glockman?"

"Yeah."

"Haven't seen you here before. You on the political staff too?"

"I cover cops."

The old guy wrinkled his nose like his tea stunk of cabbage. "You must be pleased to get in on a serious story."

"I get enough serious stories, thanks. Mine just don't go on and on with nothing ever happening."

"This great city could go bankrupt." He spoke in the voice of a headline.

"All just paperwork. The city's going nowhere."

"You're not wasted on cops."

"How long have you been covering City Hall?"

"I'm in my twenty-sixth year."

"It took a long time for the city to dig a financial hole this deep. Least I gather from reading Glockman and the rest of you. Money borrowed to repay money borrowed. Shit the banks would never let me get away with. Goes back to Mayor Lindsay's administration, even further. Where were you big-time city hall boys when all that was going down?"

"*We* didn't manage this city into a financial grave."

"No, you just *missed* the story."

"Won't be lectured by a police reporter." He huffed and turned around to be alone with his tea.

Taylor was happy to get back to the story he cared about. He called Sidney Greene at police headquarters.

"Good tip, eh?"

"Yeah, very good. Maybe something's not right there."

"That's your job, reporter-man. I'll tell you this. Big brass are all involved."

"Aren't they always, when an officer is killed?"

"Yeah, but they've spent months trying to convince people this isn't really Fear City, despite the police union pamphlets and budget cuts and layoffs. Now a cop's been gunned down. Doesn't help with the PR."

"Has the mugger been identified?"

"His name's Johnny Mort. That's from the first canvas of the neighborhood. But not confirmed. Lived around there somewhere, but no specific address yet. There was no ID on his person."

"Anything else?"

"Just the chickens doing their pretty dance."

The pressroom got word at 6:15 p.m. that the lid was on, which meant no announcements would be issued by City Hall. Taylor informed Worthless, who then told Taylor about the cop killing. Taylor said he already knew and had been at the scene. The city editor swallowed his protest. Worth knew it was an important story, no matter what else was going on. Taylor gave a deskman what he had so far, including the description of the scene, which he thought—hoped—none of the other reporters had been able to get. The real story about Dodd's killing would take more reporting, maybe days of it. Next he called the Ninth Precinct and asked for Samantha Callahan. The desk sergeant said she was *with* the detectives. Taylor could only imagine.

Outside City Hall, he headed north in the general direction of Tompkins Square and the murder scene, but swung abruptly east up the Bowery to the punk rock club CBGB. The venue—

whose initials stood for country, bluegrass, and blues, though the club hardly booked those sorts of bands anymore—had become a favorite hangout of his since Laura introduced him to punk seven months earlier. She was gone, and he still had CBGB. That didn't stop the knot of loneliness from growing in his chest as he approached the bar.

He'd hardly fit in with the crowd then or now. Funny thing, they didn't care. Punks were particularly good at that—not caring. They filled the place every night in leather, tattoos, torn jeans and T-shirts, and weird hair. He wore his Army field jacket and corduroys. No one said a word. He was an outsider and accepted at the same time. He'd even made a few friends.

However, tonight he wasn't here for friends or music. This was a good place to try and learn something about Johnny Mort, punk rocker and presumed cop killer.

He had to knock to get in at 7 p.m. Doors usually opened at eight. Frederick the Dutch, actually a German, unlocked the door and went back to stocking the bar, a Camel drooping from his mouth. He wore a leather vest and no shirt. His bald head was shiny with sweat.

Taylor slid a copy of the *MT* across the bar to Frederick, who immediately opened it to the horseracing pages, while handing Taylor a cigarette. Frederick loved to play the horses but hated paying for a newspaper. Like most punks, he believed in anarchy. It was just that his definition was a bit odd. Taylor lit up. He'd somehow survived 17 years in a newsroom, starting as a copyboy at 17, without picking up the habit. Not until he started hanging out at CBGB, which was the only place he indulged, trading the anarchist handicapper across the bar from him a free paper for a cig.

"Dammit." Frederick the Dutch slapped the paper to the bar. Interlocking horseshoes were tattooed on both his arms. "One horse off a three hundred fifty dollar trifecta. Your man Crimson said his horse was pick of de day." His English was lightly accented after years in London and New York.

"I wouldn't spend my money on anything the boys in the toy department come up with."

"What is toy department?"

"It's what everyone at the paper calls sports."

"My ten dollar bet was no toy."

"I thought money wasn't important to the punk life."

"Need and importance are different." Frederick held up a seven-ounce bottle of Rolling Rock. Taylor nodded. "I don't understand why you drink such small beers. In Germany we take it in liters."

"Maybe drinking small beers is a good way to keep it under control."

Frederick's big booming laugh bounced off the graffiti-scarred black walls of the rock club. "I've seen you drink very many of your little ponies. You'd save us both trouble if you'd order normal."

"Never normal, Frederick. Never." Taylor rubbed his thumb across the slight lift of the painted label on the pony. That sensation alone relaxed him—knowing he held the bottle. He took a swallow of the beer, which fulfilled the promise made to his thumb. "Do you know a man named Johnny Mort?"

"Name is familiar. Lots of people come here."

Taylor flipped open his reporter's notebook. "Spider web tattoo up around the neck. Also a spiral pattern on the top of his hand with an eye in the middle. Bones tattooed on his fingers."

"Yes, yes. I see him now. Tough tattoos for a gentle little man."

"The man I'm describing was shot by a cop this morning. Police say he held up a woman for her purse and was chased by the officer. They exchanged fire. Both are dead."

"Doesn't sound like the Johnny I know."

"It never does."

"I'm serious. Johnny Mort spends his days taking care of the stray dogs in the neighborhood. Scrounges food. Begs off of veterinarians for sick ones. You know some of these guys on the street hustle for change using dogs. They don't feed the dogs so much. Johnny even takes care of those mutts. He's no violent person." A small woman, also in punk garb but carrying a bucket and mop, walked past the bar. "Suze, you know Johnny Mort?"

The woman put down the bucket and inhaled from her own cigarette. "The dog guy?"

"Yeah. He was in a shoot-out with a cop." Frederick spoke like he still didn't believe it.

"Johnny wouldn't hurt a fly. Fucking cops hate us all." She waved the cigarette and walked to the back, which meant CBGB's legendary bathrooms were getting their first cleaning in months.

"See, what did I tell you?" Frederick put down another pony for Taylor.

"Don't those spider webs on his neck mean prison time?"

"No, he got his because he liked mine. Punk doesn't always mean tough, man. Maybe Johnny is dead—I really hope not—but he was no killer."

"What else do you know about him?"

"In here most nights with enough money for cover and a couple of beers. I made sure he got a couple extra. I'm a big dog lover. Often with a friend he came to the city with. Let me think." He puffed on the Camel. "No, it's not up here when I want it." He tapped his bald head. "I'll think of the name. Told me he squats over on Avenue C between East Seventh and Eighth. Didn't say the building."

"That's only a couple of blocks from the crime scene."

"Many coincidences in the world, my friend. If it is Johnny, I am very sad. A good kid. Something is not what it seems."

"Hope so."

"Why is that?"

"Makes a better story."

"You'll become an anarchist yet."

"Yeah, well, speaking of anarchy," Taylor finished off the beer, "if it is the Johnny you know, this place is going to be overrun by reporters."

"I hate reporters."

"I thought we were getting along so well."

"You're not a reporter. You're just an oddly dressed punk."

Taylor left three bucks on the bar. The excessive tip was thanks for the information. He'd love to stay and listen to the raw music that would come from CBGB's tiny stage, so different from the crap on the radio. Tonight, however, he needed to be in a cop bar.

3

———◆———

SOMETIMES THE SMALLEST favor paid off in a big way. In the scheme of things, Taylor had done a tiny favor for Jim Salvatore when Salvatore was a second-year cop. Taylor's tip about a two-bit drug dealer had earned Salvatore a nice arrest. The story didn't even make it into Metro Briefs. Still, Salvatore never forgot. He'd helped Taylor whenever he could, even when Taylor was on the outs with most other cops for journalistic sins real or imagined. So if Salvatore said Little Cindy's was the after-work bar for the cops of the Ninth Precinct, Taylor could count on it. Cindy's, on First Avenue south of St. Marks Place, had the right perfume: stale beer and cigars smoked for hours.

For the first half hour, Taylor sat at a table in the corner to the left of the door with a view of the place. A bottle of Schaefer was in front of him. No Rolling Rock. He'd been nursing it. Questioning cops after one of their own had fallen was a delicate game. They'd be angry, drinking heavily, and—though none would admit it—scared. Several groups of men sat at other tables and up at the bar. The only woman in the place was tending that bar, patting arms and shoulders maternally, though her exposed cleavage was far from maternal. Probably

Little Cindy. The bar was Formica topped, as were most of the tables, except for a folding one with a card game going and a giant round wooden table that was entirely out of place. The brands of liquor behind the bar, which lacked mirrors and instead was painted black, were limited to what you took in a shot glass.

No cocktail crowd here.

Taylor had yet to figure out the magic combination of elements that made a cop bar. He'd been in saloons with magnificent polished wooden bars and others that looked like delis serving booze. He knew the obvious requirements. The spot needed to be close to the precinct—close enough for a pop or two during the shift without anyone noticing. And the owners had to be happy serving only cops because that was the way cops liked it.

The stares he was getting weren't welcoming. Even so, he was doing okay so far. He'd been in places where "who the hell are you?" came before "what'll ya have?" The jukebox had already played a lot of Sinatra and a bit of Glen Campbell and Billy Joel. Neil Sedaka's "Bad Blood" came on. That was about as rock and roll as cops got.

Samantha Callahan, now in civilian clothes, walked through the door and headed straight for an empty table on the right side of the bar. All eyes followed, and they weren't welcoming.

Taylor almost didn't recognize her. Some guys thought a woman looked sexy in a uniform. Didn't do anything for Taylor. Callahan, on the other hand, looked great out of uniform, almost transformed, in blue jeans and white blouse with her auburn hair tumbling down her back.

She sat a few minutes. Nothing happened. She went to the end of the bar, ordered a beer and carried it to her table. She probably just wanted to fit in, on this of all days. Taylor wondered if that had ever been possible. She drank her beer and stared out the window at the people passing on the sidewalk.

Taylor walked to the bar himself, ordered a second Schaefer—he'd left the first one half full—and went over to her table.

"Okay if I sit?"

Her eyes were red. At some point since he'd last seen her, she'd been crying. How hard was it to look in control now?

"Taylor, right?" He nodded. "Sure, long as you don't mind being a pariah too."

Taylor pulled out the chair that would give him the best view of Little Cindy's. "Pariah, eh? Ever been a journalist?"

"Not sunk that low yet." A long sip of beer. "This day couldn't suck more if it tried."

Samantha stared at him with sad eyes. Did she have intelligence as well as courage? He'd only get that by talking. Some officers were smart, brilliant even, with the kind of insight you could only get from the University of the Streets. Some were dumb as posts. Those were the dangerous ones, doing with fists what they couldn't do with their heads.

"The others at the scene weren't very supportive."

"They're still not, if you haven't noticed."

Samantha suddenly got to her feet, and Taylor figured the interview had ended before it even started. She went to the bar, giving him his best view yet of her rear in close-fitting blue jeans. It was a good view and a very nice rear. At the bar, she ordered and carefully returned to the table with two shot glasses so full only surface tension and her slow walk kept the whiskey off the floor. She set one in front of Taylor and held the other.

"You want to talk with me, you gotta drink with me. No one else in here will."

I need to know why.

Taylor raised the glass, less carefully than Samantha. He didn't mind losing whiskey as it plopped on the Formica. His first rule of drinking was beer in little bottles. His second rule was no shots. Two rules down. How many more tonight? He had to be careful. The rules were important. They were meant to keep him from becoming a drunk. Like his father.

"To Robert Dodd," said Samantha loudly, looking out over the room, "a good officer and a great partner. Too good."

She put the shot away hard and fast. Taylor followed. The whiskey burned all the way into his stomach. He coughed once and chugged from the Schaeffer. The burning eased into that familiar warming sensation radiating out from his gut. Samantha stared at her own beer as if daring herself to need it.

"Dodd was too good?"

She looked away. "Was fine with having me as a partner. A rookie with a year in *and* a woman. Taught me things. That's all. I'm not saying anything about the case to the paper. I'm in over my head and trying not to drown."

"Who says you're giving anything to the paper?"

"Why are you here then?"

"Right now we're just having a drink. If you see I can help and want to talk later, great." Taylor looked around the bar. "Besides, wouldn't be so smart to do an interview in this place."

"That would be very stupid indeed. My father, the mighty Sergeant Mick Callahan, gave me one single piece of advice after I joined the force." She drank her beer. "Keep in mind, this was after he had a cow over me joining. Took him a year to finish having that cow. But The Sergeant got over it eventually. Bless him. When he did, The Sergeant told me to keep my head down. That's what I've tried to do the whole time. I'm this alien thing. A female on the force. Talking to you is *not* keeping my head down. None of this is. Just the opposite."

Don't push any harder.

"Is your father still on the job?"

"Yeah. The One-Nine."

"Upper Eastside. Classy."

"Don't get any ideas." Almost a smile. "We're from the Bronx."

"Small world. I live on City Island now."

"You're a Bronx boy?" Samantha gave her head a light turn like this surprised her.

"No, Queens."

"How the hell did you end up out on City Island?"

It was the obvious question to ask. Queens and Bronx did not mix, just like the Yankees and Mets. Add to that the fact that City Island was one of the strangest corners of the Bronx—an actual island in the Long Island Sound with houses, apartments, clam bars, and boatyards.

"Short version. I had a house in Queens. Nice place. There was a fire. When it was half done, the guys repairing it ran off with the money to finish the other half. Had to sell. A buddy at the paper has a houseboat on City Island. It's got a hole in the hull, so it's up on blocks. That's where I live while he's away."

"A house fire? That's scary. Anyone hurt?"

He paused a moment. This would test whether Samantha really wanted to have anything to do with a police reporter, particularly Taylor. It might get her to see he was the one to help. Or scare her very far away.

"No, luckily. About a year ago, I did a story on a ring of corrupt detectives on the Harlem Vice Squad. Week later, a Molotov cocktail came through my living room window. Nobody was arrested. That's probably the least surprising part of the story."

"Corrupt cops? That *will* make you unpopular. I didn't know there really were any of those." Her tone was breezy and sarcastic. She gave him an actual smile. The way it lit her pretty face, he wanted to think of ways to keep it there. "Dodd said dirty cops just about destroyed the force. He said the job was simple. You enforced the laws or you broke 'em. These guys have a bunch of convoluted excuses for why they're above the law. Pure bullshit. Dodd knew. He'd seen it all. He'd spent four years in the Four-One."

"Fort Apache. Wow. Very tough place to work. Even tougher to get out of."

"Yeah, he busted his ass and caught a break a year back. Just to get shot down on the Lower Eastside."

Samantha was up again and back with more shots.

Shit. I need more facts, not whiskey. Not a good direction.

"To *The* Sergeant. Sergeant Michael Callahan. To getting the bad guys."

The second whiskey went down easier. He was too warm and comfortable, getting ready to settle in for a good session—a very bad sign. He was going to miss something important or forget something important. Or start ignoring the bad signs. Which he did immediately, going to the bar and ordering two more beers. On the trip there and back, cops followed him closely, all dark looks and a few clenched fists. Did they know he was a reporter? Or were those just the looks they gave any outsider? Taylor didn't have to wait long for an answer.

A tall, wiry guy with medium-length brown and gray hair sauntered over from his place at the other end of the bar. The guy might be plainclothes, but didn't have to be. Some patrol cops looked pretty shaggy now. Gone were the days of neat and tidy. The man turned one of the chairs around and straddled it. "What's up, Callahan?"

"Oh you know, the usual, Schmidt. Drinking to a fallen comrade. With no one else. Will you join me?"

"You already seem to have company." Schmidt continued to stare with hungry gray eyes at Samantha. "We need to keep things in the family. Who's your friend?"

As if on cue, the conversation in the bar slowly died to almost nothing. The off-duty men in Little Cindy's watched Samantha's table. Sinatra continued singing "Summer Wind."

"He's not a friend. He's a newspaper reporter."

Samantha's eyes took on a dangerous glint that made Taylor want to be a lot more sober. He didn't know enough yet to read what was going on.

"We're worried about you. Things I'm hearing about what happened with Dodd—those things are a serious concern. Now this. Airing your dirty laundry with a fucking reporter."

"*Our* dirty laundry."

Need to cool this down.

Taylor lifted the bottle of beer. "Just having a drink with Samantha here. That's it. I know a lot of people on the force. Check me out."

"I don't give a shit who you know. I don't know you. Nobody on this patch knows you. Nobody on this patch talks to *any* reporters."

Taylor watched his hopes for the night go out the window. He'd needed to learn as much as he could from Samantha, even if he had to wait until later to get it all on the record. Tonight was supposed to be about figuring out what direction to go with the story. Have drinks with a source and get a handle on where to go next. That was how reporting worked. 'Course it didn't usually involve multiple shots of whiskey. Or violence. How was he going to learn anything more? He needed a plan B.

"The only story I'm interested in is Officer Dodd. He's a hero, and I want to write a profile of a hero. Give me something for that."

"Bullshit. We're not heroes in your paper. Not any paper. You're here looking for dirt. You're going to leave here bloody."

"Stop being such asshole." Samantha stood, sliding her chair back with her calves. The wiry cords on Schmidt's arms tightened. She went to the bar and brought back *another* round of shots and set all three down.

"I'm not drinking with the bitch who got Dodd killed."

"I didn't get him killed. But something's going on. Any idea what?"

"Be careful, little girlie. Dodd's gone, and he's about the only one round here who tolerated a meter maid."

There would be no toast. Samantha's whiskey went right in Schmidt's face. He slid off his chair and slammed her into the wall with one hand on her throat.

Taylor wanted to react fast, he really did, but thoughts moved so slowly through his brain, sludged up by booze on no dinner.

If he put a hand on Schmidt, these cops would kick the crap out of him and charge him with whatever they felt like once he got out of the hospital.

He slowly stood up. "Easy, Schmidt." He slipped the notebook out of the field jacket's pocket and opened it. "This is a bad story for everyone. Let her go. Let's sit down. Or better, the two of us can leave."

Apparently, Samantha didn't feel she needed Taylor's help— what little threat the notebook might have been. She drove her foot down hard on the top of Schmidt's, broke the chokehold, and pushed him away.

He limped sideways, groaning. "I'm going to fucking hurt you, bitch."

Samantha stood her ground. "C'mon, then. Hurt me. Try."

Two hands grabbed Taylor from behind and threw him at the table they'd been sitting at. He managed to twist around so he landed on his shoulders and slid off as the table tipped over. Without that move, he'd have ended up with more than a sore ass.

A silver blur as Taylor rose to his feet on the far side of the overturned table. Something long and metal hit the edge of the Formica. The bartender with the cleavage held the golf club— probably a nine iron—that had put a decent sized dent in the table edge. "Nobody fights in Little Cindy's. Or it's a life ban." She pulled the club back onto her shoulder.

The hefty cop who'd tossed Taylor clearly valued his time in the bar because he backed away into the crowd instantly. Schmidt straightened up, grimacing against the pain. He showed his teeth. "Stay out of this, Cindy. This isn't covered by your rules."

"Yes it is. It *always* is. Nothing gets settled in my place. Nothing. Not ever."

"She broke more important rules."

"I don't know what you're talking about, and I don't wanna know. Not on any day, but particularly not on this day. My rules, they get followed. Nobody gets hit in here. You both need to leave, and whoever you are," the nine iron pointed at Taylor, "you too. I never like it when I don't know a person."

With a slow turn of the head, Samantha took in Schmidt, Cindy, and the two dozen other off-duty cops staring at the standoff. Then she turned from the overturned table and made for the door. Taylor followed. Once on the street, he had to work to keep up with Samantha, who walked fast and seemed less affected by the whiskey. Maybe it was getting thrown on the table that had wobbled his balance. He was smart enough to give her time to calm down. She stayed quiet as they strode all the way to the Astor Place subway stop. She was about to go down the stairs, but halted. She pointed at the corner of Lafayette and East Eighth Street.

"That's where Dodd and I were. The guy did the mugging right in front of us. We heard the woman scream. How could that've happened just this morning?"

"I'm sorry about back at the bar."

"You weren't the biggest asshole in that place. I want to go home."

"Thanks, I think. I'm going to check out Mort's background. Also see if I can talk to Dodd's family."

"Knock yourself out."

"I'm going to figure out what's going on. I'll let you know what I learn. If you want to tell me what you know, that's great."

"Like I said, knock yourself out."

She stepped around Taylor and disappeared down the steps. As it happened, he needed the 6 train too. Taylor had a feeling Samantha wouldn't take it well if it even looked like he was staying with her, so he waited five minutes, went down and caught the next train, changed to the 4 and back to the 6 at 125th Street. At Pelham Bay Park, the end of line, he waited for the bus to City Island. By the time he got to the bed in the houseboat on cinderblocks, the buzz was gone, his butt hurt, and he was dead tired. In the cabin, he banged his head and elbow getting out of his clothes. The marooned vessel had all the negatives of living in a tiny boat without the positive of a gently rocking swell. He couldn't even make out the whisper of the Long Island Sound.

He was asleep before he could do his nightly ritual of running through the story he was working on.

4

———◆———

TAYLOR WOKE TO the tang of low tide, mingled with more than a hint of petroleum and some other chemicals he couldn't ID but knew weren't natural to the badly polluted Long Island Sound, which narrowed past City Island on its way to joining the dark, even dirtier East River.

Would he ever get to sleep in a real house again? When the contractors took half the insurance money with the house still badly in need of work, he'd been forced sell at the worst possible time. The real estate market was still in the crapper, like the rest of the economy. Jerry Hanson, a decent guy then working on the city staff, had lent him the *Bulldog Edition* when he was assigned to the *MT's* one remaining foreign bureau in London. Hanson would be back in six months. It was only fill-in duty. Everyone at the paper knew the London bureau remained so the Garfield kids could play at journalism *and* play in Europe. Their parents, aunts, and uncles owned the paper along with the New Haven Life Insurance Company—the increasingly impatient New Haven Life Insurance Company.

Taylor appreciated Hanson's generosity. Hell, he needed it.

But the Bronx? On City Island? For a Queens boy, it was like being shipped off to Nantucket.

Out the back window, the sun glanced off the slate gray water. A small two-humped island stuck out of the sound. Rat Island. Perfect name. No one lived there. No surprise, either.

His mouth was gummy from last night's drinking and a medium-grade headache pulsed in his temples. He swallowed aspirin and two glasses of water, showered in the boat's tiny head, and dressed in cords, plaid shirt, and Army field jacket. He walked out to the main drag, appropriately named City Island Avenue. In appearance, the island wasn't so much Nantucket as a down-in-the-dumps Jersey shore town grafted onto the Bronx. The main avenue cut the length of the mile and a half long island, with side streets leading to boatyards and four yacht clubs—each almost a century old. City Island had been all about boats for a long time.

Lining the avenue were seafood joints decorated with plaster statues of Neptune, giant red lobsters, and neon signs of impressive size. This was where the Bronx came to eat seafood and look at the "ocean." The island had no beach; it was all docks. For swimming, you had to go back over the causeway to the mainland and a mile through Pelham Bay Park to Orchard Beach, dubbed the Riviera of the Bronx. Now, it was hardly that. Like most city parks, it was a dangerous place, a casualty of gang war, drug dealing, and general neglect.

To Taylor, the oddest thing about City Island was the proximity of the elements of a dowdy seaside resort to the trappings of New York City. MTA buses ran on the avenue. PS 175 taught the kids. The firehouse said NYFD.

Taylor bought a buttered hard roll and coffee with two creams and two sugars and climbed on one of those buses for his long morning commute. Add that to the things he hated about being stuck out here. Still, free was free, and every day he tried to make the commute count. On the bus and then the subway into Manhattan, he worked out his next steps. He wanted to try and find Johnny Mort's squat in Alphabet City, or failing that, people on the street who could tell him more than he already knew about the kid. The angle about his caring for stray dogs was interesting. He needed more specifics. Mort was being written off as a cop killer. There was much to learn.

On the inside cover of his reporter's notebook, he started listing the key people in the shooting. Samantha Callahan was at the top. Bad things were swirling around her. Was she involved in those bad things? Or was she a victim? He liked the way she'd stood up to Schmidt. He liked the way she looked too, which was an immediate alarm bell. Liking the source—or the subject—of a story would send a reporter down a rat-hole. That had been one reason being in a relationship with another reporter, with Laura Wheeler, had worked out so well—for as long as it did work. He and Laura could talk about work and help each other and never end up with that sort of conflict. That wasn't the first or only reason he liked Laura so much. It had just made things easier. Life hadn't been easier since she left the paper … left the paper and him.

He pictured Laura smiling, dark eyes lit by her intelligence, and had to blink twice to see the notebook again. The notes were there, but so was the knot of loneliness he carried around every day. When a good story distracted him, the knot would shrink some, almost to the point where he didn't notice it. Another reason to push hard on this assignment.

Taylor underlined Samantha Callahan's name a second time, as if to remind himself she was a story to get, not a woman in distress to help. He would need to uncover something to gain her trust, or at least get her interested. At the scene, Samantha had said they were bringing *weight* down on her. In Cindy's, Schmidt had straight out accused her of getting Dodd killed. He put "Schmidt" second on his list as the train braked into 125th Street with a screeching that made thinking impossible. The car's doors rattled open and commuters from Harlem boarded.

Next on the list was Dodd's wife. He hated door-stepping the families of victims. He didn't need to ask Dodd's wife how she felt—the classic *Eyewitless News* line. He knew already. He'd interviewed enough relatives of victims. Still, he had to get more information about Dodd the man, and she would be the source for that.

His visit to the crime scene had left him with other questions. Since Dodd had taken a shot to the face, he must have fired first. There was nothing wrong with that in and of itself. Mort had a gun, so Dodd had every right to warn and fire. Still, Taylor wanted to know exactly what had gone down inside the building. He was no pathologist, but the bullet to Mort's chest looked like it should have knocked him down instantly and killed him very quickly. How then had Mort managed to aim and hit Dodd in the face? That was the real question. And where was Mort's pistol? It was the strangest ending to any standoff Taylor had seen. He wouldn't be happy until he had reasonable answers to his questions. Detective Trunk went on the list.

He skipped stopping off in the newsroom. He was on a legitimate story and didn't need to give Worthless a shot at sending him back to Room 9.

AVENUE C BETWEEN East Seventh and Eighth Streets was typical of the wreckage of Alphabet City. Typical and shocking. Some buildings were burnt out, some were boarded up, and some were in use. And, Taylor knew, some were all three. A shirtless man in raggedy blue pants and no shirt weaved toward him with his hand out. He was so high or drunk or both, he didn't stop or ask for change, just weaved past, leaving behind the stench of human filth.

Taylor hoped to avoid canvassing every building on the block. That would be dangerous and could take more time than he had. There was no guarantee he could even get into the most decrepit ones—the very buildings where people like Mort squatted.

Across Avenue C, two homeless people were sitting in cardboard boxes propped against the wall of a boarded-up building. A surprisingly well-fed German shepherd sat between them, wearing a thick rope. Taylor crossed the street, saying a silent reporter's prayer that they would be coherent at least, sober at best.

The dog was tied to the man, who sat on blankets in a long box. A woman was in the other box. She stood as Taylor approached, rearranged a torn red plaid blanket into a spot of sunlight, and settled back down.

"Man, you don't live on our block." The homeless man said it like a challenge.

"No. I'm a reporter with the *Messenger-Telegram.*"

The man laughed. "*The Empty.* Wannabe *New York Times.* What a piece of crap. You know you're not going to last."

Fight or flight instinct sent an electric jolt to the base of his spine. "I don't want any trouble. I'm looking—"

"Calm down, man. Don't mean you. I mean your paper. Wintertime, Sally and me were scrounging for newspaper for extra warmth. We always left the *Empty* behind. Thinnest paper in the city. Not that we found many copies. Tell me that's not true."

Taylor had to marvel at the insight. Oscar Garfield had started buying cheaper newsprint about a year ago, leaving the paper feeling flimsy, as if it were only half there. During the same period, circulation had dropped by 90,000.

"You're right about both. *I* hope we make it. I need the job."

"We all need jobs, man. We all don't get 'em. This city's biggest problem."

"Can't help but notice your dog's in good shape."

The German shepherd wagged his tail. Taylor reached out to pat his head, and the dog immediately leapt, snapping at Taylor's hand, straining the rope tied to the homeless man's leg.

Taylor pulled in his hand and took a quick step back as the man laughed. He was black, with oiled hair neatly combed.

The woman was white with hair just the opposite—sticking out everywhere—and appeared a lot younger. The man pulled in his leg to reel in the dog. "Even he don't like your paper."

"I see that. Like I said, curious how he's so well fed."

"What's it to you?"

"I'm looking for the squat used by a guy named Johnny Mort." The man and woman exchanged glances. "I hear he took care of dogs in the neighborhood."

"What do you want with Johnny?"

The woman came off her blanket and pulled the shepherd close. The dog quieted. "Probably nothing good. Probably nothing good."

They don't know. Hate this part. You have to say someone is dead for them to really die.

"I'm afraid I've got bad news. Johnny was killed."

"Ah no. Ah no." The woman's words turned into moans. She buried her face in the dog's black fur.

The man fished around in the pocket of his beat-up black-and-white checked overcoat. "I'm Rayban Lincoln. This is Sally. We don't want the paper to have *her* last name." He pulled out two thirds of a cigarette, lit it with a Bic, and looked up at Taylor. "Why's it you're digging Johnny's grave?"

"The police say he shot a cop. He was killed too."

"You don't believe New York's Finest?"

"Seems straight enough to me. I'm just trying to figure out who Johnny was and why he did it."

"Yeah, he took care of dogs. Lots of dogs. Some he kept. Others, like John-Boy here, he made sure we got food for him. He wasn't no criminal at all. He begged, badgered places for leftover food."

"He robbed a woman yesterday."

"No way."

"The cops say he took her purse at gunpoint. Was chased by Patrolman Robert Dodd and shot the cop when he was cornered."

Rayban slowly pulled on the recycled cigarette and the end glowed like a tiny furnace. "That's crazy. I mean maybe he lifted some things when he was desperate. I'm talking food for the dogs from midtown stores where they're too stupid to notice. Johnny never did violence. Not to get money. Not for anything. He could take care of the dogs, but he could hardly take care of himself on the street. People looked out for him because he looked out for the mutts. Take a look around. There ain't no Humane Society down here in Alphabet City—not for the humans or the dogs. That's all he was doing."

"Can you show me where he lived?"

"Can and will. He's got dogs in there. They must be starving." Rayban stood, untied the rope, and tied it to Sally's wrist. He patted her hair and kissed the top of her head. "We both see a lot of people go down here. Folks on the street and some in the squats too. Occupational hazard. Hits Sally hard every time." Rayban led the way north. "How come we haven't seen cops on the block?"

"I guess they don't have a lead on Mort. I got the street at CBGB. He hung out there. That's where I learned about the dogs."

"Surprised." Rayban climbed up the steps of a mid-block brownstone with boarded-up windows and an intact front door. The only thing missing was a doorknob. "Police are bad in this part of town, but they usually get their shit together when one of their own is killed. Impressed you got here first. Your paper's still doomed."

"Thanks for that."

Rayban reached over the side of the masonry steps and came up with a doorknob, inserted it in a square hole and opened the door. "It's not what you call security, but I guess it might slow down somebody really stupid. It's why I sleep outside. I can see 'em coming."

A big pile of rubbish blocked the first floor hallway, but the stairway was clear. Down from some apartment on a higher floor came barking. Taylor climbed behind Rayban, who left the stairs on the third floor, where the hallway was surprisingly clean compared with the first, and walked toward the apartment door at the front of the building. The barking turned to a cacophony as he approached.

Rayban had the doorknob with him. He inserted it, slowly opened the door, slipped inside, and waved his hand for Taylor to follow. Two small dogs ran in circles and yapped at the same time. A big black Labrador barked too, though he was sitting and wagging his tail violently on the wood floor. A fourth stood in the doorway to the kitchen, whining. Dog urine and crap pervaded the place.

"Careful where you step." Rayban moved gingerly to the left. "Poor Johnny's been gone more than a day. They couldn't hold it. This place is usually immaculate. Cleanest squat I'd ever been in."

The two little dogs quit spinning and jumped up on Rayban's leg. The Lab came over to Taylor, who was gun shy after the shepherd. The black dog nuzzled his hand, so Taylor carefully scratched his head and the tail swung even faster. Rayban went into the kitchen.

"There's no food. Johnny usually locks most of his supplies in the yard in the back of the building."

"Why not up here?"

"He figured someone might hit an occupied squat looking for stuff, but they would skip the backyard. Worried like crazy about the dogs when he was gone. I'll feed them and then see about getting them all out for walks."

"What will happen to them?"

"We'll take care of them. We owe him that. There's a bunch of people around here with dogs from Johnny. Some, he took care of *their* dogs when times got worse. They'll step forward. Bad as it looks, it's a neighborhood out there. Excepting the creeps, killers and shitbags, of course. Dogs are good company when life is bad."

Somebody better help. The city was closing firehouses and schools. Taylor didn't want to think what the pound looked like these days.

"He's got friends at CBGB. I'll see what they can do." The Lab leaned against Taylor's leg, pressing something like 75 pounds of dog against him. The tail kept going. "This one have a name?"

"Perry Mason. Johnny was a bit of a dreamer. Said the TV show reminded him of when things were good with his family." Rayban turned to the dogs as if they were a class he was about to lecture. "All right, ladies and gentlemen. I'm going to get you some breakfast."

The dogs barked even more loudly as they left. On the first floor, they had to go through an apartment to get around the garbage-clogged hallway and reach the door out to the tiny backyard, where weeds grew, along with one small tree that had forced its way up through a pile of broken cinderblocks. At the rear was a fence with a three-foot-high shed built into the corner.

Rayban lifted the combination lock. "Johnny had me feed the dogs a couple of times when he was away."

"Where'd he go?"

"Family or something. He didn't need to live this way, you know. He's one of the ones down here by choice. Gave up all the comforts because he was into that punk music."

He dialed the combination and lifted the lid, revealing brown paper bags containing dry dog food. There were also a few cans, four leashes, some rope and a well-chewed squeaky toy. Rayban took out one bag. When he lifted the second, a board shifted and Taylor caught sight of something with a dull black shine. Once Rayban had the cans and leashes, Taylor flipped up the floorboard with a squeak, revealing a briefcase in good condition.

"Johnny ever mention this?"

"Nope. My guess it's from his other life. Where he was before he came to Alphabet City."

Taylor rested the briefcase on the edge of the little shed. The latches were the one part of the case that weren't in decent shape. They were badly bent, pried free from their locks. He lifted the lid. Inside in a neat stack were certificates. No, not certificates. They almost looked like giant $5,000 bills. He read the fine, engraving-like printing on the top one. "The City of New York Serial Bond." It was numbered. The first few carried the same dollar figure: $5,000.

"What the …." That magic electric charge rolled across his shoulders. The story was suddenly a whole lot bigger than even he'd thought.

"What are they?"

"They appear to be City of New York bonds. Five-thousand-dollar bonds." He counted the stiff parchment rectangles, each the texture of currency. There were 50, all the same value. "There's a quarter of a million dollars worth in here. If they're real."

Rayban backed up, hugging the dog food. "Keep those away from me. That's bad shit. That's rich people money. No one down here can spend those. No one down here has a bank that'll take those. You're going to find *that's* what got Johnny killed."

"What was Johnny doing with these? What's two hundred and fifty thousand worth of bonds doing locked up with dog food at the back of his squat?"

"Don't know. Don't want to know. We've got to get the dogs out of here. A serious shit storm is going to come down on this building."

Taylor considered the intricate printing that looked like it was from another century. A shirtless Indian in full headdress. Blocks of words in a typeface designed to mimic old-style script. *Counterfeit? Stolen? What do I do with them?* Taylor knew he couldn't walk off with evidence like this, but he had to know more about them, and what they really meant.

He set the top certificate on the ground, pulled out his

collapsible Polaroid and snapped one picture and a second, just to be safe. Putting the bond back in the case and the case back where he found it, he closed up the little shed.

"We could get killed while you're making pretty pictures." Rayban headed for the backdoor. "I'm taking the dogs and not coming back. I'm forgetting that combo too."

Back upstairs, Rayban fed the dogs and gave them water. They were done in minutes.

When Perry Mason finished, he came and sat next to Taylor. "Who will get this one?"

"He's the biggest challenge. Someone will watch him. For a little while at least. Big dog to feed. That costs. You think maybe one of the CBGB folks will help out? Some money folks go in there."

"He's not one Johnny was taking care of for someone?"

"No, these four are all strays Johnny found. He was trying to find others to adopt them."

"All right, he can come with me then."

Rayban shrugged at Taylor's impulse. Taylor wasn't sure himself why he'd said it. He was impressed with Rayban's willingness to step in and help and surprised that others in this poor neighborhood would do the same. *Maybe because it's something I* can *do in this colossal wreck of a place.*

He had an out, after all. He could always put a notice in his own paper to find the dog a home. When his brother and his mother were still alive, his family had had a dog, a medium-sized black mutt named Josie. Somewhere along the line, he'd meant to get a dog himself, but he was always chasing one story or the next one. Maybe he'd done it now because of that knot inside and the empty houseboat on bricks.

Maybe I'm just an idiot.

Back at the cardboard boxes, Sally surveyed the dogs as the German shepherd greeted them all with far more friendliness than Taylor had received. "Where's Moon? Where's Moon?"

"Who's Moon?" Taylor asked.

"Johnny's dog. Johnny's dog. Loved her. Loved her."

Taylor turned to Rayban. "Johnny's dog is missing?"

"Yeah, guess so. Didn't notice in all the commotion."

"Odd thing to miss. The dead man's own dog."

"Hey, listen, this is all crazy, mixed-up shit. Johnny showed up in the neighborhood with Moon. A beagle, or beagle mix. Dog's not here now. That's all I know."

"Would he give that dog up?"

"Doubt it."

Taylor handed Rayban his card. "You don't need anything else in that building?"

"No way. Not going back."

"I'm going to tip the cops to the place. Assuming they don't find it first. Call me if anything happens down here."

Taylor and Perry Mason walked west, the dog wagging his tail like every day was a good day. Taylor wondered what it was like to see the world that way. It'd make him a piss-poor police reporter, he knew that much.

5

—◆—

THE WALK TO Broadway allowed Mason—Perry Mason was too formal for this smile of a dog—to finish his business. Taylor's plan had been to stop at a diner and make some calls. Not now. He couldn't go in the Bleecker Street Coffee Shop with Mason. He couldn't go anywhere until he got Mason home. *Christ, how I am getting him home?* Not on the subway or the bus. He'd have to drop a day's pay on a cab, providing he could find a cab that would take them. Make that a day and a half's pay. *What was I thinking? How was this ever a good idea?*

He bought coffee from a cart and found an enclosed phone booth. Mason sat on the other side of the door, the leash snaking underneath, staring at Taylor as Taylor stared at the phone.

Who do I ask about the bonds? It was a good bet that once word got out, the army of reporters covering the city's financial crisis would overrun him and his story. Whether the bonds were connected to the crisis or not—how could they not be?— they were too juicy an angle to ignore. The other names on his interview list would have to wait. He needed to know what he had before the whole thing blew up in his face.

Henry Novak. He could help. Taylor didn't have sources in the financial world, but Novak worked for the *MT's* business desk. Novak had come up as a copy boy at the same time as Taylor. Less ambitious, he settled for a job rewriting company press releases, going to Chamber of Commerce meetings, and doing puff pieces on executives. But they'd stayed friends since their days fetching coffee and running copy around the newsroom. Taylor knew he could trust Novak because of that shared experience. Copy boys didn't become reporters anymore. New journalists now arrived at the *MT* with fancy degrees from places like Columbia. Taylor and Novak were becoming a rarity, and that was their bond. Didn't bother Novak like it did Taylor. Few things did.

"Can you talk?" Taylor knew the answer.

"What's up?"

"You know anything about municipal bonds?"

"Who doesn't? City's going bankrupt because it can't repay its bondholders."

"Do you know what an actual bond looks like?"

"Since when do you care what a muni bond looks like? Just last week you told me you couldn't give a shit—"

"Forget what I said. Do you?"

"Yeah, I guess. They look a lot like stock certificates. Formal type with a face value, serial number, and some other language."

"So you could ID one?"

"I don't know. Maybe."

"I need more than a maybe." Taylor held one of the pictures he'd snapped. The shot of the certificate framed in the white of the Polaroid gave him an idea. He tapped its corner lightly on the phone. "Do you have file photos?"

"We've used shots. So has the front page since the city's troubles started. New York can't sell new ones to get the money to pay back the old ones."

"Sounds like a con game to me," Taylor said.

"Told you this was a story."

"I've got a story. Meet me for lunch."

"Why not? The boss is at an American Express Company reception."

"Chumley's at one. Bring the picture. Don't mention any of this."

"I can't mention what I don't know anything about."

"Thanks, man." Taylor hung up and dialed the city desk. He could easily have had Novak transfer him, but didn't want Worthless to know who he'd been talking to.

"Where the hell are you?"

"Working the cop shooting."

"You get anything?"

"I found the shooter's squat. Got some good color. He took care of stray dogs in the neighborhood. Was a one-man ASPCA. The police haven't gotten to the squat yet."

"What the heck does that do for us? We're not going to make a dog-helping hero out of a cop killer. Why are you so obsessed with homeless people?"

"Lot of people on the streets these days. I go where the story takes me."

"Well, don't let this one take you very far. Not another one of your ten-day specials. We don't have the staff for it. I've got just about everyone else on the fiscal crisis."

"There may be some other elements with the shooter." *Hint at some of the oddities at the crime scene. Maybe that'll get Worthless into it. No mention of the bonds yet.*

"Hold on." Taylor could make out another voice saying something to Worth. "You're downtown?"

"Yeah, Broadway in the village."

"Excellent. Finally somewhere where I need you. You're covering the Greenwich Village Halloween Parade tonight. It starts on West Street and runs to Washington Square. I'll send a photog."

"A parade? First City Hall, now a parade?" His voice got louder as he got angrier. "How in the hell is a parade police reporting?"

"It's not. This is coming from the top. Garfield himself. Apparently the parade is in its second year. Some big theatrical pageant. He doesn't want to get beat by the *Voice* this time."

"We're chasing the *Voice*? *MT* readers don't read the *Voice*. *MT* readers have never heard of the *Voice*."

"Don't you worry your little head about the readers. Let the thinkers around here handle that. I've got no one else. City Hall, Gracie Mansion, and the governor's New York office are all staked out full-time. I've had to send two extra reporters to Washington because the city's fate is now in Ford's hands."

"Ford already said he won't help. Even I know that. What the hell—"

"Think of it as me being nice and giving you the afternoon to chase that story of yours. You won't get much more time than that. Then go find out what this pageant or parade is and phone something in. It starts at six. Garfield wants lots of color."

After Worth hung up, Taylor sat in the phone booth fuming. Mason continued to stare up at him. The parade assignment was pretty much what Taylor expected from Worthless, which didn't make it any less galling. What really worried him was Garfield's plan for turning around the *Messenger-Telegram*, if you could call it a plan. Garfield, the great-great grandson of the paper's founder, Cyrus, oscillated between chasing hard-news political scoops the *Times* would prize and obscure features like this parade thing. The latter were supposed to bring back younger readers. Taylor had news for the editor-in-chief. The younger readers were gone for good. To the suburbs. To TV.

Taylor knew from 17 years on the paper that its readers bought the *Messenger-Telegram* for news on the city and for crime. That, and he had to admit, for articles half the length of those in the *Times*. You didn't need a day and half to read the *MT*, but could still believe you were reading—and your fellow commuters could see you reading—a *serious* newspaper. The *MT* wasn't so much a poor man's *New York Times* as a man's poor *New York Times*.

Wrong decisions. Bad decisions. Charging one way, then the other. The paper's decline seemed to be caused by the same behavior that was bringing down New York City, except that Taylor understood what was happening at the paper a whole lot better. He had the paper in his bones and knew in his bones the paper could fail. He'd watched newspapers die in the mid '60s. Die fast. *New York Herald Tribune. New York Journal-American. New York Daily Mirror.* Proud names, each with a great tradition, destroyed in a battle over pay and new printing technology. The *MT* could so easily go under and probably faster than the city ever would.

TAYLOR TOOK TWO hours getting Mason home, between taking a cab—the driver had required some convincing—buying food and dog dishes at the Ben Franklin Five and Dime on City Island Avenue, and talking to the old man who oversaw the small boatyard where the *Bulldog Edition* sat on bricks. With a squint eye and merchant marine cap, he made Taylor think of Popeye. They negotiated a buck a walk for Mason during the workday. By the way the man smiled and Mason wagged, Taylor was pretty sure Mason had at least one more friend in the world.

Before catching the bus to the subway, he used a pay phone and found Samantha Callahan doing desk duty at the Ninth. She wasn't pleased to hear from him.

"Leave me alone."

"I've discovered some interesting facts about Mort. Could be important. I'm not sure if it's connected, but there may be another crime involved. A lot bigger than a mugging."

"So …."

Hint of interest in her voice? Need to know why she said the weight's *coming down on her. Why Schmidt accused her. Ask now, she hangs up.*

"I want to sit down with you—"

"No way. Not again."

"Look, you can go off the record. I need to hear what you know. Not somewhere with guys like Schmidt listening. Have the detectives found Mort's squat yet?"

"I've no idea. They're not telling me anything."

"Think about this. Is anyone else helping you out right now?"

"Oh *yeah*. I've got a union rep. He came in, threw his card on the desk, and left the room like it stunk. Mumbled 'bitch' as the door closed."

"I can help you."

"You're not on my side. You just want a story."

"What I want are the facts. You don't want to be quoted. Fine with me as long as I can confirm what you tell me. Anyone around there treating you like that? You know, facts first?"

A long pause. "I get off this desk at five."

"Great. I'll be downtown. I'm covering the Halloween parade."

Callahan laughed in a way that sounded profoundly tired.

"What's funny?"

"Bunch of guys here are detailed to it. They're really pissed off. One of them pointed at me. 'Why can't she do it? With all the layoffs, we've got to watch fruits and goofs in costumes? It's the only thing she's good for.'"

"Meet me at Chumley's. Say five thirty? Do you have Dodd's home number?"

Samantha gave him the number, with a promise that if he upset Kathy Dodd or the three kids, not only would she refuse to talk to him further, she'd drum his head into the floor. Taylor hung up. The bus and subway gods would have to be good for him to get to Chumley's by one.

6

——————◆——————

LIKE SOME OTHER bars in New York, Chumley's had been a speakeasy during Prohibition. Unlike the others, Chumley's enjoyed the undercover look so much that it had made no effort to reveal itself after the 21st Amendment passed. The painted wood door with metal grate for a window at 86 Bedford appeared like the doors of the buildings on either side. No sign. You just had to know this was Chumley's. Taylor pushed the door open to the music, conversational hum, and warmth of one of his favorite bars in the city. The hint of smoke from cigars and the working fireplace offered an earthy welcome. The nondescript door swung closed behind him. The various rooms were crammed with stools and tables as well as booths lit dimly by small, shaded lamps.

Henry Novak sat before a cocktail at a table to the right. His hair was slicked back in a '50s look he refused to give up. Taylor admired that stand. Taylor's own hair was caught between the decades. Too short looked stupid and too long, a mess, so he'd settled for the middle ground. Novak had an open, smiling face and wore a dark suit, having adopted the style of the business staff and the men they covered. The walls behind him were crammed with photos and paintings of literary types and the books they supposedly worked on while drinking in here. Novak was one of those patrons who claimed he had a novel in him, though Taylor wondered how he would ever get it out, given the man's laid-back approach to everything. Still, he was one of the few staffers on the paper Taylor had somehow managed not to piss off. They didn't compete at any level. That helped. It was also because Novak was a plain nice guy.

"Taylor the Man." Novak smiled and slid a photo to the middle of the table.

Taylor sat down, turned the picture over and slid it the rest of the way. "Remember, I said we need to keep this quiet."

"Don't even know what *this* is." He waved at a waiter. "You getting?"

"Not now. Work to do."

"That shouldn't stop you. Since I'm the expert witness, you're buying." He rattled the ice in the glass at the waiter. "Another Manhattan."

Despite what he'd just said, Taylor heard himself order a Rolling Rock. Moments later, he held the cold bottle his brain didn't want but his tongue had requested. One couldn't hurt. He had to be focused when he met Samantha Callahan later.

He studied the eight-by-ten Novak had provided. The black and white looked much like the smaller color Polaroid of the certificate he took out his jacket, though it wasn't an exact match.

He laid the pictures next to each other. Both bonds were labeled City of New York and had the shirtless Indian. The one in Novak's picture was denominated at $10,000 instead of $5,000. The blocks of print in tight script typeface were the tough part. You couldn't read the type on the Polaroid to make a comparison, not even with a magnifying glass.

Why didn't I take a bond to get checked? Because that would be a crime. Bad enough I haven't tipped the cops to the squat yet.

He turned the pictures to face Novak.

"What do you think?"

Novak put his finger on the white frame of the Polaroid. "Looks real enough to me. I mean I'm no expert. Like I said, I've held stock certificates before. Never city bonds."

"Ever heard of anyone counterfeiting them?"

Novak laughed jovially. "Counterfeit something that's going to be worthless. Why bother?"

"So it's probably real."

"Good chance. Where did you get it?"

"It was in a briefcase with forty-nine just like it."

Novak held the glass away from his lips and whistled. "Quarter of a million dollars worth. What are *you* working on?"

"Cop shooting." Novak's eyes went wide. "I found the briefcase in the Alphabet City squat of the shooter. He was also killed."

"What the hell was a squatter doing with two hundred fifty thou in bonds?"

"You tell me."

"No idea, man."

Novak picked up the picture and looked it over closely. "Something, something." He put the Polaroid down. "Another story." He slapped the table hard. "The missing bonds."

"What missing bonds?"

"Don't you remember, a summer ago? Goldin, the city comptroller, released an audit."

"Remind me. I can't keep track of any of that stuff."

"In July of that year, this audit by outside accountants found there were five-point-four million dollars worth of bonds missing from the vaults. That is, the bonds were listed on the city's books but not *in* the vaults. Mayor Beame and Goldin threw shit at each other over it for a few weeks. A special prosecutor eventually said it was slipshod record keeping. Whole thing got left there. Too much other bad financial news. The city's accounting still sucks. What if these are some of those?"

"Big leap to make." Taylor put the Polaroid in his pocket.

"Maybe. Or maybe there are others missing that particular audit didn't uncover. Goldin really went after Beame. Remember, Beame was comptroller before he became mayor. This whole financial mess piled up on his watch. Three days later, a different audit firm found a forty-five million dollar discrepancy. I don't think that was bonds. Might have been bank deposits, but still. Bad bookkeeping. Non-existent record keeping. Who knows what's stuffed in desk drawers at the Municipal Building? Or walked out the door? You may have seen some that actually went missing. A briefcase full of muni bonds found in an Alphabet City stash is a big story."

"What would happen if word got out?"

"Washington and the banks now distrust the city so much. That could be the fatal blow. If it turns out they're actually missing from city vaults, it would crush any hope for the city getting bailed out."

"Ford already said no."

"That's not over till it's over. The governor and the mayor are still working Washington. But like I said, misplacing a bunch of bonds would be the death knell."

"Kinda what I thought. Which means Worthless will have the City Hall guys and his whole New York crisis team trampling over my story." He sipped the beer. "I appreciate the help. Stay mum on this."

"Sure thing. Safe with me."

The raid on Mort's squat went as Taylor expected. He waited down the block with Rayban, who seemed more nervous than the day before. Detective Trunk watched from the sidewalk as uniformed cops hauled garbage out of the building. *Doesn't like to get his hands dirty.* Taylor had yet to spy the briefcase. He'd been sure to emphasize the shed in the backyard when he phoned in his tip.

"Found Moon. Found Moon."

Taylor turned around. Sally was on her blanket looking down the block the other way.

"Mort's dog, you found him?"

"He's dead. He's dead."

Rayban stayed silent, just watching Sally as tension tightened his face. He had the look of a man who didn't like the subject of the conversation, like his eyes were pleading with Sally to shut up. Taylor already understood Sally said what was in her head no matter what and repeated it for good measure.

"What's going on, Rayban?" Taylor asked.

"Moon's buried in Tompkins Square Park. Sally was walking John-Boy and they found the grave. Must have been Johnny buried him."

"Can you take me after I talk to these cops?"

Rayban nodded with little enthusiasm.

"There's a sign. There's a sign."

Detective Trunk remained outside the building when Taylor strolled up. A shorter muscular detective leaned against a blue Buick.

"Found Mort's place, I hear."

Trunk eyed Taylor with small green eyes set in his round heavy face. "You hear, huh? There's always a lot of good police work going on in spite of what you read in the paper."

"No doubt." *He's not even going to admit it was a tip. Not like I can call him on it.*

At that moment, one of the uniforms came out of the building with the briefcase. It was closed. The patrolman didn't bring it to Trunk, but instead called the detective over and then walked another few steps away before whispering in the detective's ear and opening the lid with his back turned to Taylor. Trunk's jaw slowly lowered until his mouth was wide open. Two more cops huddled round.

Taylor walked toward them. They were electric with nervous energy he rarely witnessed at a crime scene. Just as he joined the circle, the lid of the briefcase came down quickly as a trap door.

"Anything interesting?"

"Everything in a murder investigation is interesting."

"I look forward to hearing if you've made a big investigative break. Or is that investigative headache?" *Careful.*

Trunk gave a little nod to the muscular detective. Taylor found his face pushed into the window of the Buick, an elbow at his neck. *Not careful enough.*

Trunk's fat face lowered itself into his view. "What is it you know?"

"I've just got questions. That's classy luggage for this neighborhood, right?" *Don't go any further on the case.* "This Mort's involvement is coming up odd. He wasn't a criminal, wasn't into violence. Did you know he took care of stray dogs, for Christ sake? There's something weird about the whole incident. Why'd he suddenly do a mugging?" The arm against his neck pushed harder with each question.

"How do you know all this, scumbag?"

Taylor closed his eyes against the pain. He didn't want to spend five hours being interviewed by one of Trunk's men. He wasn't turning Rayban over to the cops either.

"Sources. Christ, can't talk if you break my neck. Got lots of sources. If you don't get this ape off of me, I'll use every source I have to make the two of you famous in a way you won't like."

"I don't like threats." At the same time, Trunk must have signaled the other detective because he pulled Taylor off the car. Several people were now standing around to watch the cops search the building. *Probably their presence—not my threat— that stopped the rough stuff.* "I like even less anyone holding out on the investigation into the death of a fellow officer."

"I just told you what I've confirmed. What's going on with Callahan?"

"IA has her. She won't get back on the street anytime soon. Good riddance to bad rubbish."

"Why?"

"No comment."

"What's in the briefcase?"

"No comment."

"See, now you're not being helpful. Have you heard from the pathologist yet?"

"Why would I talk about that with you?"

"I don't know. How about because the shooting doesn't seem as straightforward as it looked? Dodd was hit in the face, so he must have fired at Mort first. Mort took one in the leg and one in the chest pretty close to the heart. So how does *he* get his shot off? Could have been killed instantly, or near enough. What's the reconstruction of all that?"

"Amateur theories." Trunk puffed out a short laugh. "You're not a detective. You sure as hell aren't the ME. We'll tell you what happened when we decide what happened."

Taylor walked several paces down the sidewalk, and against his better judgment—which sometimes wasn't better than much of anything—turned back around. "I get tips too. Good luck with what's in that case. If the *hundreds* of reporters covering the financial crisis get wind of it, that will loose the dogs of war on your precinct. I'll be the very last of your worries."

Taylor kept going past Rayban another block to stop and lean against a light pole. Once the cops cleared out, he joined Rayban and Sally. They all headed west, the German shepherd included, crossed Avenue B and entered the tree-shaded green of Tompkins Square Park. The grass and trees were deceiving. The park might be just this side of safe late in the afternoon, but it was bad news at night.

Sally led with long, hurried strides, John-Boy trotting beside her. Under a tree, a man and a woman lay with their heads lolling together. The man's open hand held a syringe. *Is it even safe this time of day?* Taylor sensed the small revolver strapped to his ankle in its holster. He was a terrible shot, but now didn't leave the house without the weapon. Because he saw scenes like this all the time. His late brother Billy had made him take the gun before Billy left on his final tour of Vietnam, the one he never came back from. The week before, during Billy's leave, Taylor had been threatened by a couple of mobsters over a story.

A piece of blanket, a black trash bag, cigarette packages, and garbage from lunches littered their way. Beyond one more massive tree, maybe one of the oldest in the park, they stopped at a fresh dirt mound. A sign wrapped in Saran Wrap rested on the mound. Actually, its four corners were tied to strings and staked to keep it in place.

The sign was lettered in marker, graffiti style, though these words were far easier to read than the tags that covered subway cars.

> Rest in deepest peace, dear Moon. I didn't believe he'd kill you. Now I must do worse to save the others.

Below the sentences was an eight on its side with two vertical lines through it. Taylor got up from a crouch. "How do you know that's Moon?"

"Do you see the note?" Rayban asked, aggravated and antsy at the same time. "That's Johnny's style and his tag at the bottom. We're not going to dig the poor thing up. It's Moon, believe me."

"It's Moon. It's Moon." Sally walked from the grave, shaking her head.

"You both seem awfully sure. You know something more?"

"No." Rayban switched from aggravated to angry. "We just goddamn know looking at it."

Taylor repeated part of the sign. " 'I must do worse to save the others.' Is that the mugging? Shooting Dodd?"

"I don't know. I don't want to know."

Rayban, Sally, and John-Boy were already walking out of the park.

"Don't know. Don't know."

7

———◆———

TAYLOR SAT DOWN at the same table he and Novak had shared four hours earlier. He was half surprised not to find his friend there. Novak had been working up to a pretty decent midday bender and had said, after his third Manhattan, there wasn't much work left for the day, which for Novak meant there couldn't be any at all.

The waiter stopped at the table. Taylor's brain forced his mouth to order an RC Cola. He'd told Samantha Callahan he wanted a serious conversation, and he intended to have one.

At 5:35 p.m., Samantha arrived in jeans and loose fitting NYPD sweatshirt, her auburn hair pulled back in a ponytail. She looked even younger than at Little Cindy's the night before. Maybe it was the hair. Of course, she *was* young, early twenties—close to Laura's age, now that he thought about it.

"Not even sure why I'm doing this." She ordered a beer. "I'm fucked. What have you really got that can help?"

"Did you see the bodies at the scene?"

"Spend most of my time trying to forget what I saw." She put two fingers to each temple and rubbed, as if scrubbing away those memories.

"Dodd was shot in the face."

"I *know* that."

"It's hard to shoot someone else with your face taken off."

"Mort was armed. Dodd shot first."

"The mugger takes one in the leg and one right in the chest yet still manages to aim accurately."

"It's possible."

"Possible, but unlikely. People who knew Mort say he wasn't violent. Most he ever did was shoplift to feed these neighborhood dogs he took care of."

"What can I tell you? People go crazy. He had a gun when we saw him. You're not telling me anything that's going to change anybody's mind."

Samantha's beer was already empty. He needed to convince her to tell him what she knew before the heavy drinking got going again.

Toss out the big one.

"Here's something that may change minds. Johnny Mort had a quarter million dollars worth of New York City bonds concealed at his squat. Hidden in a briefcase in a shed. I don't know if it's connected, but I'm really starting to believe Johnny Mort wasn't a mugger who died after killing a cop. Or just a mugger, let's say. There's something else going on."

Samantha whistled low. "Two hundred fifty thousand."

"That's the face value. Not sure what they're really worth. We'll see what Trunk makes of them." He tapped his pen on the notebook. "That's what I got. Until I tipped the detectives, they didn't know about the squat. Trunk got pissed off when I tried to ask some questions this afternoon. He said you're in trouble with IA."

She stared at the empty Rheingold. Hearing about the bonds had changed the look on her face. Now she seemed to actually be listening to him. "They're going to get me for breaking a bunch of regs. Probably get kicked off the force. Won't matter. I'll have to resign. Word's going around I didn't back up my partner. No one will take me. As if that wasn't hard enough before this. Impossible now."

Don't push too hard.

"Why *did* Dodd take you?"

"He never actually said. He wasn't ordered to. He sure as hell didn't spout off on feminism or any other politics. He said being a cop's a job, not a special position, just a job and you did it right. He was a straight shooter without being any sort of Boy Scout." She rolled the beer bottle between her palms. Taylor's gaze drifted from her unpainted fingernails to her dark blue eyes and back to his own notes. " 'A cop's a cop,' he'd say. 'It's simple.' Dodd didn't treat me bad and he didn't treat me special. He didn't treat me differently as far as I could tell."

"What happened yesterday?"

"A quarter million." She shook her head again. "Give you credit. You do find out things the detectives didn't. We were standing outside our car on Lafayette and East Eighth. We heard a scream from across the street—the stairs to the Astor Place stop. The assailant had a semi-automatic." *The gun that's missing.* "He grabs her purse and takes off east toward Saint Marks Place, running fast. We follow on foot. Couldn't use the car, not with the one-ways and alleys and traffic."

"Hold on. You're parked just across the street, and a man pulls a daylight robbery?"

"Yes. When we got to Second Avenue, Dodd told me to go north a block to East Ninth and sprint so we could trap him on Saint Mark's between Second and First Avenues."

Samantha eyed the waiter as he passed. Taylor had to get the rest before she had another. Sober stories were the only kind for this work.

"How fast are you?"

"City parochial champ in the mile. Our Lady of Perpetual Help. Still hold a record." The glimmer of a smile before it disappeared like wisps of smoke in a breeze. "I took off. Just as I was getting to the avenue, I heard the radio report Dodd in pursuit of an armed assailant north on First Avenue heading toward 10th Street."

Taylor frowned. The map was in his head. "They made it to the avenue and got one street north of you before you could run the same block."

"That's what the radio said. It gets stranger. I'd run two blocks north myself trying to catch up when Dodd reports he's turned from Saint Mark's Place on to Avenue B with the suspect in sight. The first radio call had sent me in the wrong direction. Dodd and the mugger kept going east one full avenue and through Tompkins Square Park while I was going north. In his last call, Dodd said the suspect was in the condemned brownstone on Avenue B. He said he was going in after. When I got there, they were both dead."

The notes about the first radio call—the wrong one—already had triple underlines.

"Someone came on the radio and sent you away from the chase."

"I guess. Unless it was mistake."

"What do the detectives think?"

"That there was no such call."

"How could there be no call?"

"No record of one. I'm going to get written up for failing to back up my partner, for not pursuing a chase. Basically, for being a coward. They don't have a reg for that, but that's what it means. That's what's being said. It's so awful. I can't describe...." She paused, picked up the beer, realized it was empty, and set it down. "Then I think of Dodd and his family and feel even worse for thinking about myself. I'm not dead. I'm not missing my husband. I went round and round like that in my head, sitting at the desk all day today. This is the worst."

If Samantha Callahan, New York police officer, really were going to break down, she would have then. She didn't.

"Why would someone put that on the radio?"

"Don't know. I'm starting to think I imagined it. That I *am* a coward."

"No. Someone wanted the chase to end without you to back Dodd up." Taylor did the obvious math. "Means someone set Dodd up, someone on the force."

"Good luck proving that. The detectives think I invented the call after leaving Dodd to die."

"Who are Dodd's enemies at the Oh-Nine?"

"Didn't have any that I know of. Sort of kept to himself. The usual work talk with most guys. Although Schmidt—the guy in the bar last night—had been pestering Dodd about something for the past few weeks. Didn't hear what was said. Dodd was never in a good mood after those talks."

"Had they been pals before?"

"Not at all. Schmidt's a dick. Nothing like Dodd."

"A lot of loose ends in this," Taylor said.

"Exactly. Doesn't help either of us."

"No, loose ends are a good thing. They lead somewhere. There's definitely something going on." He closed the notebook, put it in his field jacket, and smiled. "I told you I've been given the prestigious assignment of covering the Greenwich Village Halloween Parade. Some kind of pageant, apparently. Care to join me?"

"I'm tired of talking about this. Tired of thinking about it."

"No more questions. We'll have a couple of beers before the parade steps off. In fact …." He waved down a waiter and ordered Samantha a Rheingold and a Rolling Rock for himself.

"Oh, why the hell not." The sentence ended in a sigh. "My dad doesn't know what to say to me now. You saw what happened in Little Cindy's last night. That was a mistake. I just wanted to show them I could still go in there. Probably my last time." She lifted her beer. "Why not check out what the fun folks of the Village do on Halloween."

"Excellent. Let me just call in to the paper."

The *MT's* operator gave him one message from a sergeant on the Upper Westside. Taylor was pretty sure what that meant. His father again.

He made the call.

"Dr. Taylor is throwing handfuls of candy at the kids, throwing it hard, and screaming at them. We've warned him twice. A parent's going to slug him."

"Got it. Thanks. I'm on a story now. I'll try to get up there later tonight."

"I can't promise anything."

"I hear ya. He's a grown man."

Yeah, the grown man who'd moved to the Upper West Side from Queens two years after Taylor's mother died of emphysema. He'd said he wanted a new lifestyle. He was ready to swing. He'd swung all right—from barstool to barstool, to the floor, to his apartment, and back to the barstool again. Tenure at City College was the only reason he still had funding for his full-time drunk. Another sign, albeit small, of how screwed up the city's institutions were.

Taylor and Samantha finished their beers and walked over to the Peculiar Pub on Bleecker Street for a couple more at the bar.

"Two hundred fifty thousand dollars." Samantha spoke to her beer. The revelation had clearly gotten her attention. "That's huge. What could it have to do with Dodd?"

"What did Mort have to do with Dodd?"

"Nothing that I know of. How are you making that connection?"

"I can't yet. Too much unexplained. Which is why I said the shooting maybe isn't what it seems."

A mythic beast, maybe a lion with a snake's tail, floated past the pub's window, a giant puppet held by two men manipulating sticks. Taylor hadn't expected that. He'd need to find a parade organizer to interview. He might be stuck with a shitty story, but he wouldn't do it badly. Never could.

8

———◆———

SKELETONS IN THE lead danced the parade toward Washington Square, cavorting in head-to-toe black costumes with white bones painted on them. They looked like figures from a newswire picture of the Day of the Dead. One spun and offered his hand to a chubby lady on the sidewalk next to Taylor and Samantha. She joined in the dance at the exact same moment a child on the other side of them burst into tears. Friday night was always busy in the Village, yet this was something different—organized and chaotic at the same time.

The puppets followed. Towering, articulated things, they appeared to move of their own accord, floating over the street. A dragon in the Chinese style. A bigheaded man with a grin so wide it was threatening. Humpty Dumpty cracked in half and a yellow silk yolk whipped over the heads of the spectators on the sidewalk. Laughter and applause.

Farther back, music from a group that sounded more Dixieland than marching band set a cadence no one could really march to, but some were trying anyway. The sweet burning-hay perfume of pot tickled Taylor's nose. He wondered what all this would look like if you were under the influence of a hallucinogen. It was crazy enough sober. Well, sort of sober. No other New York parade—St. Patrick's, Columbus Day, Easter—came off like this one. Even with its lurching drunks, the St. Patrick's Day parade seemed very much a part of New York City. Greenwich Village had come up with a march that was from some other world. Perfect for Halloween. Perfect for the Village.

At the door of a hole-in-the-wall bar, a waitress held a tray of beers.

Taylor pointed. "How much for two?"

"Just say trick or treat."

He did and she handed two over.

Across the street leaning against a light pole was a uniformed cop. He was tall with arms that looked too long. The cop's eyes caught Taylor's through the marchers then slid over to Samantha. His I-don't-give-a-shit mask turned to one of startled anger. He left the pole and walked along parallel to them as Taylor and Samantha continued toward the rear of the parade. Taylor wanted to see as much as he could, as fast as he could.

He nudged Samantha with his elbow. "You know the one across the street?"

"Saw him. Carmichael. A bastard. He hit on me when I first got to the Oh-Nine. As he explained so romantically, 'If we got to have you here, we ought to get something out of it.' Like the rest, blames me for what happened."

Carmichael reached the next uniformed cop and they both walked together, becoming their only little police parade. The second had an ugly face and was giving Samantha an uglier look. Taylor stopped to let some marchers pass, jotting down descriptions of the costumes. When he looked across the street again, the two officers were gone. This made Taylor more nervous. With the stares they were giving Samantha, he'd rather know where they were.

As it grew darker, streetlights, neon beer logos and store signs lit the parade, which moved like no other. Instead of marching in even files, groups of people jumped and swirled. Paraders continued to beckon costumed trick-or-treaters to join in.

A giant elongated head with a pointed nose and red pyramid of pimples stooped down toward Taylor. A red tongue slowly emerged and ran rough papier-mâché up Taylor's cheek.

Two college-aged women and a man on the sidewalk laughed hard at this. Samantha joined in.

"I think you made a friend."

"Yeah, it's a friendly parade. Let's go back to the square."

He found a woman with a megaphone by the stage in Washington Square making loud, garbled announcements no one could understand.

"You with the organizers?"

"A volunteer."

"How'd all this come about?"

"Do you know Ralph Lee?"

"No."

"Well you should." A snobby Greenwich Village look of disappointment. "He wanted to create a mile-long theater of the street for Halloween. As you see, performers, giant puppets, and music. Last year was the first. He's an incredible puppeteer in his own right. He put a hundred puppets and masks from other productions into this parade. People are supposed to join in."

As the parade flowed into the square, more revelers had indeed joined in, such that you couldn't tell the official marchers—if *official* was the right word—from the people who didn't know they were going to be in a parade until half an hour earlier.

Samantha had stood a few paces back while Taylor talked to the megaphone lady. He rejoined her as she was finishing her beer and dropping the cup in a garbage can. "Interview for the story?"

Taylor nodded.

"So reporters don't just make it all up."

"Many of us actually ask questions. We're not allowed to beat the answers out of people either."

She hit him in the arm, but smiled. "Not much you could get out of me. I told you everything."

The triumphal arch of Washington Square, looking like something dropped there from a European capital, towered over the stage. Several uniformed patrolmen were at the perimeters of the square. None were the pair they'd seen, and this detail nagged at Taylor.

The vaudeville show that concluded the parade was as ragtag as they came. One comedian, in the heart of hip and groovy Greenwich Village, was determined to do a routine that must have played back in the days of actual vaudeville. A lot of groans. A ukulele duo was followed by a decent magician—baffling card tricks—who was followed by a tumbling, juggling trio.

As the performance went on, Samantha and Taylor drifted farther from the stage and the crowd. His buzz was gone. He could use a bar and more of those little beers. Would Samantha be interested? Her face was thoughtful. She'd been this way most of the time they'd been in the Square, except to groan along with everyone else at the comedian's string of jokes about his wife's girth.

She turned to find him looking at her. "You did tell me a lot. You said you would. I don't know what to do about it."

They were now several yards from the back of the crowd under trees partly blocking the streetlights. A breeze flipped the leaves and moonlight flashed on their reds and golds for an instant.

Three Halloween revelers came from the even darker corner of the park behind Taylor and Samantha, having emerged it seemed from the gloom. They wore street clothes and masks—Frankenstein's monster, Dracula, and the Wolfman—the great horror-movie triumvirate of Taylor's youth. The masks were store-bought plastic, oddly old fashioned after all the artistic stuff this evening. They made him smile.

"Enjoying the parade?" Taylor reached for this notebook to get a couple quotes from the group.

Dracula brought a Billy club from behind his back. He slapped the stick into his palm in that cop way. A meaty sound. "We need to talk to the little lady here."

"Those sticks look pretty regulation. Got regulation badges?"

"Shut up, shithead." With both hands on the stick, Dracula shoved Taylor hard in the chest back toward the dark corner of the park. He almost fell on his ass, except Samantha grabbed his arm and steadied him.

"That's really nice. She's taking care of him. Didn't take care of your partner. Talking to the press. How many ways can you turn traitor?"

Samantha didn't answer. Instead, she reached behind. The nightstick was faster, swinging onto her forearm with a crack. Her off-duty gun clattered as it fell, and Dracula kicked it down the walkway into the gloom. Grabbing her arm, Samantha clenched her jaw like she was trying not to make any sound at all. Still, a quiet groan escaped.

The men backed Taylor and Samantha farther and farther into the dark. Three bad guys who it was a fair chance were dirty cops, Samantha disarmed, and his gun a long way down at his ankle. Why even consider it? Terrible odds. He needed to negotiate their way out of this.

He held up his hands. "All right, enough with the stick. What do you want?"

Negotiation apparently wasn't on the agenda.

Dracula hit him hard on his right side, and the air rushed out of his lungs. He sunk to his side, his ribs howling in pain, and rolled onto his back. That's what you were supposed to do when you got the wind knocked out of you. Even if it felt like you were never going to inhale again. Like right now.

Breathe. C'mon breathe.

Samantha stepped toward Dracula. "You bastard—"

"Shut up. If we wanted to take you out, we'd have done that already. Here's what's going to happen. You're going to stop talking about this made-up radio call—"

"Didn't make up the fucking call."

Dracula's stick cracked on the side of her left thigh. Samantha cried out and dropped to her knees. "Goddamn you." The words hissed through clenched teeth. With great effort, she stood back up, putting her weight on her good leg.

"See, that's your problem. You don't listen. That's the problem with all of you. You come on the job thinking you know how it's done. Like you can *do* the job."

"What I don't know how to do is *lie*. Why was Dodd set up to die alone? What's going on?"

Dracula brought the nightstick up for a backhand to the head, and Wolfman spoke. "You knock her out, how's she going to hear how it's gotta go?"

Dracula slowly lowered the club. "You're going to admit you left your partner on his own to take on the mugger. You're going to take whatever punishment comes your way. *Do you understand*?"

Samantha stood silent, leaning on her right leg, her face set. Taylor, breathing again, slowly sat up. His ribs burned every time he took in one of those breaths. Dracula pointed the nightstick at him as a warning to stay where he was.

Frankenstein's monster stepped over to Samantha and pressed against her, the plastic mask up against her face. "How about we take a little taste of police lady?" His voice had a slurpy lisp. She tried to back away. He grabbed her belt with his left hand and rubbed the end of his nightstick roughly under her chin. "We deserve a little something for this shitty detail."

"You know, you really do." Samantha's voice was sexy. "How about this?"

She slammed her knee into his crotch once, twice, the

second time even harder, wincing herself at using the leg that had been hit.

She doesn't give up. Ever.

As the man bent over, her knee came up again, crashing into the Halloween mask. The cracking noise wasn't just plastic. Frankenstein's monster fell with a hoarse cry. Dracula's nightstick swung at her head, and Samantha just ducked. The movement put her weight on her hurt leg. She lost her balance and went over. Dracula and Wolfman crowded in on her, sticks raised.

They're not watching me. Ignore the odds. Samantha did.

He pulled the pistol from the ankle holster and climbed to his feet, his ribs complaining all the way up.

"That'll be enough." They turned to see the gun. *They'll have backups too.* "No moves, fast or slow."

He stepped to Samantha's gun in the dirt, picked it up and stuffed it in his jacket pocket.

"Get away from her." They hesitated. He flicked with the gun. "Get the fuck away from her."

Dracula and Wolfman moved. Frankenstein's monster couldn't. He was still moaning on the ground, blood leaking from his mask's nose holes.

In two steps, he was in front of Samantha and out of striking distance of the men. The gun was shaking in his hand.

Dracula laughed. "You're out of your league, bub. She knows what she needs to do. We're not the only accident waiting to happen."

Samantha reached the hand of her good arm to him. Taylor gently helped her up while keeping the gun trained on the men. She held the injured arm to her stomach.

"Let me have my gun." Samantha spoke slowly through the pain.

Taylor handed her the .38. Limping, she stepped over to Dracula. With the gun in her left hand and held at arm's length, she put the barrel in the eyehole of his mask.

"Maybe I settle this here. Maybe I spread blood all over the inside of that mask."

Taylor kept his gun trained on Wolfman, who squeezed his nightstick. Wolfman was within reach. He could easily swing at Samantha. Taylor didn't want to have to shoot.

"Let's just get out of here." He backed down the path. "C'mon, Samantha."

She followed slowly. When they came out into the light, they put the guns away and walked faster. The crowd was breaking up after the show, costumed revelers moving in every direction.

He eyed her injured arm. "The way you walloped that one guy, they're going to come after us."

"We don't even know how many of *them* there are. But I'll make it."

They trotted toward the southwest corner of the park. Adrenaline eased the pain in his ribs. For now. Samantha grimaced the whole way.

9

———◆———

At Sullivan and Washington Square South, two uniformed cops watched them pass. Their radios crackled and one yelled, "You two, stop!"

They weren't going at much more than a jog. Somehow, Samantha managed to pick up the pace as they ran toward Bleecker.

Taylor glanced over his shoulder. The two in blue were coming up fast. As he crossed West Third with Samantha next to him, three more men came flying around the corner from Thompson, one block east. Street clothes. Masks gone. Nightsticks gone. Guns out.

"Shit. We've got to get off the street."

He reached his right hand for her left to encourage her. She squeezed it, cried out in pain or because of the effort or both and urged herself to go a little bit faster. Her breathing was ragged. At Bleecker, Taylor led them left so they were out of the line of sight. Line of fire, really.

"Is everyone in the Oh-Nine crooked?" He panted to catch his breath. The pain in his ribs was already back. Maybe none were broken, but he had to be pretty badly bruised.

"Doesn't need to work that way. The guys in masks just had to call our descriptions in for something. The whole precinct could be after us."

"That doesn't make me feel any better."

Where to go? Think.

He scanned up and down the block, caught sight of a name on an awning. He tugged, and they ran down the street to the front door.

Samantha read the awning. "The Other End. Yeah, the end. That's what's coming."

He pulled open the door, let her go in first, and turned to peer out as the door was inches from closing. The three in street clothes ran around the corner onto Bleecker as the door slipped shut.

Taylor led Samantha to a table in the back of the crowded rock-and-roll club. A six-piece band was in the middle of something that had as much jazz as thumping rock in it. They ordered drinks, both with an eye on the front door for anyone checking for them. Samantha deflated into the chair, and real fear registered on her face for the first time.

"It hurts so much." She held her right arm tightly to her belly. "I've got to get away. I can't do this."

I'd probably be in tears after the crack she took.

After half a set, they squeezed back through the tables to the front door. The cover had been steep and the drinks expensive, but the outlay was worth it to lose their pursuers. Taylor held up his hand, checked the block in both directions, and went to the curb. A cab dropping off a couple likely headed for the second show at The Other End was exactly the thing he needed. He waved to Samantha in the doorway.

The cab took off with both of them slumped in the back.

"We'll figure this out."

"The next time they come, it won't be a warning. Who can I trust? They'll kill me. I can't. I can't." She was almost whispering. "I'm sorry. I need to think. What to do. I'm taking the cab home. I need to get my arm checked. I want to be safe. I don't know how that's going to happen."

"Do you want me to come with you?"

"No. No thanks. I just need to think."

He honored her request, getting out at 14th Street. From a payphone he dictated the story on the Greenwich Village Halloween Parade to one of the assistant editors on the city desk.

The editor read it back to him. "Sounds like a fun night."

"A real blast."

His side sure hurt like hell. Didn't matter. There wasn't anything you could do for bruised ribs. The lobby of the 20th Precinct stunk of ammonia and puke. Taylor walked out with his father trailing behind him. The man refused to let Taylor help, so his father weaved a wide slalom to the front door. He was wearing beat-up blue pants and a gray T-shirt the cops had provided. Gray hair fell down into his eyes. He didn't seem to notice. When they'd finally arrested Professor Taylor, he had been in the apartment hallway, hurling candy everywhere. The sergeant said he was yelling too, but wasn't making any sense. Taylor knew why. Poetry. Samuel Taylor Coleridge. "Christabel," to be exact. The poem was his father's favorite to recite when he was shit-faced. They'd let Taylor take him home because it was too busy a night for the patrolmen to bother with the paperwork.

Taylor led the way down Broadway to 78th Street, their walk narrated by the slurred invective his father hurled at Taylor's back. In the apartment, the professor stumbled through the clutter of the living room to the bedroom. The springs squeaked as he collapsed onto the bed.

"Bring me a drink." It was a command.

"You've had enough."

"I've enough? The scribbler thinks I've enough." The mattress squeaked again as he tried to get back up and louder when he fell back. "Always lecturing. What does the scribbler know? Do you ever read literature? Do you even read?"

Taylor pushed aside academic journals, magazines, and newspapers to clear a space on the couch. Student papers were scattered over the coffee table. Did they ever get graded? Returned? At one corner was an empty bottle of no-name vodka. Here was why Taylor's second rule of drinking said no hard stuff. He'd broken *that* rule just last night with Samantha. But there was the interview to get.

Are those the kinds of excuses my father made to himself? Back when he needed excuses.

The room was hot and sticky from steam heat. The stink of old cigarette ash and rotting food hung in the air. He unwrapped a stick of Teaberry and chewed it.

"Get me a goddamn drink."

"You've had more than enough."

"Your brother would do it."

"Right. Do you remember the last thing you said to Billy? 'You're a fascist fighting a fascist war.' Then he was out the door. Gone. Gone forever."

"Miserable little scribbler with your miserable little quotes. There's no truth in that. There's only truth in literature. 'Tis the middle of night by the castle clock, and the owls have awakened the crowing cock.' " The first of the 671 lines of "Christabel." No matter how much he drank, the professor's diction somehow improved when he recited. "My son's no cock. He's a dick. Enough of the scribbler. On with literature. 'Tu-whit! Tu-whoo! And hark, again! The crowing cock.' "

Taylor rose and approached the small kitchen, kicking another empty bottle as he went. The bottle stopped when it hit a brown grocery bag of garbage that hadn't gotten farther than the living room. The rotting smell was worse in the kitchen. On the counter was a case of vodka delivered by the friendly corner liquor store. Five bottles were left. To the cadence of the lines, he poured each down the drain. He was absolutely certain his gesture would have no impact on his father's drinking. It made the scribbler feel a little bit better just the same.

He pulled the front door shut with a click. His father was still saying the lines. He knew they were supposed to be beautiful. He hated each and every one.

As HE ENTERED the houseboat, Taylor was greeted by Mason as if he had returned from the wars, which he pretty much had. The tail wagged. The dog jumped up, and its front paws landed right where the nightstick had.

"Ouch, ouch. Okay, Mason. Down, down. I'll take you out."

Popeye's note said, "Fed good, new water, walk at six bells." Taylor wondered if six bells was six o'clock or some other time on the nautical clock.

He put the leash on and Mason led him down King Avenue to Fordham Street. The dog did his business quickly, but was so happy to be out and about, his tail swinging so fast it was almost a blur, that Taylor kept on going, tired, hurting, but allowing the air to clear his head. On the main avenue, he turned toward the end of the island. There was nothing like a look at the ocean, even the narrow end of the Long Island Sound, to lift the spirits at the end of a tough day.

He considered the story he was stumbling around the edges of, stumbling badly. The police might announce the discovery of the city bonds, and that would go off like a bomb in the media. He could have written a story about finding them—maybe even gotten himself arrested—but a hunch told him to wait, to let the police recover them and see what happened next. He sensed a much bigger story, and he hated grabbing a little headline only to bring in all the other papers. Wasn't that going to happen anyway?

Samantha still hadn't told him everything that was going on at the Ninth Precinct. Or all of what she knew about Dodd. He was sure of it.

She was a beautiful woman and tough at the same time.

Nothing wrong with that. He liked the way she'd gone against the grain by deciding to be a cop, by not taking the shit that came her way, by fighting back. Now she sounded ready to give up. He wanted to help her. How could he do that and get the story? What if the facts went against her? Was he willing to make one person more important than the story?

The little waves of the sound quietly lapped the pilings and bulkheads. The oily chemical odor wasn't as strong tonight, allowing the salt air to break through—the perfume that made being by the sea so nice.

Two things required more reporting. The radio call that had sent Samantha the wrong way. That, and of course, tonight's attack by three men—they must be cops—who demanded she deny the story about the call and admit to abandoning Dodd. Someone wanted the shooting to go down the way it looked—Dodd killed by a mugger, who died in the exchange of fire.

So what had really happened?

He shook his head and scratched behind Mason's ears. The story already had too many leads. Usually it was just the opposite.

He also had to talk to the families of the two dead men. Would Dodd's widow know something about what was happening on the job? Maybe not, but it was still worth a shot. Johnny Mort had a family somewhere that he'd visited. Maybe they could explain the bonds. Maybe that was his allowance. Taylor chuckled to himself.

Mason looked up at him, and that reminded Taylor of one of the weirder facts in this story—the sign on Moon's grave. Someone had killed the dog and that had forced Mort to "do worse to save the others."

The "others," he assumed, were the other dogs, including the one staring at him right now. The "worse," well that might have been the mugging or the shooting. Or both. He needed to know for sure.

Taylor gave the leash a tug. Mason led the way back to the houseboat.

Popeye must walk him all over the place. He knows the island as well as I do.

The little refrigerator held seven ponies. After the visit to his father's apartment, he considered not having one. Not for long. He took a bottle and opened it. He and his father were nothing alike.

In the cassette player of his all-in-one Emerson stereo was the new album by Bruce Springsteen. *Born to Run*. Springsteen wasn't punk, but like punk his music did for Taylor what all the crap on the radio didn't. Springsteen reminded him of the rock and roll that had gone away. The rough music of passion, hard luck, and blown dreams. But Springsteen's music wasn't old or in any way nostalgic. "Thunder Road" wasn't a story for 1966; it was a story for now, for darker days.

10

———◆———

CEMETERIES SEPARATED NEIGHBORHOODS in Queens. Cemeteries were almost the defining feature of New York's largest borough. They were an archipelago strung across the county, accounting for the religions of the various populations that had settled here. Catholic, Lutheran, Jew, Methodist, godless. They were the landmarks when driving the expressways and riding the subways. One, St. John Cemetery, separated the neighborhood where Taylor had lost his house, from Middle Village, the neighborhood where Robert Dodd's home was located. Middle Village was, in fact, an enclave with cemeteries on three sides—St. John, Mount Olivet, and Lutheran All Faiths—and a park on the fourth.

This Saturday afternoon, the first day of November, Taylor sat on a couch in the Dodds' small living room, which was filled with large cops. All of Dodd's brothers were cops, except for one fireman, who happened to be the biggest of the group. There were others squeezed in too. Taylor, after being ordered onto the couch between two brothers, was offered a beer by the fireman.

The two-story attached home built of brick and aluminum

siding was a mirror image of all the others on the block. No driveway, but a front yard and a backyard. Off in three directions: headstones. This view was what owning your own place in Queens often meant.

Twenty minutes passed with the men talking to each other and ignoring Taylor. Nothing was said about police work. Not one word. The discussion revolved around the miserable season the Jets were having. They'd lost 45-28 to the Baltimore Colts at Shea last weekend. Most of the men were Jets fans, which was no surprise here in Queens. Two were for the Giants, and since their team also had only two wins, they didn't have much to say. The discussion got most heated when one of the Jets fans complained about having to share Shea with "the fucking Giants."

"You're lucky to have a real team in there."

"Go fuck yourself."

"C'mon? You kidding? The Yankees and the Giants are the best that shithole is ever, *ever* going to see."

"You guys screwed up the entire schedule. Four teams sharing. Why? So *yours* can get a better stadium."

The conversation went on like that. Profane, genial sports talk. No shoptalk. That was okay. Taylor could wait. His job was about waiting. The wall opposite was crowded with family pictures, some old black and whites and a bunch of Kodachromes with colors that didn't occur in the natural world. Many taken at the beach. Could be Montauk or Fire Island, or even Rockaway here in Queens.

Sitting with those sand-covered kids, smiling. He didn't expect to die. She didn't expect to lose him.

The hulking fireman stepped aside, and a brunette stood in the doorway that led to the dining room. The woman was petite anyway but looked positively miniature with all the big bodies around her.

A gray-haired man, tall, angular, and muscled, went over to the woman. He leaned in a moment, whispered, and turned to Taylor. "What do you want to know?"

Taylor addressed the woman directly. "I'm very sorry for the loss you and your family have suffered. I know this is a difficult time. I'm looking into your husband's death. It may not be as straightforward as has been reported."

The gray-haired guy shook his head. "If it's not, the detectives will figure it out. You'll get a press release."

"Sometimes the detectives don't figure it out."

The man crossed the room in two big steps and pulled Taylor off the couch. He had a badge out, a gold badge, and pressed it into Taylor's cheek. "I'm a detective. What *exactly* are you implying?"

The badge hurt. Taylor was going to lose the interview before he could make his case.

Go for broke, bonehead. If they're going to toss you out anyway. Once the long blue line closes ranks, I get nothing.

"I think Officer Dodd may have been set up."

"You fucking think *what*?"

"I'll see him." Kathy Dodd's voice was a little above a whisper, but the detective let go immediately.

"Are you sure?" He turned back to her. "You never know what these vultures are up to. Remember that *Eyewitness News* asshole?"

"Let him through, Davey." She left the doorway.

Davey stuck his face very close to Taylor's. Budweiser mingled with Old Spice. "If you mislead her, if you hurt her in any way, if you do even the smallest thing I don't like, I will break you into pieces and these guys will spread you all over Queens."

"That isn't going to happen. Might even be able to help."

A dark disbelieving laugh as Davey stepped out of the way, shaking his head.

Taylor walked through the dining room. Candles on the table burned, though it was midday. They gave off a waxy lemony scent that mingled with coffee and cake. Seven pairs of eyes followed him into the kitchen. If it was possible, the ladies at the dining room table looked more suspicious than the men in the living room.

In the kitchen, the screen door to the backyard banged closed. He opened it and stepped onto a small wood deck with just enough room for a rubber welcome mat and a cast-iron hibachi on a round white aluminum table. The hibachi held gray ash still in the shape of charcoal briquettes. Their last cookout?

Kathy was already sitting on a folding beach chair—aluminum piping and green plaid plastic strips woven to form the seat and back. The dark shadows under her eyes jumped out from her washed-out, beyond-pale skin. In the pictures, she smiled at the world as a good-looking woman. Now it was hard to see past the exhaustion.

Taylor took the other chair. The back half of the small yard formed an intricate garden. A waterfall trickled out of a miniature mountain on the right and became a lazy little stream that ran around the outside of the garden all the way back to a pond at the foot of the mountain. A wooden bridge arched over the stream from the yard just in front of them. In the middle of the garden was a maze created with foot-high shrubs. On the left, a forest of tiny trees, or bushes cut to look like trees. The whole thing was a tiny world in itself.

A breeze on this surprisingly warm autumn day caught Kathy's dark hair and flipped it. She didn't seem to notice.

Taylor took out his notebook and made a list of what was in the garden. "That's amazing. I've never seen anything like it."

"Robert loved doing it. He was a city boy who should have been a country boy. *Wanted* to be a country boy. Talked about moving us way up to Mahopac." A brief chuckle and shake of the head. "I'm sorry you had to wait. The boys insisted on making calls."

"To who?"

"Apparently you don't hate cops. Do pretty well by them. You're lucky. They wouldn't even let the *Times* guy in the house."

"Sounds like the Channel 7 reporter didn't treat you so well."

"He just wanted to get me to cry for everyone watching. Asked me about meeting Robert. What the kids are going to do. So I cried. He got here before the boys started looking after me. He got what he wanted."

"I've no interest in making you cry, but what I've learned may not be easy for you to hear."

She blew out air. Lipstick was her only makeup. "I don't know how I can hurt any worse."

"I'm hoping you might know something that will help."

"Like what?"

"Was there anyone who had it in for your husband? Anyone on the job?"

She turned toward him with a look that was serious, but not surprised. Her dark brown eyes were clear. The breeze continued to whip her hair around. "Why do you ask that?"

"Can you keep all this between us for now? Too many holes." *I also don't want a cover-up. Check that. More of a cover-up than already is underway.*

Kathy nodded gravely.

"Johnny Mort wasn't a criminal, wasn't violent at all. That is, until someone threatened him. I think to get him to do the mugging. The shooting itself … well, there are some holes there too. Samantha Callahan was diverted from the chase by a fake radio call. Could be so she wasn't on hand to see the shooting. Now she's being threatened to drop her story. Cops are making the threats."

"Oh God, Samantha. The boys wouldn't let me talk to her, either. She called yesterday. I'm sorry for that. Robert had no problem with her as a partner. You're sure? She didn't abandon him like they're all saying?"

"As sure as I can be. Like I said, a lot of missing pieces. They didn't find Mort's gun after the shooting. I'm still waiting for news on that. There are a few other elements that don't make sense. What was happening on the job?"

"I was so afraid something like this would come up. So afraid I didn't want to think about it. The past couple of months have been awful. A year ago when he moved to the precinct, Robert pretty quickly figured out there was a group of patrolmen taking bribes. Robert wasn't a Serpico or anything. He just wanted to be left alone to do the job. Always said, if he wanted to be a crook, he'd have been a crook. Or a banker."

She took a sip of water.

Similar to what Samantha said.

"That's one reason he was okay with Samantha as a partner. He figured he'd get left alone if he rode with her. They'd never trust her to know. It all worked until late in August. He'd been in the precinct too long, they said. They didn't like that he wasn't a part of *it*. Funny, they never say exactly what they're doing. It's like they're embarrassed. Still, they take the money. A new Internal Affairs guy had arrived at the start of the summer. That had them all jumpy. They needed to tie up loose ends."

"What's the name of the IA officer?"

"Christian Slive."

"Did your husband talk to Slive?

"Told me they talked, but couldn't say what about."

"What did your husband do about the approach from the corrupt guys?"

"Said no."

"They don't like it when you do that."

"I know." She intertwined her fingers. Her knuckles whitened. "I asked him if they came at him again." A pause. "You know, threatening. He insisted it was only the once. Everything was quiet." She shook her head. "He said that because he knew how scared I got after the first approach. Robert became so unhappy—anxious, and Robert was never an anxious guy. He didn't have any patience with the kids. Even stopped working in the garden. That was his retreat from the job. He'd putter around in there every day he could."

"Did he mention any names? A cop named Schmidt?"

"Wouldn't. Didn't want it to touch me. I know that doesn't leave you with much, but you seem to have more pieces than anyone else. If what you say is true." In her voice was sadness, like she knew it was. "I was wrong that I couldn't hurt any worse. I'm afraid of your story. I'm crushed already. I don't know that I can take any more bad news."

Taylor handed Kathy Dodd his card. "I'll let you know what I find out before I write it."

"I'm not sure I want you to."

11

———— ♦ ————

Taylor sat on a stool at the Oddity, the name the regulars gave to the Odysseus Coffee Shop, his grandfather's place at Madison and 75th. Grandpop adjusted the rabbit ears on a small black and white. The TV was a big deal. Grandpop rarely allowed it in the dining area.

"I'm not running a saloon here in this place," he'd say. Today was different. Governor Carey was going to answer President Ford's charges against the city. Grandpop permitted the TV only when history was being made.

Taylor forked off a piece of cheese and bacon omelet. "It's all just politics."

"It's *not* just politics. What would happen to this city if it went under?" His grandfather, barrel-chested with a full head of white hair, topped off Taylor's coffee.

"Business as usual. Isn't it already a financial swamp?"

"This small business of mine will be dragged down with it. The state. Everything between. Carey has said this. So will other cities and states. It'll be a financial calamity."

He's worried. Maybe the threat's real. Not just paper and talk. But hadn't the city been spending more than it collected in taxes since Mayor Wagner? Maybe. He couldn't remember. Things definitely got worse with the oil shock and the recession. At some point, Taylor had figured, things would get better again. He thought about the briefcase full of city bonds, his first direct connection with the crisis. What had the cops done with it? He'd follow up on that after the speech.

One thing Taylor liked about working Saturdays—and he did it a lot—was that he owed Worthless nothing. His workweek was Monday to Friday, unless he was covering for someone on the weekend. Today, he could pursue the story as he pleased.

Carey's long Irish face with its bushy dark eyebrows appeared on the screen. The governor started by slamming Ford's plan to create a way for the city to go bankrupt. Bondholders would lose billions. Billions more by the U.S. Treasury—that is, U.S. taxpayers—as investors wrote off their losses and the government had to make unemployment and welfare payments. Carey refuted Ford's speech point-by-point, winding up to an emotional conclusion, a call to battle that left behind the numbers and the technical details of finance.

"For New Yorkers, a final note: our city is often abrasive and arrogant, sometimes cold and unfeeling, always challenging. For a lot of reasons, it has incurred the scorn of some of our countrymen—because of our pace and tone of voice, because of the colors of our skins and the accents in which we speak, and our tradition as a magnet for the disaffected, the dispossessed, the dissenters.

"Whether we shall escape fiscal default, I do not know. Our fate is in the hands of people who, for now, appear determined not to let facts get in the way of what they want people to believe—and who are seeking political advantage by kicking the city when it's down. But whatever happens, New York will survive. We will remain a home for the exiled and oppressed. And perhaps we will have learned the lesson of fighting among ourselves, instead of standing together to wage a common fight for each other. Come what may, we will win that fight."

Led by Grandpop, the five guys sitting at the counter applauded, prompting those in the booths to turn their heads to see what was up. Carey *had* described the city Taylor loved—what he loved about it. Maybe the city the rest of the country hated. The speech was an exhilarating reply to the president. At the same time, it put a nervous twist in Taylor's stomach as he thought about those damn bonds. He put down the next forkful of omelet. He wasn't hungry anymore.

He couldn't shake the idea he'd made a big mistake holding off writing. Problem was, the bonds were a lead with no story to go underneath. He needed the police to say what they were doing there and how they were tied to Johnny Mort. He went back into the kitchen and used the wall phone to call Novak at home.

"Cracking speech, huh?" Novak asked.

"Yeah, a good one. How long does the city have?"

"You ask the best questions. Two weeks, three. Maybe a bit longer. Here's the problem. No one knows for sure when the blade will drop. The city and the state juggle money to make a payment at the last minute. The banks make another short-term loan. Public employee pensions swoop in and buy some bonds. The shell game goes round and round. It's got to stop soon. The city's probably been technically bankrupt more than once this year. If Ford doesn't get out of the way, it'll be the real deal."

"Explain to me again how the bonds Mort had will make things worse."

"Let me be clear. On the numbers, they won't. The city's got fourteen billion in outstanding debt. A quarter million is a molecule in a drop in a bucket. Ford, the Republicans in Congress, all the upstaters in the state legislature, they think the city's finances are run like my daughter's lemonade stand. Worse, actually. They'd have evidence they were right if it turned out even *one* briefcase of missing bonds was floating around. That could wreck any chance of a bailout. But only if the bonds were the city's. Unsold securities or something like that. You see, someone else could own them. Then this might just be simple theft."

"Pretty big for simple."

"Sure. The briefcase would get some attention because of the crisis, but it wouldn't play into the hands of those opposed to helping New York. You need to discover who owned those bonds."

"I gotta find Mort's family. You know, Novak, I'd say you should consider covering cops, but the beat's too quiet for you."

Novak laughed, calling Taylor an asshole, and said he had to get off to mix cocktails.

Grandpop sent Taylor on his way with the instruction to do something to help the city. The old man was proud of everything Taylor did at the *Messenger-Telegram*. Customers might bring other papers into the Oddity, but the only one Grandpop displayed on the counter was the *MT*. He was, in fact, the opposite of Taylor's father, and so it was his mother's father Taylor came to for family.

He was sad, nodding his assent to Grandpop as he left the coffee shop. The story he was working on was hardly the kind his grandfather had in mind.

DETECTIVE TRUNK ATE fried chicken out of a Colonel Sanders bucket. He was in the middle of pulling apart a wing with the gusto of Henry VIII when Taylor sat down at the desk opposite.

Trunk frowned and finished tearing the wing in two. Odor of greasy chicken. "Who the fuck let you in?"

"I told the desk sergeant you wanted to see me. Badly."

"You've got a real sense of humor." He chewed as he talked. "You'll be leaving even faster. I've no use for you."

"You *seem* a smart guy to me. Might want to listen."

"Oh fucking marvelous. Compliments from the press." Trunk cleaned off the middle wing bone and picked up a biscuit as big as Taylor's fist.

"I figure you're not going to ignore reports of corruption. Cover-ups aren't the rage anymore."

"What are you talking about?"

"Dodd was invited to go on the pad and refused."

Trunk put the biscuit down, wiped his hands deliberately with a yellow paper napkin, and sipped from the straw sticking out of a large soda. "You ought to be careful what you allege. If you want to leave by the door you came in."

"Something else that ought to be in your picture. Officer Callahan says she received a call that diverted her from the chase, diverted her long enough for Dodd to be murdered. Maybe killed in a way that's different from how things look."

"Where's Callahan now?"

"I've no idea."

"You better hope not. She didn't turn up today. She's not at home. She's not anywhere. Looks like she's running. We're putting out a warrant."

Christ, last night really rattled her. Running is the worst thing she can do. If she has nothing to hide.

"For what?"

"We'll think of something."

"If I heard that, I'd run too. She says no one will believe her about the radio call."

"Don't flack for her." Trunk rose, slamming his hands down on the desk. The stained red-and-white chicken bucket leapt three inches. A couple of detectives nearby looked up. "No one else heard the damn call. No. One. I'm working on the murder of a brother officer. I'm not interested in the shit that's being made up."

"Why make it up?"

"Makes me think police girl failed her partner. Or worse."

"That's a theory. Here's something you haven't heard yet. Last night Callahan and I were jumped in Washington Square. Three guys in Halloween masks carrying nightsticks—the regulation type they don't sell at your local costume shop. She was threatened. They told her to stop talking about the radio call. Her only option was to admit to what you just suggested. We got out of it, but were chased by the three, plus two in uniform. Who's trying to shut her up? Why?"

"You got proof?"

"Callahan was there."

"She's not here. In police work, we call that an admission of guilt." Trunk sat back down, eying Taylor. News of the attack seemed to have gotten a little of his attention, at least that part not claimed by his appetite. He reached in the bucket and pulled out a drumstick.

"Track down Mort's gun yet?"

"No comment."

Taylor wrote in the notebook, mouthing just *no.*

"Any leads on Mort?"

"You're going to tell me you've got one."

"Don't know where he's from, but a source says he came to the neighborhood from somewhere outside the city. Had a family he visited. Well off. Didn't need to squat."

"We only found dog shit in his place."

Taylor flipped back in his notebook to the pages from yesterday. "Mort's own dog, Moon, is buried in Tompkins Square. Was killed before he was. There's a sign on the grave. Reads, 'Rest in deepest peace, dear Moon. I didn't believe he'd kill you. Now I must do worse to save the others.' "

"What is this, puzzle time?"

"Sounds like Mort was being coerced."

"Sounds, huh? You get a lot from a little sign. How do you even know there's a dead dog there? Now you *are* wasting my time."

"Anything of value in that briefcase?"

Trunk put down the drumstick. He didn't turn his head. Instead, his eyes, which now had a worried look, checked behind Taylor and to either side. He picked up a pen, wrote on a small piece of paper and pushed the paper toward Taylor while keeping his greasy fingers on it. The boxy cursive read, "Above my pay grade. Leave it if you're smart." He pulled the paper back, tore it into little pieces, and sprinkled them into the bucket.

"You tell pretty little Samantha, if she's got any brains in that redheaded skull of hers," Trunk raised his voice for the benefit of the room, "she'll get in here and explain herself. *Yesterday.*"

As he walked down the stairs, Taylor wondered at the worry that came into Trunk's eyes when Taylor hinted at the bonds. That was the most important thing he'd gotten out of the interview. For the moment, at least. The corrupt cops. The attack. Telling the detective about all that had been designed to shake something loose. He just hoped whatever it was didn't drop right on his head.

12

———◆———

TELEVISION WAS THE band on the bill at CBGB that Saturday night. Taylor liked the group well enough, but they'd have a hard time topping the three shows the Ramones had put on last weekend. Each night he'd stood at the back of the small performance space. The punks had pogoed in front of him—something Taylor would never do. Instead, he'd let the raw rush of sound wash over him and rattle the buzz from a whole bunch of ponies. The Ramones, leather jackets and shaggy black hair, rocketed through the show. The song "Blitzkrieg Bop" said it all. The Ramones' bop was a blitzkrieg of sound.

It was probably a good thing the Ramones weren't in their regular New York home tonight, or he might have been distracted from what he needed to get done. As Frederick the Dutch dealt drinks to Television fans, Taylor waited to get more information on Johnny Mort. Punks in leather with hair sticking at odd angles poured alcohol down their throats. They were a tough looking tribe. They smashed into each other hard and called that dancing. Tonight, as every night, they left

Taylor in peace, and from what he could tell, did the same with any newcomer.

Frederick the Dutch opened three Schlitz in quick succession—*fitz, fitz, fitz.* "Everything I knew of poor Johnny I told you. But I remember after you left who you need to talk with. His friend Billy—" Frederick waved over Taylor's shoulder. "Billy, get over here!" A tall, lanky man in his twenties squeezed through the crowd, his hair a copy of the shaggy mops the Ramones wore. "Taylor's a regular." Billy looked at Taylor, from his faded cords to his field jacket, with surprise. "He's also a reporter. He's doing a story on Johnny Mort."

"Pigs killed him." Billy's light brown eyes dared Taylor to challenge that declaration.

"You knew him well?"

"We came to the city together. From Chap. Johnny would never use a gun, much less shoot a cop. Shit, I had to get him off the floor when the dancing really got going because he'd get hurt. Didn't have a violent bone in his body. Just loved the music and those dogs. He was set up, somehow, someway."

A setup, yes. But both Mort and Dodd?

"Chap?"

"Chappaqua. Couldn't wait to get out of that shithole."

If Chappaqua's a shithole, the Waldorf's a flophouse.

"Did you two share the squat?"

"About a month. Then I met Lacey. We moved in together."

"When did you last see him?"

"Two nights before the shooting. In here. Kind of quiet for this place. We were talking about those fucking amazing Ramones shows. He'd missed one 'cause of lack of dough. Both our dads cut us off. Pricks. Lace's old man gives her tons of cash. She just has to say she loves him and out comes the fat wallet."

"Do you have the family's address?"

"Mohegan Drive. Number forty-two. His name was actually John Mortelli. Took the new one when he came down here.

Mort is some kind of word for death. Johnny was smart that way. Always playing with words."

"Does Johnny's family know?"

"Dunno. I haven't told them. I don't want to get near his father. I'd do something Johnny never would."

"What's that?"

"Smash him in the fucking face."

A young blonde woman with a Blondie haircut tugged on the leather sleeve of Billy's jacket. They both walked away. Taylor flagged Frederick for another pony, then sat to consider the new break in the story. Two men in their twenties had come down to join the punk scene from Chappaqua, a plush Westchester County suburb culturally a million miles from the Lower Eastside. A chill walked down Taylor's spine as he worked over the knowledge. It was good for the story, but it meant he'd have to go grave digging again. This wasn't something you did on the phone, if for no other reason that he only had Billy's word on the ID. With this kind of news you had to be very careful and very sure.

He usually gave himself Sunday off. It was a tough day to track anyone down, including cops and criminals. He'd be working tomorrow.

TAYLOR SPENT THE better part of three hours getting to Chappaqua. He was forced to take two buses, the subway, and the New York Central's Harlem Line to the Chappaqua station. The trip put him in a foul mood. Taylor was a man of the subways, which whisked him wherever he needed to go. The catastrophic noise, dirt, and graffiti didn't matter. The subways still ran, more or less, and they'd take you anywhere quickly, more or less. Anywhere in New York City. Today was one of the few times he wished he owned a car. He and Laura had used one of her father's when the need arose. That thought layered a familiar sadness over his sour mood. Waiting for the local cab service—which appeared to have one car—took another 20 minutes.

The house at 42 Mohegan Drive didn't disappoint. A big white colonial with black shutters on a lot Taylor imagined you could farm. The neighboring houses, which weren't very neighboring given the lot sizes, were similar in appearance, as if the owners all wanted to impress, but in exactly the same way.

Taylor rang the doorbell at 1:40 p.m. A man with slicked back dark hair answered. He had on a pink polyester shirt and flared pants the same color. His cologne of musk and pine trees greeted Taylor first.

"Mr. Anthony Mortelli?"

"We're not buying anything, and we're not Jehovah's witnessing. Go away."

"I'm from the *Messenger-Telegram*."

"My wife takes care of the paperboy. She's down at the club." He moved to shut the door.

"I'm a reporter. It's about your son, John."

The door swung open. Mortelli stepped out, looked back into the house, let the door close behind him, and stood on the big front porch of his big house.

"What's the little shit done?"

"I'm sorry. This may be very bad news. He may have been involved in a police shooting. A man using the name Johnny Mort was killed three days ago in an exchange of fire with a police officer. You probably read about it."

"No, no." He shook his head. "I stopped reading. Too many shootings. Why the hell do you think I live out here?" Mortelli slumped into a red-cushioned, white whicker chair, which squeaked as it gave under his weight. "You sure it's him?"

"No I'm not—"

"Then why are you coming around telling stories?" The chest puffed out. "The police should be contacting me."

"The Johnny Mort who was killed didn't have ID. I tracked him down to a squat where he was living with several rescued dogs."

"John claimed he was taking care of some mutts the last time he asked for money." Mortelli spoke like it was a revelation. "I said no."

"I got your address from a friend of Johnny's. Billy. He said Johnny was actually John Mortelli."

"Bill Wilkerson?"

"He said they moved to the Lower Eastside together."

"Bill's the little fuck who ruined John. Got him into that music and the drugs. If he's dead, it's because of Bill Wilkerson."

"I'm very sorry. The police will want you to identify him. Can I see a picture?"

Mortelli reached for his wallet, stopped. "No, I took it out."

The screen door opened and a teenaged girl joined them. She wore a T-shirt like a dress, with a thick white belt around her waist. Long slender thighs ran from the T-shirt to knee-high white boots. Taylor had seen the same outfit on a member of one of the disco bands. It was in a wire service picture. ABBA, maybe?

The girl put a hand on one hip. "What's goin' on?"

"Go inside and get me the picture of John from the piano."

"What's he done now?"

"Just do it."

The girl left, swinging her hips like she'd learned how to do it yesterday and really needed to show off the skill. When she returned, she handed the framed picture to her father.

"I'll be inside in a minute."

"I want to know what's going on." Her voice stretched to a whine.

"If you don't go inside now, you won't get a ride to Lorraine's when I head to the club."

"Christ, everything is threats around here."

The hips swung back into the house. Mortelli passed the picture to Taylor. He'd gotten a good look at the dead punk in the abandoned building. The picture was that man, minus the spider tattoo. He nodded. "I'm very sorry. Do you want me to let the detectives know?"

"I don't care. Do what you do. His mother's going to blame me. It's *all* going to be my fault. She said we should give him money. What for? To flush down the toilet. That's what. It started with the music and trips to the city. Then he drops out. I said it had to stop. I've got a good job at the bank. I've got connections. In this economy you need connections. He wants nothing to do with it. Drops out of Marist College. Lives here for two years mooching off us then leaves. He prefers stray dogs and living in some wreck and listening to noise."

He put his head in hands. He groaned briefly like he hurt and got up.

"I need a drink."

The father disappeared inside the house. The door shut, and the sound transformed into the lock clicking at the apartment of Taylor's father Halloween night. He'd spent the hours since then trying not to replay the professor's ranting. He couldn't help it now. This father's reaction brought it all back. The drunken insults about Taylor's work. The lies about his brother thrown in for good measure. Would his father be as cold as Mortelli if Taylor died? Or would he get so drunk he wouldn't know what had happened? That's what he'd done after the telegram about Billy. MIA in Vietnam. Still MIA, and the war over and forgotten.

Taylor was certain of one thing. Now he wouldn't stop until he found out what happened to John Mortelli. And why. The more a victim was alone in the world, the more Taylor wanted to tell their story. That was the legacy of his brother's loss. That and the way he missed Billy. The gloom was always somewhere in the back of his mind, shifting around, roaring forward at moments like this.

He had more to ask. Was Mortelli really the gentle young man who would need to be coerced to take up a gun and mug a woman?

But here was another problem with grave digging. He'd confirmed the victim's identity, which would make a good follow-up story, but he wouldn't be able to ask any more questions today. He had to leave the family in peace.

WHEN TAYLOR GOT to the newsroom, he found three guys in sports. One was working on the Jets' loss to Buffalo at Shea. Most of those cops at Kathy Dodd's house weren't going to be happy. The weekend editor was at the city desk.

Taylor called the Ninth Precinct. Trunk wasn't in. He told the detective he reached about John Mortelli. The cop went from bored to disbelief to anger when he realized Taylor was ahead of the investigators. He hung up when Taylor asked for a quote. Typical.

Taylor wrote a story profiling John Mortelli, including his gentle nature, his family in Westchester, the stray dogs, and the odd death of his own dog, Moon.

Turning in the story to the weekend editor reset the internal reporter's clock that made him more anxious the longer he went without a story in the paper. A story on Sunday was a special gift. He was all but guaranteed good play.

Again, he left the $250,000 in bonds out of the story. He'd thought about that a long time. He'd seen them and he could say he'd seen them. He had no context for them. No, it wasn't that. If you knew something, you could put it in the story, and to hell with context. Trunk's note worried Taylor. Novak's advice worried him even more. He may have ignored the financial crisis as not his beat, so not his business. But New York *was* his city. He didn't want to be the one to push the city off the cliff, at least not until he understood the reason for the push. It was a tough call. Stories almost always came first.

13

———◆———

MASON LED TAYLOR on their morning walk down City Island Avenue. This was his new routine, and he was getting to like it. He got up and moving a little earlier in the mornings. On the days after he had a few too many little beers, the walk cleared his head that much quicker. At the corner diner—the only place on the island owned by Greeks—he bought a coffee and bacon-and-egg on a hard roll to go.

Three days had passed since his story on John Mortelli had run. The *News* and the *Post* both followed with their usual zeal. The *Times* ignored it, which was pretty standard. The Gray Lady would do as she would, which usually meant writing a story when she could be all-encompassing. That was assuming a double killing in Alphabet City was something she cared about at all. The financial crisis and Ford firing his defense secretary and CIA chief had dominated the *Times* this week. The only crime story had appeared way back on Saturday, when the paper played the murder of a fifteen-year-old girl named Martha Moxley at the very bottom of page one. The killing occurred in Greenwich, Connecticut. At the *Times*, it was all about geography.

Taylor didn't care. His little scoop might actually have made Worthless happy. Not that the city editor had said anything. No, that was asking too much. But he'd stayed off Taylor's back for two full days. Might also be because Worth was so distracted. He'd been in lots of meetings with Editor-in-Chief Oscar Garfield and the other department heads. Rumors were whipping around the *MT's* newsroom at the speed rumors can travel only among journalists—close to that of light. Taylor heard them all. The paper's financial problems were deepening. Layoffs were coming. Another merger. Taylor, working his sources close to Garfield as hard as anyone, couldn't confirm any of it. The *MT* had had a lot of close calls in his 17 years. Things had really gotten scary when four other New York dailies closed in the middle of the '60s. Somehow, the Garfield family had pulled through, merging with the *New York Messenger* and bringing in the New Haven Life Insurance Company as an investor.

Were things really worse this time?

Taylor tried to look to a future where he wasn't chasing police stories for the *Messenger-Telegram*. Nothing. The emptiness of a direction never considered. His gut tightened like a hand was squeezing it. What would he do if he didn't have this job? He hadn't made any connections with editors at the other papers. He wasn't that kind of schmoozer. Cops, lawyers, and a fair number of villains. Those were his contacts.

No point in worrying about what hasn't happened. The hand squeezed tighter still. *Get the story. Then get the next one.*

The sandwich he carried was supposed to be for back at the houseboat. Now he would have to get his appetite back. In the end, that didn't turn out to be the biggest problem of the morning. He and Mason turned the corner at Reville Street onto King Avenue, which ran along the small Pelham Cemetery, City Island's only place of burial. The dead had a great view of the sound.

He'd called Samantha Callahan's place every day since

Sunday. He'd wasted last night going to her apartment in the Bronx. Sidney Greene at 1 Police Plaza was good for the phone number and address of anyone on the force. The plainclothesmen in their car had been parked halfway up the block when Taylor arrived, convincing him Samantha wasn't there and wouldn't be coming back. She really must be on the run. After the attack in Washington Square, he understood her instinct, but it wasn't doing her much good. The department had suspended her, and unnamed sources quoted in the other papers had spread the story on Tuesday that she'd abandoned her partner. Taylor hadn't received *that* call, which was galling because he wanted to know who was spreading the story. More importantly, the next story he had to break was about what really happened to Samantha during the chase. He needed her for that. He was crazy enough to also want to learn the names of the masked cops from Halloween night, though without getting clubbed or shot in the process.

The crunching of a car stopping on the gravel should have attracted Taylor's attention and brought him back to the present, but he was too busy with his story's dead ends.

A rough grip on his shoulder did get his attention. He was spun in a half circle. His coffee flew out of the cup, forming, for an instant, a creamed-coffee-colored sculpture in the air. Time sped up again and two hands pushed him hard in the chest, slamming him into the front quarter panel of the car, a shocking reminder his bruised ribs were far from healed. The blow had enough force to flip him onto the hood.

When Taylor regained his feet, Mason looked up from sniffing, and as he did with every person and thing he encountered, wagged his tail. It was the detective who'd muscled Taylor in front of Mortelli's squat. The cop extended his revolver at the dog and pulled the hammer back.

"He's wagging his tail, you fucking idiot."

The gun swung to Taylor. "You need to be more respectful. Thought I made that crystal the other day."

The gun held steady. Taylor prayed Mason wouldn't jump up to say hello. Too many trigger-happy cops in New York right now.

The car's back door opened. Detective Trunk sat there with a satisfied grin. He took a bite out of his own sandwich and got out. Grease dripped on the sidewalk. Trunk jerked his thumb. The other detective holstered the gun and got in behind the wheel. The guy clearly wasn't along for his prowess at detection.

"We each have a dog." He tore off a piece of sandwich and tossed it to Mason. "Yours is no attack dog, though. Not like mine." He nodded at the car. "I enjoyed that. The look on your face. Worth it to come out here just for that. After you ambushed me in my own precinct. You looked scared."

"Glad it was fun for you. Says something that yours doesn't know what a wagging tail means."

"He doesn't know what anything means unless I tell him. I need somebody like him. The job's gotten like that. You should know that much, at least. Some things don't fit in Dodd's killing. It bothers me." *Here come the excuses.* "But it's not my worry anymore."

"Why's that?"

Trunk pushed the last piece of his sandwich into his mouth, chewed, and swallowed. "Christian Slive with the Internal Affairs office at the Oh-Nine took over the case."

"He had the corrupt cops in the precinct worried."

Trunk shrugged. "Me, I generally try to stay away from corruption. You either get a bullet in the face or indicted."

"You came out here to tell me *that*?"

"The case isn't mine anymore, but that doesn't mean I want it handled badly. Dodd was killed in the line of duty. He deserves our best effort."

Outside Internal Affairs everyone hates Internal Affairs.

"If it's corruption we're talking about—"

"I'm not talking about corruption. Where you look is your business."

"Something I've been wondering … you know, let's say in general. The gangs of dirty cops are supposed to be all gone. The Knapp Commission finished three years ago."

"There is no *all* in my world. You turn on the light, the cockroaches scurry for cover. Eventually the light gets turned off again. People forget."

How could that be possible? There had been so much wrenching change since Knapp was set up in 1970 to investigate bad cops. Arrests, indictments, jail sentences. How was this happening at the Ninth now?

"What's the story on Callahan?"

"The shooflies are on her now. No one gets out whole. She's running from something. Are you going to interview Slive?"

"If he's handling the case—"

"I said he is."

"Then yes, I'll talk to him."

"Good. Someone needs to."

"What does that mean?"

"Means what I said. I had this case covered. I should still have the file."

"What about the briefcase? What about the bonds?"

Trunk lowered his backside to the seat and swung his belly around. "What bonds?"

"You can't make a quarter million dollars disappear."

"No, I can't. I can't do anything. Not on the case. I'm just thinking what's in the best interest of our city. You should too."

14

———◆———

TAYLOR TOOK MASON to the boat, went back and ordered a replacement coffee from the diner and sat at the counter to decide what to do next.

What is in the best interest of the city?

His work had never floated at such airy heights. *Report the story. Write the story.* The more people knew about the crime around them, the better off they were. They could take precautions. They could demand better policing. He'd never ignored a crime, though Christ knew there were hundreds he hadn't covered because there wasn't the time. Felonies got ignored just because of their zip code. Older reporters talked about sitting on stories during World War II. They did that in the best interest of the country. Everyone was on the same side then. All of it went out the window with Vietnam, Watergate, and institutionalized corruption. He couldn't keep the bonds in his notebook much longer. He had to nail down the facts and get a story in the paper. If anything, Trunk's oblique warning had only spurred him on. Slive or the Ninth's commander were the folks to grill. And he would. But right now, the story on the fake radio call was most important. Since Samantha was in the wind, he figured his next stop ought to be her father, Sergeant Mick Callahan.

Later in the day, Taylor took the 6 train to the Hunter College stop and walked over to the 19th Precinct on East 67th Street between Third Avenue and Lexington, a postcard version of a police station, three stories of clean old stone, windows trimmed in blue and a flag hanging over the arched doorway. A sparkling clean firehouse was right next door. Even in the worst of times, the best neighborhoods did okay.

Callahan—short, burly, with wavy gray hair—was just coming off shift at three o'clock.

"Sure, let's talk." He signaled to the other side of the street. "Over there."

They crossed the street and walked past apartment buildings. "Samantha doesn't understand how dangerous things are," Taylor said.

"She's not the only one."

For the second time that day, a cop slammed Taylor into the side of a car.

"Goddammit," said Taylor. "This is getting old."

Callahan delivered a shot to his ribs, landing close enough to the spot where Taylor had been hit Halloween night. The pain had only just started to fade. It returned like blinding light. He couldn't help but cry out.

"Bad enough they're spreading stories about my daughter. I've got the shooflies all over me. Now you? I'm going to spread *you* all over this concrete."

"I didn't … unh …." *God it hurts.* "I didn't spread any rumors."

"You're a fucking reporter. Enough for me."

Callahan held Taylor against the car.

"Really wasn't me. The *Post* and *News* did those. Check the *MT.* Held off. "

"I'm not checking shit."

A hand fell on one of Callahan's forearms. "He's telling the truth." The hand and arm led to a figure in a bulky hooded sweatshirt, too-large blue jeans and Keds. The voice was a woman's.

Callahan turned his head while keeping Taylor pinned. "Jeez, I said not this close to the house. You know they're watching me too."

"I was careful." The woman pulled her hood back a little and the shadow underneath shifted enough to reveal Samantha Callahan's pretty face. Her right forearm was wrapped in a short cast that ended at her wrist. "What about you? This isn't being careful *at all*. Leave him alone."

The sergeant let go of Taylor grudgingly. "You're lucky. My daughter vouches for you. That's another thing makes me question her judgment."

"Thanks, Samantha." Taylor's ribs hurt with every breath.

"Let's get away from here before someone notices." Samantha started east toward Lexington Avenue. They got to the corner and turned uptown when movement back down 67th caught Taylor's eye. Two men in suits and trench coats ran straight at them from the precinct.

Taylor touched Samantha's shoulder. "Don't think that's good."

"Not for them," said her father.

"Dad, remember. Careful."

"You get away from here fast." Sergeant Callahan strode back toward the two men. "I don't get fucking chased off my patch."

The two in trench coats made to run around Mick Callahan. They didn't care about him. Unfortunately for them, Callahan did care if they got past. He bulled into the man running on the left and knocked him sprawling to the sidewalk.

Samantha took a step back down 67th, back toward her dad, and froze. The second pursuer raced past the sergeant, bearing down on Samantha and Taylor.

Callahan turned to chase the second one, but the first grabbed his ankle and brought him crashing to the cement.

"Stay the fuck out of it," the man said. "Or there's trouble for you."

Taylor pulled at Samantha's arm. "You need to get out of here."

"My dad."

"Lead them away from him, and you get away at the same time."

She looked at her father, then up Lexington, and took off north. The lunch crowd was pouring from the office buildings along Lex, turning the sidewalk into an obstacle course. This was a good thing, since their pursuers would have a hard time keeping sight of them. A bad thing, too, since Taylor had no idea if the plainclothesmen were a block behind or right on top of them. After three blocks of just barely keeping up with Samantha, he stopped at 70th to check. Every breath was a stab in the side.

Damn. Too close and gaining. We need to disappear.

He caught back up with Samantha, grabbed her hand and pulled. She yanked back as he tried to cross Lex against the light.

"No!" Taylor insisted, "got to go now."

He pulled again. They dodged between two cars—honking—sprinted behind the rear of a bus, and would have been flattened by a cab if Taylor hadn't pulled up suddenly in the middle of the avenue to let it pass. One more lane. As they raced for the curb, a blue-and-white police car skidded to a stop with its bumper inches from their legs. Inside, two patrolmen, furious.

"That won't help."

Taylor kept going, sprinting as hard as he could, his ragged breathing a shock of pain with every gasp. Samantha was out in front of him again, so he had to grunt "left" when they made Park Avenue. A block and a half later, he pushed for one last little bit of speed and signaled to her to turn into the North Building of Hunter College. He stopped for an instant to check behind them. They'd made enough distance. No one there to see them go in.

They plunged into a crowd of students and joined one current heading farther into the building. Hunter College was part of CUNY, which meant the population was as diverse as it got. Working class city kids. Punks. A few unrepentant hippies. Professors, some the most unrepentant of the hippies. Taylor and Samantha didn't stand out because no one really stood out. Taylor just wished he wasn't huffing like a steam engine. Samantha, the ex-track star, could easily have come in from sitting on a Central Park bench.

When they passed a small student lounge, Taylor turned in and headed for two seats in the corner.

He slumped into one. "Who were those guys?"

"Probably IA. IA's on the Dodd case. They're on me."

"I heard that." Her eyebrows rose. "Had a breakfast visit from Detective Trunk this morning."

"What'd he want?"

"He's off the case. He wants me to ask questions."

"What kind?"

"That's what he didn't tell me."

Taylor checked the room to see if anyone was paying attention to them—no one was—and lowered his voice anyway. "What if they weren't IA? What if those two are connected with the three from Halloween night?"

"They wouldn't do that in broad daylight in front of a precinct. I don't care how bad things have gotten in the Oh-Nine. Though, after the stories the other papers ran about me, they could be friends of Dodd." She shook her head. "Sorry. Black humor. Only kind I can come up with lately. They were official. I'm sure of it."

"Where have you been hiding out?"

"Stayed at my parents' in Woodlawn until they put a car on the house. Crashed with some friends. None of them cops. All housewives, actually. We went to Catholic school together."

"They're homing in on you. We need to confirm your story and get it out there."

"You don't believe me?" Her eyes caught fire as she switched from flight to fight in a heartbeat.

"That's not the problem." *Good way of not answering.* "We have what we call in the news business a he said/she said. You say you heard the call. Everyone else they interviewed—"

"*Claim* they interviewed."

"They all say there was no call. We need someone or something to back you up."

"Where do we get that?"

"Let's get somewhere off the radar and figure it out. You visit the Upper West Side much?"

"Never."

"Perfect place to go then. My third-or-so cousin has a place."

The Lighthouse Coffee Shop at 84th and Broadway was actually run by his *grandfather's* third cousin. Coffee shops ran deep on the Greek side of Taylor's family. The man wasn't there when they arrived, which was fine by Taylor. Disappearing was about not being seen by anyone.

He ordered a coffee. Samantha asked for tuna casserole. She hadn't eaten since breakfast and smiled around a forkful. "Almost as good as Mom's. The potato chips on top are the key."

"So why'd you decide to trust me?"

"You didn't print the lies." *I really hope we can prove they're lies.* "What's it matter, though? I'm still screwed. When Internal Affairs gets involved, they assume everybody's dirty. Slive doesn't get me, then the thugs from the precinct will. They're going to set me up or take me out."

"Is there anything you didn't tell me about the radio call?"

"Told you exactly what I heard. It was on the local channel."

"How many people would be listening?"

"The chase had just started. Could be a handful, a dozen. No way to know. It wouldn't be the whole precinct."

"No idea who was talking?"

She laughed. "Broke in without an ID. Muffled sounding too."

"If I have to, I'll interview everyone who worked in the precinct that day."

"They won't talk."

"Good. Printing a bunch of 'no comments' and assorted evasions will shake something loose."

Samantha looked impressed. "Why would you do that?"

"That's how reporting works. One interview after another. As many as it takes. It's the only way to get the facts. Which brings me to a possible why for what happened to Dodd, assuming we can figure out what actually did happen in that condemned building. Kathy Dodd told me her husband had been approached to join a group in the precinct on the take. Happened in late August."

"News to me."

"How about Dodd's mood since then?"

"Definitely more tense in the past few weeks. I asked him if I'd done something to piss him off. He said no and really clammed up after that. I started to think maybe he regretted partnering with me, even though he claimed I wasn't the problem."

"Did he *do* anything odd?"

"One thing was pretty weird. Actually, he asked me to do it. He read off a description of a woman. Wanted me to check for a missing person's report. Didn't say why. The mood he's in, I'm not asking. But this was like detective work. I went through the reports and found what looks like a match. Gave him the woman's name. That was it. He clammed up again."

"Do you have the name?"

She pulled out a cop's leather notebook. "Don't know why I'm carrying this thing around. Not like they'll listen to the facts if I ever do go in." She thumbed up pages. "Her name was Kristy Copper. Report filed October 10th by Jim Nichols of 270 East 10th Street. Her roommate. Profession listed as entertainer. Missing a week when I found the report. Nothing had been done about it yet."

"Meant nothing to you?"

"Not a thing."

"Had you heard anything about the corruption from him? Or anyone?"

"No. The boys never let me in on any of their secrets—legal or illegal." She finished her lunch and nudged her plate a few inches away. "The thing I can't stop thinking about is the money you found."

"They're bonds."

"Whatever they are. It's a shitload of dough."

"That angle's gotten a little weird."

"Just what I need."

"Actually a lot weird."

"Even better."

He told her about Trunk's note and what the detective had said that morning. "I need to find out if they're still checked into evidence. Were they ever?" Taylor shook his head. "You know I never sit on a story like this."

"That I truly believe." Samantha smiled at him. "You either talk about it or write about it or both."

"Funny."

"I kinda like. The stoic, silent types bore me. But think about it. If the shooting was set up to get the bonds, you'd never have found them. Right? They'd have been taken. It wasn't about Mortelli and his bonds."

"So Dodd was definitely the target. You believe that?"

"He said no to bribes. Dirty cops don't trust you, then usually they shoot you." Samantha stood and pulled the hood back onto her head. "Thanks for lunch."

"You're leaving now?"

"Got to keep on moving. That was too close."

"Stay. We'll figure something out."

"Can't. Already got The Sergeant in trouble. That I swore I wouldn't do."

Taylor took out a business card and added his home number

to it. "Be careful and be in touch. Let me know if you need anything. We'll need to talk again before I write this story."

She walked out of the Lighthouse. The loose bulky clothing did a depressingly good job of camouflaging her curves. More of a downer was that she left so quickly. He enjoyed talking with Samantha, in spite of the trouble chasing her. He'd like to keep doing it. Learn more about her than the details of the story he was after.

From the phone at the back of the Lighthouse, he dialed Directory Assistance and got the home number for Jim Nichols. The lead might be out of left field, but Taylor wanted to know right away if it fit in the story or was a dead end. He had time now before heading down to the Ninth.

Jim Nichols got angry fast.

"I don't fucking believe it. We just buried her last week."

"I'm very sorry, Mr. Nichols, I didn't know—"

"That's the problem. Nobody knows. Nobody knows anything. She was already dead two days when I filed the missing person's report, but the cops didn't fucking know. She'd been dead three weeks before they figured it out. They had her in the morgue and my report and it took three goddamn weeks. The whole city's going down the shitter."

"You have my deepest condolences. I didn't mean to upset you. Her name came up in connection with a different crime. The shooting of a cop in your neighborhood."

"Yeah, read about it. Why should I give a shit? The cops didn't give a shit about Kristy."

"Was there foul play?"

"Foul play?" His voice cracked. "Are you kidding? They pulled my Kristy out of the East River. She'd been strangled. They're not doing a goddamn thing about it. They won't. She won't get justice because they think she doesn't deserve it. That's the worst part. Someone she was working for did it to her."

"Where'd she work?"

"She acted in adult films. So do I. Ready to hang up?"

"Not all. You're saying she was killed by someone in the film company?"

"*For* a film—a snuff film. They were getting rougher and rougher. We knew of someone else who'd disappeared. I was more worried than she was. That was Kristy. Nothing worried her. One day she didn't come home. And no one's doing anything about it. Neither will you. I've got to go. Her parents are in from upstate. There's too much to deal with right now."

"Last question. When was her body taken out of the river?"

"October eighth."

What in hell was Dodd doing researching a missing person's report on a porn actress? One who might have died in a snuff film?

Samantha didn't know any more. She'd said that. He didn't remember a report of a strangled floater in the East River in early October. Not that it would necessarily be a story for him, but he tried to take notice of all the murders that hit the blotter. Some days there were just too many.

TAYLOR WORKED THE front of the Ninth for an hour and a half. None of the cops would talk about the chase that ended with Dodd's murder. Eventually, he made such a pain-in-the-ass of himself that he was roughly escorted off the block. That was fine. If he wasn't going to get interviews, he might as well get some theater for the story.

By seven thirty, he was back on City Island Avenue walking Mason. To his surprise, Samantha approached from the direction of the mainland bridge.

"I hope you meant what you said." Her face was serious, and there was a quaver in her voice. "I called your home number a couple of times. No answer. Knew City Island isn't that big."

"What's wrong?"

"Seems I've run out of friends. Word got round the housewife network that I was trouble. Tried to meet my dad in Pelham

Bay Park. He'd picked up a tail. This time I think it *was* the guys who want to shut me down. Weren't dressed for IA work. Just barely got away."

She bent down to scratch behind the dog's ears. Her face softened. Mason was a natural tranquilizer.

"Mortelli was taking care of Mason here."

"Cops reporter Taylor is really a soft-hearted guy who takes in strays. Does your paper know?"

"Oh, they think even worse. I get lectures for writing about the homeless too much."

"For shame."

They walked Mason to the houseboat and went to have their second meal of the day together, this time at the Sea Shore Restaurant, on the island since 1920 according to the red neon. Samantha had swordfish, while Taylor had a plate of oysters and the Captain's Platter. They both drank a lot of cheap white wine.

On the stroll back, Samantha checked out the restaurants. "Dad brought us here Sundays in nice weather. If you listened to him, you'd have thought we were driving five hundred miles, not ten minutes in the Falcon. Place doesn't change." They reached the boat. Mason bark-whined from inside. "A boat not on water. How romantic." Her eyes dropped to the gravel. "What do you really want from me?"

"You're not being treated fairly. I want to help."

"That's it, huh? What about your story?"

"There's a story in the shooting on Avenue B whatever happens. I'll admit, a better story with what you've told me." He climbed up the ladder first "You can sleep in the main cabin. There's a couch amidships I'll use."

"Listen. I may be desperate. I may be out of friends. But don't get any ideas."

"It's been a long day. I'm too tired to have ideas. Believe me."

He handed her a pair of pajamas, took four Rolling Rocks out of the half-sized fridge and pulled the cabin door shut.

He went up on the roof deck, which had the only real view of the water, and sat down on a beach chair he'd picked up at the Ben Franklin. Mason, who couldn't climb the steep stairway, whined at the bottom. He was going to keep Samantha awake.

"Damn." He carried the dog up, despite his sore ribs, almost losing his balance. "I'm going to have to rig a hoist for you." Mason circled and lay down.

A bottle of beer later, Samantha climbed the stairway. She'd put the sweatshirt back on. The pajama bottoms showed off the lovely shape of her rear better than the baggy jeans. The air was still oddly warm, more of the late Indian summer fluke. Taylor figured that meant that any day, winter would descend and not let go until March. He opened the other beach chair, which gave a loud, complaining squeal. He went downstairs and found a bottle of white wine he'd bought for Laura. The last one he'd bought. His selection of glasses was poor. He filled a plastic tumbler and returned.

They drank in silence. Taylor considered putting on music, but thought of Samantha's warning about getting ideas. Music would probably give him an idea. For that matter, so would her rear end. He wondered about her legs, the legs of a former track star. His head was suddenly full of ideas.

Taylor watched the water. Samantha leaned back and stared at the sky. They had talked themselves out. His head was pretty fuzzy from the wine at dinner plus the beers now. He was too tired to think about who or what he needed to follow up on. Bonds. Lying cops. Christian Slive in Internal Affairs. The phantom radio call. He couldn't put them in an order that made sense. He closed his eyes.

Taylor started, awake again. Samantha was standing above him, her glass empty. Mason looked up. She patted the dog's head.

"Taylor, the reporter who takes in strays." She bent down and he thought she was going to pat him on the head too.

Instead, she kissed his cheek. "Thanks for the help. Not sure what it's going to get you."

"We'll figure out a plan tomorrow."

She disappeared down the ladder. Now fully awake, he wished he had another beer. He was too tired to go to a bar on the avenue. He wanted to play "Born to Run," but that would wake Samantha. Going to bed made the most sense. He fell asleep quickly on the couch, but not before he and Mason almost got killed. With the strong buzz messing up his balance, he brought the dog back down the steep stairway and slipped, only to catch the handrail at the last moment.

15

———◆———

TAYLOR LEANED IN close to Novak at his desk. "Have you said anything to *anyone* about the bonds?"

"All's quiet here. I think *that* debt is the least of your worries right now. The least of any of our worries."

What Taylor didn't need right now were additional worries. He'd somehow convinced Samantha to stay at the houseboat today. He was worried—no, not worried, panicked—that if she went on the lam again, the cops or the villains—who also happened to be cops—would get her. Still, he wasn't sure she'd keep her word and stay out on City Island.

Taylor couldn't help asking, "What's going on?"

"My boss was called in really early. All the editors were. They've been meeting ever since."

"That's been going on all week. You hear anything solid?"

"No, just something big. Today."

"Heard that before too."

Novak's face was relaxed as always. Nothing flustered him.

"Let me know if anything comes your way."

Novak rolled a sheet of typescript into his Selectric. "I think we're all going to hear at once. We're not going to like it either."

"You're not helping."

"Must keep my nose to the grindstone." He picked up a press release. "Exciting soap news from Proctor and Gamble."

"Don't know how you do it."

When he'd come through the cluttered newsroom—a floor that once held insurance salesmen—only about half the staff was in at 9:45 a.m. No surprise there. Reporters and editors on a morning paper worked late into the evening and so started late in the morning.

A big announcement really was the very last thing he needed. He already knew he wasn't in any way prepared to look for a job, knew it so well that he'd actively tried not to think about it. For Taylor, the best-case scenario—*not* getting laid off—wasn't even appealing. A merger or reorganization would be followed by weeks or months of confusion. Editors would fight turf wars while stories got missed. He'd been through that before. Nothing was more frustrating than having news he couldn't get in the paper. After the previous merger, he'd approached newsstands with fear, expecting every time he'd see the story that was stuck in his notebook on another paper's front page. He'd lost a great one on a Westside drug ring when the *Messenger* and *Telegram* were slammed together.

Taylor wove around chairs, bookshelves, false partitions, desks, and low walls made out of file cabinets. Those at desks who caught his eye had the same anxious waiting look. Too many of them had watched New York newspapers sink to put on a journalist's cynical pose. On purpose, Taylor for once circled back past the city desk. Only a copyboy sat there fielding calls. He looked clueless rather than worried.

The long orbit brought Taylor to his desk. He flipped through the three other papers, found nothing that embarrassed him, and better, nothing at all on Dodd or Mortelli. Mayor Beame blamed Ford for the city's difficulties. It was nowhere near as good as Carey's speech. The mayor had been forced to the margins, yelling at Ford and Carey and all the other players with the real power.

There was a little good news for the city in the *Times*. New Jersey's governor said his state faced a crisis because bond issues were defeated at the ballot on Tuesday. This was good, Taylor figured, because New York was no longer alone in the bailout boat. In fact, the *Times* said most bond issues had gone down in the elections across the U.S. Voters were reacting to the crisis in NYC.

Maybe that'll get Washington off its ass.

He killed 30 minutes with the papers, including looking over stories in the *MT* he already knew about. The editors remained in their meeting. His phone rang, and he answered. The caller had a high-pitched male voice with a strong New York accent, like deepest Brooklyn, or maybe even the oddly stretched strains of Staten Island.

"You were at the station asking about the radio call Callahan heard."

"No one wants to talk."

Here it comes. Some officer from the Ninth reaming me out for questioning his cops.

"I do."

Taylor, who was slouched back in his desk chair, sat up so fast its springs gave a loud complaining squeak. He flipped open his notebook. "You work at the Oh-Nine?"

"I heard the call."

"Got a name?"

"I'm a cop and that's all you're going to get."

" 'Anonymous *maybe* cop says call no one heard actually went out.' Not going to help me much."

"You're work's not my problem. Now you know the truth."

Keep him on. Get as much as you can.

"Why tell me?"

"I liked Dodd. He was a solid cop. What's happening to Callahan isn't right. Not sure I like having *them* on the force, but no cop should get put in a frame. There's a right way to do the job. But the dirt's getting back in. Too many have their hands out."

"There are a lot of officers in the precinct. How come you're the only one talking?"

"Weren't a lot on the local channel to hear it. Don't know for sure how many. Already told you about the dirt. Maybe some others just don't like having Callahans around the shop."

He hung up.

Damn.

Taylor couldn't use the interview in a story, but he could use it to jimmy out some more information. He didn't hesitate. He flipped to a clean sheet in the reporter's notebook, dialed the Ninth Precinct and asked for Detective Slive. To Taylor's surprise, Slive took the call.

"This is going to be quick." Slive's voice was the opposite of the anonymous caller, smooth and deep, cultured even. "I'm not investigating this in your paper. That's already done enough damage. We've got an officer down. We've got another officer up on charges and on the run. I'll talk at length when I've concluded my investigation."

"Just talked to a source who heard the same radio call as Officer Callahan."

"Got a name?" Slive didn't sound fazed.

"I don't reveal sources."

"Then you've got *nothing.*"

"You're going to ignore a legitimate claim about the call."

"It's not legitimate unless someone comes forward to talk. If they don't, then it's the same cowardice that led to this tragedy. Dodd was murdered while pursuing a dangerous suspect. The rest is ass covering."

"Mortelli dangerous? Have you interviewed anyone about him? Did Trunk?"

"We're done."

He knew he shouldn't, but Taylor couldn't help himself. "What about the bonds?"

Slive didn't miss a beat. "Don't know what you're talking about."

Too fast. He answered too fast. I didn't give him enough for a denial.

"Really? The two hundred fifty thousand in New York City bonds recovered behind Mortelli's flat. Now, it seems, gone missing in your precinct. That's an internal affair if there ever was one."

"Fiction won't do in the newspaper. Have a nice day."

That's what I needed. Taylor had watched the briefcase go into police custody. Slive's denial had to be enough to say the securities had disappeared while in police custody. *He's IA after all. Who better to know? That's a story.*

He stood up as soon as he set the receiver on the hook. He'd held off too long, but now he needed to talk to Worthless about the briefcase. That the city editor would throw Taylor under a subway train at the first hint of real trouble with a story never made him confident. But he had to get this in the paper and that wouldn't happen without Worth's backing. As he approached the city desk, the door to the page one conference room opened. Worth was first out.

"Need to talk to you about the Dodd shooting." Garfield was right behind Worth. "If you and Mr. Garfield could just give me some time—"

"There is no more time, you idiot." Worth pushed past.

The editors went to their various sections and came back trailing their reporters. Everyone—three quarters of the newsroom was in now—crowded around the city desk and clogged the aisles leading to Garfield's office, which had been built right in the center of the newsroom next to the city and national desks. Garfield climbed on Worth's shiny maple desktop.

"I'm afraid the news is very bad. The paper is closing."

The collective intake of breath sounded like the whole crowd had been hit in the stomach. Several moans.

"Shit, knew it."

"Oh god, no."

"This is the saddest day of my life. For my family. As you all know, the paper goes back one hundred eighteen years to the *New York Telegram*'s founding by Cyrus Garfield. We have tried to weather very difficult times in our economy, our city, and our industry." Garfield could barely project his voice. He sounded exhausted, like a man who'd been up for nights. He probably had been. People pressed in to hear. "I could not have asked more of all of you. When the *World Journal Tribune* folded eight years ago, I really thought we had a chance to be one of the survivors. We couldn't find a buyer. There was some interest from Australia, but that faded. My family's resources are exhausted. The New Haven Life Insurance Company will not provide any more cash. They have a substantial holding in New York City bonds and are worried about their own survival.

"We must close up shop today. We bargained, fought, even begged to the bitter end, and this is that bitter end. You'll all get two week's pay. I'm sorry; that's it."

Garfield looked around at the faces below him, lowered his head, and got off the desk.

This being a crowd of journalists, many had questions. People pushed toward Garfield's office. Taylor turned and moved against the surge. There wasn't an answer Garfield could give that would help.

Crossing back to his desk, Taylor felt numb. The *MT* was family. It had taken him in, taught him the job he loved, and become his home when he lost his mother, then his brother Billy. He hadn't felt this hollow since receiving the telegram informing them that Billy was missing in action. Some others figured out what Taylor already knew and returned to their desks, shaking their heads, frowning. Two reporters were crying.

The presses wouldn't even run tonight. The *Messenger-Telegram* would go out with a whimper, not a bang.

Taylor went to another floor to get a cardboard box for

his two Rolodexes and the notebooks containing stories he was working. He'd thought people might hang around and reminisce about the paper. He was wrong. The newsroom cleared quickly. As Taylor left with his small box, Worthless was still cleaning out his desk.

People did want to reminisce, it turned out; they just wanted to do it while drowning those memories in booze. The paper was waked at Keen's Chop House on 36th Street. The bar-restaurant, one of the oldest in New York, had been a favorite of the staff from the time the *MT's* offices were in a garment factory building on Seventh Avenue.

Reporters and editors filled the bar and spilled into the saloon, where Taylor stood with his second beer. Above him, hundreds of clay churchwarden pipes lined the ceiling, as they did throughout the dining rooms of Keen's, one sign how far back the place went. Taylor wondered if ancient Cyrus Garfield had dined here. Had kept his pipe here. How long did *he* hope his paper would last?

Probably forever. Publishers are never short for ego.

He found he couldn't drink as fast as the others. Some were already pounding shots. A lot of beer *might* help with the emptiness inside. Fill the hole with Rolling Rock. He imagined the ugliness of waking up with a hangover *and* no job. Something more than that held him back. Two women from the features desk and a sportswriter were already so sloppy they were hanging on to one another. He didn't want to go out that way. That was his dad's way. Samantha was still back at the boat. He hoped. He wasn't showing up there trashed.

How am I going to tell her I've got nowhere to run the story?

Novak, a whisky on the rocks in hand, smiled into Taylor's face. "Journalists have fun at the worst times."

"Occupational hazard. What are you grinning about?"

"Not here. What are you doing tomorrow?"

The question was ridiculous but he gave it a serious answer. "Working on the story, I guess. Don't know what else to do."

"That's Taylor. Always on the story. How about sometime in the afternoon at your grandfather's place?"

"Sure. Two o'clock."

They both watched more people arrive, including journalists from the other papers as it got toward lunchtime. The wake of a newspaper was a big deal in the business and always a well-attended affair. The guild of scribblers never wanted to see a title go under, but knew the importance of properly drinking it into the grave. The newcomers bought drinks for the *Messenger-Telegram* staffers. After a while, a few ended up in quiet conversations in one corner of the saloon. Faces were serious. The *MT* people were the ones who anyone would consider the stars of the dead paper.

Before walking off, Novak nodded in that direction. "Looks like a job fair. See you tomorrow."

Taylor went up to the bar, already rethinking his desire to stay on this side of sober. Tom Sabatini, an older reporter from the huge cop shop at the *Daily News*, stepped up next to Taylor.

"Really sorry." Sabatini signaled to the bartender. "I got that."

"Thanks."

Sabatini also studied the impromptu meetings in the corner. "It's like they're pawing over the body."

"Don't blame people for trying to land a job. Things are bad."

A silence opened between them, filled with the question Taylor couldn't bring himself to ask.

"Listen Taylor, if things weren't what they are, I'd go to the boss ...." He trailed off.

"I know. I get it."

Sabatini polished off his martini. "You probably already know. You've got a rep, man. A loose cannon. Great stories, you know. But editors are such control freaks."

"Aren't they always?"

New plan. Time to start drinking seriously.

Before he could order, Laura Wheeler walked in the door. Here was a way his day could go badly that he hadn't even anticipated. She looked down the bar with dark brown eyes. Black hair. Beautiful. Her eyes found his.

Shit.

She came straight over. "I'm so sorry."

"Yeah, thanks. You made the right move. Clearly. Where's Derek?"

"On assignment in Israel."

"I see." *Sounds so much better than on assignment in Queens.* "Can I get you something? Glass of wine?"

"Shouldn't I buy?"

She should because she still had a job, but he ignored the question because she also still had a piece of his heart. Taylor ordered Laura the red wine she liked. He backed up his beer, looking longingly at the bottles of whisky, each a rule ready to be broken.

Laura lifted her glass. "You still get the best scoops. The ones no one else knows what to do with. I'm going to talk to one of my editors."

"How *many* do you have?"

"Lots. My paper has lots of editors." She didn't exactly sound pleased with this.

"*The Times* is never going to hire me."

"Why not? You're the best. Give the place a shot."

"I don't have the degree they want. I don't write the stories they want. A dead teenager in Greenwich?"

"Think what you'd do with that."

"Run away screaming. If I'm the best, why Derek?"

Laura blinked twice at the change in subject. "I don't want to go into that here. We talked."

"Let's talk more."

"Today's bad enough. Don't."

Bad enough for me. It was the snappy comeback he couldn't make himself say. There must be another one. He just couldn't think of it with the paper closing and the beers and Samantha back at the boat. He couldn't think of anything nasty to hurl at her. Asking about Derek was the best, or worst, he could do. He wasn't the type. He liked her too much. Still. He was saved from the stretching silence by two *MT* staffers who came over to talk to Laura. She'd been popular in the newsroom, far more than he was. Which, for Taylor, only served to remind him the newsroom was gone forever.

He left his half finished beer on the bar.

TAYLOR CLIMBED THE ladder to the top deck of the houseboat with a case of Rolling Rock, full-sized bottles.

Samantha sat on one of the beach chairs with a half empty bottle of wine next to her. "Having a party?" she asked. She had on her baggy jeans and his sweater.

Mason gave Taylor his traditional tail wagging, circling welcome. "How you'd get him up here?"

"A bit dicey. Had to do something after half an hour of crying. Oh, and the old guy who walks him was pissed off. Said he should get word ahead of time if he's not needed."

"Great."

"Why all the beer?"

"An Irish wake."

The pretty smile faded from Samantha's face as he settled into the second chair, scratched Mason's head, and opened a beer.

"Who died?"

"*The Messenger-Telegram.* Yesterday was the final edition."

"I'm so sorry. You've worked there a while, right?" She filled her glass.

He waited for her to ask about the story that was supposed to help her out of one serious, life-threatening jam. Instead, she did the very generous thing and didn't say a thing about her own problems. She drank her wine and waited for him to talk.

Through three beers, he told of his arrival at seventeen, time spent as a copy boy, the move up to reporter and then how he landed the job covering the police beat, the only job he ever wanted to do. Taylor wasn't the type to brag. He let his stories do the talking. However, she was a willing listener, and as it was a night of endings, he told her about a couple of the scoops that made his name. The corrupt vice squad in Harlem and the murder of the McNally teen back in March.

"Not sure what I'm going to do now."

She put her hand on his arm and leaned toward him. "You've got a dead paper. I've got a dead career. We're a matched set."

He closed the rest of the distance and kissed her. Her mouth was sweet from cheap white wine. She pushed her hand through his hair. They stood because they couldn't get any closer in the beach chairs. They kissed as a three-quarter moon lit the deck and the Long Island Sound. Taylor reached his hand down and grabbed her rear, pushing her hips toward him. She let out something between a sigh and a moan.

They necked. He ached for more of her. "There's no romantic way to get down these steps."

She laughed. "No there isn't."

"Plus I've got to get this idiot down."

She laughed again. "Shall we meet downstairs in the bedroom? But Mason stays—what'd you call it?—amidships."

"Definitely."

Samantha disappeared down the stairway. Taylor considered the implications of leaving Mason up here. Really annoying whining. Or taking him down after having consumed six beers. Possible drop to the blacktop. He'd risk that rather than the noise.

As he entered the cabin, Samantha dropped her bra to the floor and slid into the bed. He undressed and joined her. They kissed again. He reached down to slide off her panties and found frills and lace.

"This hardly seems regulation."

"I'll show you regulation."

She rolled on top and kissed his lips, chest, nipples, then slid herself down onto him. They made love like two people with nothing to lose.

They lay together entwined, their breathing still coming quickly. Taylor volunteered to go upstairs and retrieve the booze.

After he got back, Samantha lay on top of him—the bunk wasn't much more than a single—resting, occasionally rising on one elbow to sip her wine.

She finished her glass. Taylor set down a beer unfinished for the second time that night. It was a strange evening indeed. They made love again.

16

———◆———

THE *DAILY NEWS* had the best headline. Of course. It wasn't the masterpiece of eight days ago, but it was still pretty good.

THE MT
IS EMPTY

The subhead gave the details. "Insurance Co. Gives Up on Daily; CEO Cites Concern Over City Bonds." Taylor would have to wait for the *Village Voice* to read the blow-by-blow on the behind-scenes efforts to save—in the end, actually kill—the *MT*. The *Voice* was the only paper in town that covered what really happened at the other papers. For Taylor, that was the only reason to read it. The hippy-dippy stuff was getting old.

His hangover glowered out at the world from behind his eyeballs as he sat in a booth at the Oddity. He hadn't been able to sleep after Samantha dozed off. Back on the top deck, he'd put away another six. He'd woken up in the beach chair, shivering, with empty bottles around him and the sky still dark. So much for his self control at Keen's. He'd gone downstairs and fallen onto the couch and into blackness until Samantha woke him around ten. She'd laughed darkly and declared them both train wrecks.

Samantha was across from him now. Grandpop refused to let Taylor sit at the counter when he had a guest in the place. He hated that. It made him a customer, which he certainly wasn't. He'd worked in the Oddity from the eighth grade on, first for the fun of it, then for the badly needed cash money of it. He'd probably be working here again in two weeks when the money ran out. The one nice thing about a booth was that Grandpop could only hover so much. As surrogate father and only surviving grandparent, he took it on himself to worry about Taylor's romantic future, all the more so since he'd convinced himself Laura Wheeler *was the one*. Laura was gone. Now, the *Messenger-Telegram* was gone. The old man took that personally, very personally. He acted more upset than Taylor.

"They close the paper that my grandson works at?" The rhetorical question came in his heavily accented English.

Taylor answered anyway. "I don't think my working there had anything to do with it one way or the other."

"What do you mean? Best reporter in all of the city. Best cops reporter in all of New York." Grandpop stood at the booth with the round glass coffee pot. He wore his work uniform of white apron over T-shirt and dungaree overalls.

Samantha smiled at this as she ate her hash and eggs. They'd both ordered greasy breakfasts as a hangover cure. She was a woman after his own heart. He knew from long experience the food would cut the hangover's symptoms, but the effect would be temporary. The headache and stomach flips would come roaring back, worse than ever. The only real cure was sleep. That or hair of the dog, maybe after he met with Henry Novak. What else did he have to do today? There was also the problem that hair of the dog was number five on his list of rules, right behind don't drink your breakfast. How much did the rules matter now?

"The end of the *Messenger-Telegram* was a bit more complex than that."

Grandpop slapped the *Daily News*. "They dare to call it *Empty*. I offer no papers in The Odysseus. Nothing replaces the *Messenger-Telegram* until your new job." He topped off their coffee cups.

"Suit yourself." Taylor poured in lots of half and half and added two packets of sugar.

"I go on too much. I will let you sit with your nice friend." Grandpop's concern for Taylor's love life trumped his concern for Taylor's career. "Please let me know if you and the miss would like anything."

He wanted an introduction. This time, Taylor had to be rude. Samantha was still on the run, and there were a lot of ears in the Oddity—cabbies, truck drivers, even cops who worked the Upper Eastside, maybe some from her father's precinct.

After his grandfather gave him one last concerned glance and left, Samantha leaned in. "He reminds me of my dad. The way he worries. How am I ever going to survive on the job? Will I ever meet someone?" She sipped her coffee. "Guess we know the answer to the first."

"We don't know any answers yet. That's what we're missing."

"What are you going to do with those answers?" She looked meaningfully at the *Daily News*. "Or don't you read the papers?"

"I'll freelance it. I get a story on Dodd's killing that no one else has and someone will buy it. Believe me."

"How about you write it for me?" Henry Novak stood at the booth. "May I?" Without waiting for an answer, he pulled a chair over from one of the tables and straddled it.

"You're working already?" Taylor didn't mean to sound surprised, but he was.

"I am. I've got a job for you too. Don't know about your friend."

"She's set. Where?"

Henry looked at Samantha, realized there was no point in

asking anything more and took a piece of bacon from Taylor's plate. "I'm starting a local wire service. The City News Bureau. Very small at first. I've already lined up four radio stations as clients. They want fresh stories, stories they're not getting from the AP, which as you know, come from the newspapers anyway. They're tired of hand-me-downs."

"You're starting ...." Taylor was now pretty much stupefied. "When did you do this? Last night at the wake?"

"No, of course not. You know I go to all those meetings of business leaders." Taylor nodded. "Met several station managers. They started complaining about their news coverage, and I started thinking." Taylor continued to look at Novak in amazement, and Novak read the look. "I know, I know. I didn't really put much effort into interviewing and writing. Any of the work at the *MT.* Too damned boring. What I learned I like is cutting deals. I goddamn love selling people on an idea. Best thing is, I know people like you who will do the stories better than I ever could. Started working on it about three months ago. The writing was on the wall at the *MT.* We'll get more stations. Most of them don't have reporters. With scoops like the ones you get, like the one about the briefcase—"

Taylor hissed, "I told you not to say anything."

"Calm down, man. I haven't. When our radio clients get a story like that—money and corruption, not in any of the papers—they're going to eat it up."

"How are you paying for this City News Bureau?"

"My dad. He's got money. You know that. Small pharmaceutical company in Jersey. In his immortal words, 'This is real business. Better than that bullshit you've been wasting your time on.' Say yes. It's a paycheck and someone's going to run your stories."

"Reading them between Top 40 songs."

"Just come over to the office and talk about it. The Paramount Building, 1501 Broadway."

"Times Square? You're not squandering the old man's money."

"Right in the middle of the city's top crime district. Perfect for you, no?" Novak stood up. "I'm only talking to five other people. A couple others from cops, a GA guy and a rewrite man. Like I said, small."

"I'll think about it."

What else is there?

"You'll come through, Taylor. You always do. Worth never got that. I hear he's begging for a nightshift over at the *Post.* See ya."

Taylor shook his head. He'd have bet any money nothing would top yesterday's surprises. Henry Novak becoming a businessman and offering Taylor a job did just that. His whole world had been turned upside down. How could he get excited about this offer, though? He might want a paycheck, but what a huge step down! His stories read out on a handful of radio stations rather than a byline in the *Messenger-Telegram.*

I'm a beggar. Can't be a chooser. Least it's a step up from freelancing.

Samantha, who'd stayed quiet during Novak's pitch, shook her head slowly. "I guess *you* do have a job."

"We'll see. Whether I do or don't, we've a story to get."

"We?"

"You got anything better to do?"

"Only avoid arrest and death."

"We still need to figure out what's going on in the Oh-Nine."

"That doesn't sound like a great way to avoid arrest and death." She took in a breath. There was no humor in her voice. "Listen, I need to know something now. What happens if you have to choose between the story and me?"

"You."

He'd said it without hesitation—a surprise in itself. In the past, he'd have had to think about it or hemmed and hawed or maybe even picked the story and lost the woman. But the Garfields and the New Haven Life Insurance Company hadn't picked him.

"Why? Doesn't seem like the right choice for a top reporter."

"And look where that's gotten me."

There was something else, something talking to Laura last night made him realize. Samantha was like him in a lot of respects. They had more in common. She'd grown up in one of the boroughs and come up the hard way. Harder even than Taylor, he had to admit. She'd overcome so much to get through the academy and make it on to the force. He was enthralled by the doubled bravery of working a dangerous job for a department that didn't want her. The only thing he and Laura had in common was a dead newspaper. Sources. Stories. Worthless. Those were the things they'd had to talk about. He and Samantha had each fought harder, for more, and so maybe had more to share.

He sipped his coffee. *A bit of Irish whisky would be so nice in this.* "Without getting arrested and killed, is there someone there you know we can interview? Someone who will talk without bringing Slive down on you?"

She lowered her own cup and looked at her reflection in the black liquid. A small smile turned up the corners of her mouth. "Donald Priscotti asked me out a bunch of times. He might be desperate enough to meet me for a drink and not tell anyone."

"How desperate?"

"Lives with his mom. Hasn't had a date in years, if ever. Desperate. He's the clerk in the precinct on the dayside."

"Sounds promising."

"Promising that I have to go on a date with a desperate guy?"

"No, that he's the clerk. He sees and hears everything. And it's an interview, not a date."

"We'll see what he thinks it is. It'll have to be me alone. I'll tell him I'm trying to clear my name."

"I watch from somewhere in the place. With bad cops involved, you need a witness." Interviews were supposed to be on the up and up, no made-up stories, no undercover stuff. The *MT* was gone. People were trying to get Samantha. The precinct had dirty cops and two people were dead. *I need to break the rules just to get by.* "I've got a source from the Knapp Commission indictments. He's a cop hunter and knows all the other cop hunters. I'm going to ask him about what's going on."

"Cop hunter. Pleasant term."

"I'm afraid that's what we're doing now. Slive said he wants to close the case fast. With the conclusions he's already come to, it'll get a lot harder for us to figure out what really went down. The judicial process flattens everything. People shut up."

Samantha took two minutes to arrange drinks with Priscotti at a nondescript place, Freddie's Grill and Saloon, on East 43rd near Grand Central. Taylor planned to get there a half hour ahead of time.

PRISCOTTI WAS A fat man, fat beyond the stereotype of the overweight cop, his uniform stretched tight across his gut, his back and all sorts of other places. His chubby face lit up like he'd spied an all-you-can-buffet as he approached Samantha. She smiled back. The smile was fake. Taylor had known her long enough to be sure of that. So was the laugh that followed. Priscotti ordered whiskey. She ordered wine. Taylor was too far way to make out what was being said but could tell things were going well. This bothered him.

Stupid to be jealous. She's playing him.

He forced himself not to stare. He gave the room the occasional look round to check for possible cops and then went back to reading the papers. *The Times*, of course, wrote the longest obituary for the *New York Messenger-Telegram*. Column inches and inches on the Garfield family, going back more than a century. The two other dailies did well enough by the *MT*. Journalists knew how to bury their dead.

He chanced a look. Samantha and Priscotti were leaning in close, their faces very serious. Now Samantha's intensity didn't appear feigned. Priscotti slid his big ass off the stool and threw cash on the bar. Samantha got up and followed him to the door.

Shit, that's not part of the plan.

Samantha didn't give him a look.

Now what? Shouldn't follow or I'll blow it. Whatever it *is.*

He got up.

Too dangerous not to.

The yellow cab pulled away from the curb as he reached the sidewalk. He sure as hell hoped Samantha knew what she was doing.

Taylor's meeting with Jersey Stein was set for nine o'clock. He'd planned it so Samantha could trade roles and be the watcher. There was nothing to do but go see the investigator from the Manhattan DA's office. This was going to be tough. In an interview, there were so many things to pay attention to. Question. Answer. Follow-up. Hint. Mistake. Sign of a lie. Everything that lived between the lines. How was he supposed to concentrate when he didn't know what was going on with Samantha and an officer from the precinct where just about every cop wanted a piece of her?

17

———◆———

"SURPRISED YOU MET ME SO QUICKLY."

Stein finished his glass of Royal Crown Cola. It was said he never drank booze. "Your paper's dead, right?"

"Killed before we could put out a last edition."

"Then you can't do me any damage."

"You're a sentimental man."

He was the opposite, in fact. As well as being a teetotaler, Stein pursued corrupt cops with a single-minded zeal. That was still a dangerous business, even with the revelations of the past five years.

"Sentiment will get you killed. You've always operated under the romantic misapprehension your stories bring about some kind of justice. Justice comes with a conviction."

"A few of mine helped."

"Helped, hurt. Who knows? What is it you want?"

"I'm working on the cop killing in Alphabet City."

"Are you now? *Who* would you be doing that for?"

Stein signaled for another RC. Here was the time for Taylor to keep things under control. Keep off the booze. Stay focused. The hangover headache pounded against his forehead. He ordered a Bloody Mary, extra spicy. Stein's face, with its prominent cheekbones and clear hazel eyes, remained impassive. How to answer Stein's question? Desperation was a sour tang on his tongue. The drink wouldn't help with that. *Haven't said yes to Novak yet. No sense muddying the waters here.*

"Maybe I'll freelance it. A guy's gotta eat."

"Probably shouldn't have met you so quickly then." He shook his head ruefully. "All this is off the record."

"With you, it's always off the record."

"That's right. Quotes are for guys running for office. Or idiots trying to get knocked on the head."

"The Dodd shooting is pretty messy," Taylor said.

"That's a broad generalization."

"Is the mugger's gun still missing?"

Stein nodded. "So I hear. A little odd that is."

"You're not helping much."

"Ask me something smart, and maybe I will."

Taylor sipped vodka, tomato juice and horseradish through the thin plastic straw. The unpleasant grinding of the hangover slowly began its transformation into a comfortable little buzz. He thought through everything he knew. Some things—the briefcase, the threat on Halloween—he wasn't ready to give to the DA's office.

He was distracted. Why had Samantha left without a signal? What if he had her all wrong? *Maybe she's playing* me. The ache from the end of the *MT*, behind all his other worries. When would that go away?

Focus, dammit. Looking into a Seagram's Seven mirror, he remembered the crime scene.

"Dodd was shot in the face. Mortelli caught one in the leg and one in the chest. Must have knocked him down. May have killed him instantly. How does that play out as a gunfight?"

"See, I knew you could get to specifics." Stein reached into both outside pockets of his green suit jacket. He pulled out the little three-inch spiral notebooks he always carried. There were six—no, seven—on the table. Stein sorted through them, looking at their bright-colored covers. He picked up one that was Halloween orange and flipped its pages. "Dodd still might have shot first. Mortelli points the gun at him and Dodd fires, catches him in the chest, and Mortelli fires back before falling."

"Yeah, I know that's a possibility. Do you believe it happened that way?"

"No. More importantly the ME's office doesn't. John Mortelli died instantly. Shot through the heart. They both hit the ground corpses."

"Will they confirm?" Taylor asked.

"That's your job."

"What have you heard about Officer Callahan?"

Stein leafed through the little pages some more. "The gal who was his partner? Somehow got lost when it went O.K. Corral for Dodd."

"She got a radio call sending her the wrong way."

"A call no one else heard."

"I've got an officer who says he did."

Stein's thin black eyebrows moved up. "Name?"

"Anonymous tip."

"Anonymous, shit-on-i-mous. What the hell can I do with that? Nothing."

"We're trying to confirm it with another officer."

"Who's we?"

"People have to work. I've got help."

"Really? Be careful. Callahan's a fugitive, you know."

"Everyone keeps telling me to be careful. This isn't a business for caution. You should know that. How come you've got one of your notebooks going on this case?"

"One never knows when the District Attorney for the County of New York will seek justice."

"My source on the radio call said …" Now it was Taylor's turn to flip pages covered with the scrawled stutter-step attempt to solve a crime. " 'There's a right way to do the job. But the dirt's getting back in. Too many have their hands out.' What's going on in the Oh-Nine?"

Stein put his hand over Taylor's notebook. "You and I never met, right?"

"Sure, whatever you say."

"There *is* a gang operating out of the precinct. As far as we can tell, they're just grass eaters taking nickel and dime bribes to look the other way on street-level stuff. Uniformed officers, it appears. Plainclothes and detectives may be clean."

"How many?"

"Haven't nailed that down yet."

"Dodd wouldn't join. Is that why he's dead?"

"Think that through. If the two shootings *are* more than they seem, then your theory is a bunch of low-level grass eaters murdered a fellow cop. The result? More heat on them. If it is a setup, it's awfully sophisticated for this group. They're not the brightest of lights. Maybe this is about something else—assuming someone can prove the whole thing was staged to kill Dodd."

"Like what?"

"That's our sixty-four-thousand-dollar question. How do you know Dodd wouldn't join the pad?"

"His wife told me."

Stein chuckled as he wrote with a golf pencil. "They always make that mistake. They never talk to the wives. Expect them to stay in the kitchen and cry. Sometimes they know the whole story. Or a neat little piece of it."

"Why is Trunk out and Slive from IA in, if it's not about the dirty cops?"

"I don't know."

"Ah c'mon. You must."

"I mean it. I know Slive. He's the son of some deputy chief or assistant deputy chief. That's important by itself. He went in and cleaned out three precincts after Knapp. I mean went through like a storm. That's just as important as who his father is in these days of clean hands. Your shit-on-i-mous source got one thing right. The dirt always gets back in."

"Why aren't you coming down on the gang in the Ninth? Just because they're small time? Not like you."

"Waiting for it to play out. Not the time yet to turn on the lights. We will."

A black man in a blue suit stopped behind Taylor and Stein's barstools. He was tall and broad and could pass for a Jets linebacker. *Check that*, Taylor thought, *not with the way the Jets are playing*. More like the Steelers. He knew James Brent as Stein's partner at the DA's office for the past two years. He'd joined after working for the FBI doing difficult, dangerous and maybe even crazy work down south, where Taylor figured everything was crazy anyway.

Stein slipped off the stool, lithe for his fifty-plus years. The many colored notebooks disappeared into pockets.

Taylor swung around on the stool to Stein's partner. "I'm still looking to do that feature on your time with the bureau."

"And I'm still not talking to reporters. Stories don't help investigators."

Stein tapped Taylor lightly on the shoulder. "You see. James is a very smart man. He knows to avoid journalists. *Just* like I do. Now we've got to go talk to some politicians who never *ever* take bribes. Given the city's finances, we're pretty sure that's the only place they could be getting the money. Call again if you stay out of work." He shook his head and repeated Brent's words. "You're a smart man. Too goddamn brave for your own good, but smart at least."

"I'm not the one who tells cops how many years he's going to put them away for," said Brent.

"Like to set their expectations."

They were gone.

Taylor sucked every drop of Bloody Mary from around the ice cubes. He used the men's room and then was stopped by the sight of the payphone. The black handle of the receiver looked like the exclamation point on an insult. He had no one to call. There was no city desk, no cop shop, not even the warm voice of the night operator at the *Messenger-Telegram* with the phone messages that were the lifeblood of his work. Officials. Interviewees. Sources. Tipsters. Readers with conspiracies. Even angry officers. No paper, so no way for all that information to get to him. For the first time that day, Novak's offer came into clear focus. He couldn't be a reporter unless he had somewhere to be one. The editors at the *News* thought he was a loose cannon. It'd be the same at the *Post*—worse, if Worthless ended up there. A suburban paper? He couldn't go to one of those rags and chase DWIs and burglar alarms. He'd die.

The chill night air hit his face. The suburbs. He did need to go out there tomorrow, though. To the Mortellis. The death of the *MT* had interrupted his plans to do a story on the bonds. Now he'd take one more day on this, the strangest sort of loose end he'd encountered. As much as he'd like to know where the case had gone to, he needed to know where it had come from. Maybe he'd get something from the father.

He went home in the hope of finding Samantha. He wanted to know where she'd gone. He wanted to know he could trust her. He just plain wanted her.

18

———◆———

HIS SECOND VISIT to the Mortelli house was very different from the first. This time, the dead man's mother had picked him up at the station.

He sat in an overstuffed chair in an over-furnished living room with a coffee cup on a saucer. The shag rug was the same color as the coffee. A mantle clock donged three.

Cecilia Mortelli smoothed the fabric of her black dress across her legs. "Thank you for taking an interest in John's death. No one else seems to care. Not even the ones who should. You asked to see my husband on the phone. He's not here. I threw him out." She kept smoothing the already smooth fabric. "John's life should never have ended the way it did."

"You have my condolences, Mrs. Mortelli—"

"Cecilia, please."

"I'm trying to find out what really happened. People who knew John say he acted totally out of character. I'm sure this is difficult, but I need to know. Did your son have a violent side?"

"No, no, no." She shook her head with each *no*. "He was never in a fight in his life. He couldn't stand seeing anything hurt. He volunteered at the dog shelter. He was going to veterinary school until all the music stuff happened. I never understood this punk thing. My son wasn't a punk."

"When did you talk to him last?"

"I visited him four days before he …." Her index finger and thumb, nails lacquered a dark red, rubbed the bridge of her nose. "We met in Grand Central. I gave him forty dollars. It was the most I could manage." She shook her head. "I had to take it out of the household fund. My husband doles out the money in little drips and drops. There was a big change in him. When I'd gone down three weeks earlier, he'd been happy. We'd had lunch at a favorite place on Park. We got lots of stares because of his clothes and crazy hair. I didn't care. He'd talked all about the dogs he was taking care of and some of the people he'd met. Some men need to sow their wild oats. I thought if he was happy, he'd get through this. Maybe even taking care of the dogs would bring him back to what he was supposed to do. But my last visit was totally different. He was frightened. Someone had scared him. I told him to go to the police. He said he couldn't. It *was* the police."

"Who on the police?"

"He wouldn't say anything else. Ran out of Grand Central. That was the very last time I talked to him." Tears ran down both cheeks. Pulling tissues out of a silver box, she cried for a couple of minutes, blew her nose and smoothed the dress again. "I'm sorry. For the first few days I couldn't stop. Now it comes all of the sudden in waves like that."

"Are you okay for a couple more questions?"

"Yes." Her chin rose.

"He also owned a dog. Did he mention Moon?"

"That name tells you everything about my son. He nursed a dog with the same name at the shelter here in town. This Moon had been badly beaten and didn't make it. John was inconsolable. He cried for days, cried like I've been crying since he died. This poor little injured mutt dies, and he can't leave his room for two days."

"The dog he had in the city was killed by someone. John buried her and put a sign on the grave. Says, 'I didn't believe he'd kill you. Now I must do worse to save the others.' I'm sure whoever killed the dog is important to the case." Maria's eyes opened wide. They were dark brown and suddenly lively. "Would your son act differently if the dogs were threatened?"

"I … I don't know. He would do a lot to protect them. Shoot someone? I don't see how he could ever shoot someone."

"One last question. John had something very valuable stored behind his squat. A briefcase with two hundred and fifty thousand dollars in New York City bonds."

"I don't understand."

"Municipal bonds. The kind sold by the City of New York."

"The police didn't say anything."

"Yeah. There's something going on there too."

"John begged us for money from the time he moved down to the city. He couldn't have …." A pause. "You see my husband works in the bond department at the bank."

Here was the connection. Taylor asked the next question without changing his tone. It took some effort. "Which bank is that?"

"First National City. Anthony's always talking about the city's problems. That whole catastrophe. Never makes any sense to me."

"You're not the only one."

She smiled. "Anthony's been so worried for months. You'd think he was the one going bankrupt."

"Where is he right now?"

"He's staying at the Howard Johnson in Elmsford. I don't know how long. We won't get divorced. Can't. We're good Catholics. I don't know what I'm going to do. I just can't look at him."

Cecilia drove him back to the train station in her Country Squire. Taylor got out and leaned on the passenger window.

"Thank you for seeing me."

"Did the bonds have something to do with John's death?"

"Not sure. Be careful who you say anything to. There's a reason the police aren't asking questions. Problem is, I'm not sure what the reason is."

The best interests of the city? That's what Trunk hinted. Or something else.

On the train ride back to Manhattan, he made an attempt at planning his next steps. He failed. He couldn't get Samantha out of his head. He hadn't been able to since he'd found only Mason at the houseboat last night. No calls this morning. As the train bounced along, he alternated between anger and anxiety, chasing his emotional tail, changing directions every few spins.

THE DESK WAS half in and half out of the door of the nineteenth floor office in the Paramount Building. Novak had the end on the inside and Cramly, one of the most crotchety of the *MT's* rewrite men, had the other. With Cramly groaning louder than a shooting victim, the two moved it into a small two-window office already crowded with four other desks. There'd be very little room to move around in the new headquarters of the City News Bureau.

"Couldn't be *that* heavy," Taylor said.

Cramly, scarecrow thin and wearing a battered blue suit, lit the stub of a cigar. "You fail to understand why I went into journalism."

"Why was that?"

"No heavy lifting."

"Here I thought it was to fuck up my copy."

"You were never funny, Taylor."

"I'm not the one telling the oldest joke in journalism."

Novak faced them from the windows. He spread his hands out. "You like?"

"It's intimate." Taylor sat down in the nearest mismatched desk chair. "Where'd you get the furniture?"

"Dad. They redid the typing pool at his company, and this stuff was available. He's also sending over the typewriters."

"The ones they replaced?" Taylor asked cautiously.

"It's so groovy," Novak said. "We're going back to manuals."

Taylor grimaced. "We're going back in time is what's happening."

Cramly exhaled blue smoke. "That IBM Selectric didn't make a better writer of you."

Novak squeezed back through the desks, smiling at his new empire. "It's all great. The building is great. You know, two Broadway shows have their offices on this floor, and I swear to god, a for-real private detective. You need to meet him. Might get some good tips."

"On midtown divorces and shoplifting gangs."

"I also met this old press agent. Ancient. He's been promoting shows since vaudeville. I told him what we're doing, and he asked if he could pay to send stories on his clients to our radio stations."

"That's not journalism."

"Can't be too picky. A business needs money. If we can get both the stations and the sources to fork it over, why hell, then we've really got something going."

Taylor shook his head. Novak was already off in the wrong direction. They'd be sending out PR puffs and news at the same time. His byline would never appear in New York again.

Novak waved Taylor into what looked like a closet. Turned out to be a very small office—not much more than a closet really—with one desk wedged inside.

"I know it's a Saturday. Thanks for stopping by on moving day." Novak sat down. "Speaking of money." He pushed the door shut, and it banged on the corner of his desk before it closed.

"This is the executive office?"

"Yeah, miniature. And no window. I need some quiet to talk

to clients. I know some of this stuff sounds like a bit of a dodge to you.

"Worse. You don't let people buy coverage. You *can't.*"

"All right, all right." Hands up in surrender. "I'll say no to the old boy. We'll figure other ways. I can pay you three-quarters what you were making. Don't tell the other guys. They're getting half. I'm not taking anything at this point."

A twenty-five percent pay cut. Hurts bad. Hundred percent would hurt worse.

"How are you going to get by?"

"I've got some savings. Plus, Dad agreed to pay for my apartment. You wouldn't believe it. He's so pleased I'm doing this. Newspaper writing was a waste of my time. Starting a business. That's worthwhile. Even if it's still journalism. My dad's weird."

"You're lucky. At least he likes *something* you're doing." Taylor had never been able to find that one thing for his father. Now it didn't matter. The professor's happiness came from one source only. "All right. I'm in. But none of this press agent crap. What's up with the other guys?"

"All thinking about it."

"Are you kidding? Don't make me regret this."

"You won't. How's the story?"

"Police corruption is probably involved. I've got more on John Mortelli."

"Juicy. Come in Monday. Let's get up and running. We need to start sending out the stories—" The phone rang and Novak answered. He quickly put his hand over the mouthpiece and bounced his eyebrows. "A radio station manager calling from the *country club*. I've got to take it."

Taylor left Novak's office still wondering if he'd done the right thing. Cramly unpacked a grocery bag of papers and office supplies into the desk nearest the window, which meant if Taylor wanted a view, he'd have to sit next to that cranky old man. Nope. He slumped into the chair at the desk near the door. He had a spare reporter's notebook in the side pocket of his field jacket. He wrote *Taylor's desk* on a sheet, placed it in the middle of the desk and put the notebook in the top drawer. *There. Moved in.* He pictured this little crowd of desks dwarfed by the *MT's* newsroom. When would he work in a place like that again? Or was this it? Had he peaked?

Glum, he stood up and turned to the door and almost walked into Samantha, standing there in blue jeans, tight long-sleeved sweater, and windbreaker. These clothes were definitely cut for her. He was close enough after hitting the breaks to catch the hint of a light floral perfume.

"How'd you find me?"

"I called Henry and he said you planned to stop by after an interview."

Cramly rose with a grunt. He looked Samantha up and down a couple of times. He'd been one of the paper's leading letches. "You working here too? We need a typist to get all the copy out."

She opened her mouth to answer, but Taylor shook his head. "Let's go get coffee."

"You have a coffee in your hand."

"Let me buy *you* one." He stepped past her into the hallway.

She caught up as he headed to the elevator. "I've got some good stuff."

"That's nice." He pressed the elevator button.

"What's wrong with you?"

"You had me freaking out. Wasn't part of the plan for you to go off with that cop."

"I was improvising."

"Oh yeah. What did that entail?"

The brass needle rose slowly to the number nineteen as Samantha's face fell. "You don't trust me."

"We had a plan."

"My plan played out better." Her cheeks reddened. "I don't work for you. If you're one of these guys who thinks he owns me because we slept together, you can fuck yourself. I'm not taking orders from you. Too many people already think they're in charge of me."

Doing it again. Screwing things up.

19

———— ◆ ————

AFTER HE APOLOGIZED, they rode the elevator in silence. He thought she might storm off. Instead, they walked to the Howard Johnson with the all-male burlesque theater on the floor above and took a booth.

Samantha ordered a patty melt and seltzer. Taylor asked for a second coffee and a grilled cheese.

Instead of getting himself into deeper trouble, he stayed quiet and tried to think of something else. The first thing that came to mind was how disappointed Grandpop would be if he knew Taylor was at HoJo. His grandfather despised chain restaurants as a black enemy of the corner coffee shop. (There were many types and kinds of black enemies.) Maybe they were. Taylor kept coming to this Howard Johnson because of the brave stand it was taking by maintaining its bright orange-and-white presence at the city's intersection of sex and crime. Even ten years ago, it had made sense for HoJo to be here. For decades Times Square had been a family destination, with several great places to eat. But Child's Restaurant was long gone, and now the Horn & Hardart Automat had closed, replaced by a Burger King. He missed the Automat most because of its old-timey vision of an automated World's Fair future. One wall of the Automat had been taken up entirely by little doors with glass windows, behind which you'd see fresh-made appetizers, main courses, and desserts, all constantly replaced by the cooks in the back. Popping coins in the slots in the doors purchased the dishes. All that had been obliterated in favor of the Whopper.

Taylor crunched into the sandwich. The aroma of the melted American cheese carried him further back in time to the kitchen of his childhood. Mom would have been there with Billy, while the professor was at work or a faculty cocktail. There had been lots of faculty cocktails.

His focused back on the present to find the anger still in Samantha's gunmetal-blue eyes.

Better deal.

"I said I was sorry."

"Maybe that won't be enough."

"I was worried. When you left with Priscotti I didn't know what—"

"Did you think I was dirty too? Going over to the other side? Going to bed with him?"

"No, no, and no. Just didn't know what was going on." He chewed the inside of his lip after telling the lie. He *had* thought she might be dirty. *No way I'm admitting that now.* "This is dangerous work. Then you don't come back …." He trailed off and nibbled at the grilled cheese. He needed something to do before he dug himself into a deeper hole.

"I don't have to check in with you. I don't have to come back to your place. I don't have to tell you what I've found out. I'm trying to save my career. My life. This is *not* a story for me."

This is going so well.

He sipped the coffee.

"You're right. You don't have to tell me. Even if you don't, I'm still going to try to help you. *You*, and not for the sake of the story."

The fire in her eyes banked from solar flare to smoldering.

The anger tightening her face let go a little.

"I just hate the assumptions. The fat slug insisted we go to dinner. Wouldn't talk about anything but the Jets until I said yes. We went to this crappy place in Little Italy he claimed is owned by a cousin. Spaghetti for tourists. After a bottle of Chianti, he finally gets chatty. There's ten of them in uniform taking money. To protect numbers and prostitution ops. They stay away from drugs. Too hot after the Knapp busts. No one cares so much about whores or numbers runners. They call themselves Top Deck. Something about where they all sit at Mets games."

"Good, good. That's more than Stein had, or was willing to give up. What about the other cops in the precinct?"

"If they know, they look the other way. That's Priscotti's view, at least. He can't know what everyone's thinking."

"Who are the ten?"

"He wouldn't give names. After the second bottle, I asked pointblank about Schmidt, and he admitted Schmidt's in charge."

"He knows a lot for an outsider. If he is. What did he say about Dodd and Schmidt's relationship?"

"According to scuttlebutt from others, tense all summer. Got worse after Slive took Dodd aside for a long serious conversation that a few guys saw. After that, Dodd met with Slive in his office several times. Priscotti's sure that panicked Top Deck. They had to think Dodd was giving them up."

"When did the meetings happen?"

Samantha took out her police notebook. "Wrote it all down after I got rid of Priscotti. Moron had it in his head we were going home after dinner. What makes guys think that? Slive and Dodd started talking four and a half weeks ago."

"Stein made an interesting point. Why set up this elaborate murder to take a guy out over a nickel-and-dime racket? This was no big conspiracy. You know, the real meat-eater corruption where cops are actually running drug rings and protection."

"Depends on your point of view. A cop gets sent up to Attica or Ossining, and he's looking at beatings, rape, and death. Won't matter what the size of his take was. The big chiefs downtown want the dirt swept up fast as it appears. If Dodd was talking to Slive, that would look bad to Top Deck."

"Okay, so they set up this shooting to kill Dodd. We still don't know how, exactly, Mortelli fits in. Was he the killer? Or the bait? Where's the gun?

"Nothing from Priscotti on that."

"He gave us lots to work with. Really nice work."

"I'm a police officer."

"Could be journalist."

"Don't be insulting." The hint of a smile.

"Stein told me Slive is some kind of hotshot at nabbing bad cops. Cleaned up three station houses. Why would he let people see him talking to Dodd? The wrong people. Not the subtlest way to conduct an investigation."

"Not safe for Dodd at all. Deadly, in fact."

"That and Mortelli are the big question marks. What was Mortelli doing? What, why, and for who?"

"Can't interview a dead man."

"No you can't. But maybe he talked to someone. A guy named Rayban in the neighborhood seems to know a lot of Mortelli's business. Rayban didn't tell me Mortelli's dog was missing. Pretty sure it wasn't an oversight. Maybe he knows more." Taylor finished his coffee. "What did you do after dinner with your fat friend?"

"Why's it any of your business?"

"I ... I just care. Never mind. I don't want to argue anymore."

She grinned. "That's how you get me, Taylor. You care. I met my dad up in Westchester, then stayed at a motel in Hastings. No one here would think to look *waaaay* up in the country."

"Don't they still have a car on your father?"

"He lost them this time. Really hurt his pride he led them to me the first time."

"I hope you're being careful. Those goons from the park must be Top Deck. They won't escort you to a departmental hearing."

"Got my thirty-two for that. Had to see Dad. The Sergeant is really worried. If I don't keep him calm, he'll do something crazy. That won't help either of us."

They walked back to the office. Cramly had gone. Novak was hanging a big calendar on the wall for tracking assignments. Taylor used the phone to call Mrs. Mortelli and give her his *new* office number.

"Let's go downtown and see if we can find out more about her son."

As they walked to the subway, the call to Mrs. Mortelli again brought up Taylor's anxiety about all the sources who wouldn't know how or where to find him. Probably thought he'd disappeared with the paper itself. It might take weeks to reconnect with people, if ever. A dizzying sort of anxiety. Maybe he had disappeared with the paper. Maybe it was more than a home. Maybe it was his identity. Would he have to invent a new one?

The R train took them to Union Square, and they came above ground into the cool autumn evening. The sky was a deep blue and darkening. Clouds moved in as they walked, and a misty rain started. Taylor put on his beat-up wool hat and Sally pulled up her hood, and they hustled east into the heart of Alphabet City, which looked far more dangerous in the dark. Abandoned buildings with their windows yawning like black mouths made the sidewalk a gloomy place. Worse, many of the streetlights were out. A ragtag man shambled by, followed by a guy who was better dressed and somehow more threatening. He had his hood up and darkness hid his face.

Taylor thought of Samantha's back-up piece. He sensed the leather straps of his holster around his ankle. He had to be honest. Samantha's was the gun that would save them.

No one they passed was using an umbrella. Those were for

uptown folks. At Avenue A and the corner of the park, the *clop, clop* of heavy steps behind them, closing as they reached the next intersection. They stopped. Samantha, thinking the same thing as Taylor, reached behind for her revolver and kept her hand back there. They crossed the street. The steps again. Taylor turned, could only make out a long coat and broad hat in the misty rain. When he looked again, the long coat was going up the steps of a brownstone with warm lights on in the windows. Home and dry in Alphabet City.

Why not? People do live in this neighborhood.

On Avenue C, Rayban's encampment was still in place. The boxes were closed up. The rain eased a bit.

Taylor knocked on the one Rayban had been sitting in the day he'd led Taylor to John Mortelli's squat.

"It's Taylor from the *Messenger-Telegram*." It came out automatically, before he could correct himself. No answer. He knocked again and there came a *thump, thump, thump* that was probably the German shepherd wagging his tail.

Two flaps opened a crack. "There ain't any *Messenger-Telegram* no more. Told you your paper was doomed. Now leave me alone."

Sally's box stayed closed. From inside came a muffled voice. "Want sleep. Want sleep."

"Yeah, Sally, we all want sleep. Just some people won't leave us alone."

"I'm still working the story. I want to talk to you about Johnny Mort."

"Decided he's not someone it's good to talk about."

"Is there something you didn't tell me? Something to do with the killings?"

"Decided I need to go back to bed."

"How about getting something to eat?"

"We ate. Was a good day for us."

"A drink then?"

The flaps opened more as Rayban sat slowly up. The dog's

head also popped out. "I could do with a glass of red."

Sally's box shook. "No wine. No wine."

"It's okay, Sally. John-Boy can stay with you."

The side flaps of Sally's box opened and Rayban stood and brought the dog into her open arms. Taylor and Samantha let Rayban lead them north to a place he said he knew. Behind them, Sally's voice receded. "No wine. No wine."

Rayban's dive bar two blocks up welcomed them with all the ambiance of a construction site. The place looked like it might have been converted from a bodega. Shelves were pushed into the back of the space, and the bar was made up of plywood laid across two sawhorses. At one end three punks drank straight vodka. This actually made Taylor relax a little. For some reason, the punks made him believe they were safer.

Rayban ordered red wine, which the bartender, a short man in a dirty T-shirt, poured from a jug with a glass loop. Samantha didn't want anything. Taylor used that to bolster his willpower and waved the man away.

Rayban sipped. "Ah, that's it. Stomach's a mess. Can't take spirits anymore. The red red wine still goes down nicely." He hummed a little of the Neil Diamond tune. "Who's your friend?"

"She's helping with the story—which now hinges on the trouble Mort, actually John Mortelli, got into. What was going on?"

"Everyone knows he was in trouble. That's how he got dead."

"You *knew* Moon was missing and didn't say anything to me. If Sally hadn't said—"

"We'd all be a lot safer. Same if she hadn't found the damn grave."

"Someone killed Moon for a reason. They wanted Johnny to do something. I can guess, but it's just a guess. Guesses don't help us now. I think you know who and what. Did he tell you?"

Rayban's eyes widened. He polished off the glass and stared

at it like he needed Taylor to buy him the courage to talk. Taylor plunked down another buck.

Rayban drank more, swaying back and forth to a steady beat that he heard, singing more of the song. He took a big gulp. "We watched this guy casing the block for about two weeks. He was a cop. No matter how hard they try to hide it, you can tell. End of two weeks, he grabs Johnny. Johnny shakes him lose, but not for long. The guy chases Johnny down, hits him hard a couple of times and forces Johnny to take him to the squat."

"And?"

"I wasn't there, man. This is dangerous territory."

"Johnny told you."

Rayban nodded. "The cop tossed everything in the flat. Wrecked the place."

Taylor lowered his voice. "Was he looking for the bonds?"

"If he was, Johnny didn't say. Johnny *never* mentioned those to me. God's honest. He said the cop wanted to scare him. Out of the blue, he pulls his gun and shoots Moon between the eyes." Rayban shook his head. "Such damn cruelty to a poor dumb thing. And to Johnny."

"Why didn't you tell me before?"

"Because people are getting killed. I wanna stay off that list."

"He killed the dog to make Johnny—"

"Do the mugging." Rayban bottomed the glass of wine. "The most important thing was Johnny had to make sure this one cop chased him into that building. Bad cop told him where the officer would be. After that, Johnny could go on his way. Didn't work out like that. Probably was never gonna. He was really scared. Which is why I've been keeping my mouth shut about things he told me."

"The cop have a name?"

"None that Johnny gave."

"What's he look like?"

"Ah man, you're putting me in a mess of shit."

"I will keep you out of it."

"You better. Lives on the line here. He was tall, skinny, with a bullet-shaped head. Hair was black, streaked with gray. Sorta long. Cop, cop, all goddamn day a cop."

Taylor looked to Samantha for confirmation. She didn't seem surprised. "That's Schmidt."

20

———— ◆ ————

TAYLOR BANGED THE phone down hard.

Cramly turned from his desk. "Easy on the merchandise." The rewrite man had planned to retire from the *Messenger-Telegram*, RIP. Now he was as worried as a mother with an infant that the City News Bureau wouldn't last until he made 65, worried down to how the equipment was treated. "How's the story coming?"

"I'll get it to you."

Taylor had arrived at the offices Monday morning to find Cramly was the de facto city editor of the new operation. He'd handed Taylor a front-page story from the *New York Times* reporting 15 of Manhattan's subway stations had lost more than a third of their passengers in the past ten years. Times Square station alone experienced a 40 percent drop, from 40 million to 25 million riders. No wonder the crossroads of the world had turned into a shithole. Or was it the other way around? People stopped coming because the crossroads of the world had turned into a shithole. Cramly had told Taylor to interview riders at the station for a quickie to go out to the radio stations for their noon newscasts. The urge to argue rose in him like instinct. He was going to complain about following the *Times,* that it wasn't cops, that he was on a bigger story—all the things he'd have said to Worthless. Novak had been on the phone in his office, jiggling his leg nervously. He'd given Taylor a little wave. The clipping had wavered ever so slightly in Cramly's hand. In that moment, Taylor had checked himself. Cramly wasn't Worth and this wasn't the *MT*. Novak had taken a huge risk on all of them. He needed to pull his weight. A quick man-on-the-street story wouldn't slow him down much, after which he'd head to the Ninth Precinct in search of Slive to try and nail down the last piece of the story on the killing of Officer Robert Dodd.

That was why he'd slammed the phone. The Internal Affairs detective was never there when Taylor called. Slive was ducking him. He knew it.

As he looked over his interviews from the subway riders, Taylor counted one small blessing. Next to the subway piece, the *Times* had run a story on Ford repeating his opposition to a city bailout, which caused Carey to cancel meetings with state legislators. Some agency or the other was going to default by the end of the week.

Thank all the gods Novak and Cramly don't want me to chase that.

Not that he didn't now believe the city's financial crisis was a real threat. He did. He also believed he had no way of untying that Gordian knot of numbers, estimates, claims and counterclaims. He wouldn't even know where to start.

Before typing the rest of the story, Taylor looked up. "When are the others getting here?"

"Later. Applying for unemployment first. Double dipping. Smart."

Why didn't I think of that? I need to get my shit together. Story can't always come first. My finances are a ruin.

He banged hard on the Olivetti manual. He needed to just to move the keys. His knuckles ached halfway through the story. He'd gotten soft using the Selectric at the paper. They said newspapers were going to switch to computers any day now. Taylor's career was going in the very opposite direction. What else was new?

Still, he *was* closing in on the story. So very close. Between Priscotti, Stein, and Rayban, he and Samantha had collected great material. Problem was, it was either off the record or had to be sourced anonymously. Add to that the one thing he needed that he didn't have. A real link between the corrupt cops and the killing of Dodd and Mortelli. That would be a real scoop. He didn't give a damn if it only ran on four radio stations. The story would be a coup for Novak and the new City News Bureau. All the papers in town would pick up on it. They'd see Taylor hadn't disappeared.

Slive was the key. If anyone, he was the one who could confirm the connection.

He can deny it all too. Then what?

He pulled the last sheet out of the typewriter and dropped the story on Cramly's desk. "I'm getting lunch."

"Awfully early. We're going to need something for the afternoon newscasts."

"Got to work on the cop killing."

Cramly held up another clipping like he hadn't heard. "There's concern these new super-high voltage power lines are frying people's brains."

"The *Times* wrote that?"

"Well, you know, in their way. 'Emissions' blah blah 'potentially harmful' blah blah. Nice sort of story to scare Top 40 listeners."

"How am I supposed to get it?"

"You're the reporter. Call people upstate who live under them. You know, Westchester, Putnam. See if their brains are on fire."

"Right. When I get back."

* * *

SAMANTHA WAS WAITING at the Howard Johnson as they agreed. Her face was sunburned. She glowed like a summer postcard, and he couldn't help kissing her big on the mouth before sitting on his side of the booth.

She'd gotten the color yesterday. The temperature had climbed to 72 degrees, the very strange November weather continuing one last day, and she'd convinced him to put a blanket down on the top deck and lie in the sun. She'd also banned shoptalk—nothing about the police, the news bureau, *the* story, none of it. She wouldn't even let him buy the Sunday papers. They both needed a break, she'd insisted. Taylor didn't know what to do with this break. Samantha did. Stories. She'd told him about summers growing up in the Bronx. Her family had gone to Lake George every year and visited a now defunct Bronx amusement park called Freedomland U.S.A. As she'd talked, Taylor found himself wondering about Laura and Derek. Had they discovered common interests outside the news business? Imagining them together didn't hit him hard the way it usually did. Not the usual pang.

Samantha had shaken him from his reverie when it was his turn to tell a story. He'd struggled. Each of his seemed to start with the *Messenger-Telegram*. Finally he'd talked about going to a Greek Orthodox Church in Queens with his mother. He wasn't religious now, but the memories were mystical. Icons covering the walls of the church. The priest in the long robes and the long beard. He'd told her of the wall separating the worshippers from the altar, with its three special doors. He couldn't remember their Greek names anymore, nor their specific purpose, but knew one was called the Beautiful Gate and another the Angel's Door. Doors to other places. What kid wasn't captivated by magical doors? Samantha had listened, rapt. She was a Catholic and still went to mass. The church of the East was strange to her, she'd said, and his version made it sound even stranger. They'd walked Mason around the island, eaten clams, mussels, and a lobster he couldn't afford and gone to bed, making love and falling asleep early.

"What's that for?" Samantha asked after the big kiss.

"You're beautiful."

"You are the poet, aren't you?"

"Never bury the lead. Remember that, if you switch professions. Priscotti take your call?"

"Of course." That confidant smile. "Slive's at the precinct. Has been all morning."

"Goddammit. He *is* dodging me. Got to talk to him. It's that, or confront Schmidt."

"That would be crazy."

He shrugged and tried not to sound like he was boasting. Or actually crazy. "I've interviewed bad guys before. It's never smart to kill a reporter. Turns the whole thing into a much bigger story."

"That was when you worked for the *MT*."

"Good point. Least I've got you for backup."

"Don't know if that's smart either. I'm just as likely to shoot the bastard as wait for his answers. Kills Dodd. Sets me up. I might not have gone into hiding, knowing what I know now. I was sure they were going to fit me up and fire me. Now they will anyway. Fire me at least."

"Schmidt's still innocent until proven guilty."

"Such a stickler. Want me to wait until he fires at you?"

"No, definitely shoot first. What's Slive's schedule?"

"Priscotti says he's like clockwork. He leaves every day at twelve twenty-five for lunch. Walks somewhere, but Priscotti doesn't know the place. Tan trench coat, blue-gray suit. He's tall."

Taylor looked at his watch. "Crap. Quarter to noon. I gotta move if I'm going to join the detective for lunch."

"Let me back you up."

"Too dangerous for you to be near that precinct."

"I don't want to sit around the damn Howard Johnson waiting."

"All right. Meet me at the Acropolis Coffee Shop on Sheridan Square. That's Westside. Far enough from the Ninth. We can take the 1 back up here. But be careful. They're all looking for you."

He kissed her again and left.

Taylor was breathing hard when he pulled up from a dead run at the corner of East Fifth Street. The precinct was in the middle of the block. In steady rain, he walked the rest of the way. A delay on the subway had forced the sprint. His watch said 12:22.

Three minutes later, a tall man in a blue-gray suit and tan trench coat came out. Slive quickly put up an umbrella. Taylor followed at a safe distance, using Slive's umbrella to keep him in sight. The detective walked like a man who never expected anyone on his tail. He wound his way to a small Italian restaurant at the corner of Thompson Street and West Houston.

Taylor watched as Slive was seated, then pulled open the restaurant door, walked in, and took the other chair at the IA man's table.

"Thought it would be more productive if we met in person. You're so very hard to reach."

"Who the fuck are you?" He said it casually, like he was talking about the weather. His eyes stayed on the menu.

"Taylor. I've been calling you."

"Ah, the *ex*-reporter."

"Work for the City News Bureau now."

"Never heard of it." The waiter stopped at the table. "Chicken cacciatore with pasta on the side. Tomatoes and mozzarella for an appetizer. The gentleman *won't* be joining me."

Slive was sleek and muscular. Where did he put all that food?

"You'll know about us soon enough. In fact, soon as I write the story on corruption in the Oh-Nine and the murder of a police officer to cover it up."

"You can prove this?"

"I have a source who talked to John Mortelli. Mortelli said he was being forced to do the mugging and draw Dodd into the abandoned building. The man who threatened Mortelli fits the description of a Ninth Precinct patrolman named Schmidt. He's part of a group taking bribes. They call themselves Top Deck."

Slive looked at Taylor evenly as the salad was set in front of him. The tomatoes were blood red against the milky white mozzarella, making Taylor think of a wound. Slive's gray eyes shifted off Taylor's face to his salad. He had a long face and salt-and-pepper crew cut. He began cutting the salad into red and white cubes.

Red and white salad met white teeth and red tongue and mouth.

"Interesting."

"Then there's that tip I got that the radio call Callahan heard was real. You weren't interested in that then. Now, perhaps? Dodd was set up, murdered to protect cops on the take. Mortelli was an innocent killed as part of the plot."

"Interesting."

"If I'm wrong, then tell me what the fuck *is* going on. Why did you spend so much time talking to Dodd? Because that probably made the Top Deck guys think he was going to report them. Not very subtle."

Slive reached across the table with his knife and gently set it next to Taylor's hand. He put another forkful of tomato and mozzarella in his mouth, chewed and swallowed. "What will happen if you come at me with that knife?"

"I'm not going to."

"When you do, I'll pull out my revolver and shoot you. In the kneecap. Probably both knees. Dead assailants are messy. I'd want you alive."

"I said I'm not picking up the knife."

"That's not what I'll say. Or any of the wonderful staff here at Marco's. You need to understand, just because someone says something, that doesn't make it true. My word against yours. It's important whose word you're relying on."

Slive reached for the knife, and Taylor couldn't help but pull his hand quickly toward his lap. Slive smiled tightly, thin lips and no teeth.

"You know, I work a lot of cases. You might think there's just your big story. Not so. I did talk to Dodd, but not about anything at the precinct. I wanted Dodd's help with another investigation. There's a serious corruption ring working the Upper Eastside. This one's committing real crimes. Running drugs. Extortion. Guess who heads it?"

"No idea."

"Michael Callahan. I was trying to get Dodd to work Samantha Callahan for me. I'd hoped we'd get some information out of her."

"Was he?"

"He was good. I was thinking of recruiting Dodd into IA."

"What did you learn?"

"I can't comment at this time."

"Of course. What about the Oh-Nine?"

"You have some interesting information. Some. Let's say you're warm in places. Cold in others."

"Give me a direction to go in."

The waiter removed the salad and put down the chicken dish with a side of pasta.

"Not my job. Please be careful, though. This is more complex than you understand. I will clean it up. And I'll rip through anyone who gets in my way."

HE LEFT MARCO'S. The sidewalk gave off the odor of a storm just passed. The rain had stopped. Taylor turned west toward Sheridan Square. His hope had been that Slive would confirm some important piece of the story—the Schmidt connection would have been ideal. Admitting there were open questions about Dodd's killing would have been a start. But the IA investigator's warm-cold crap didn't give him any direction to go in. Worse, Slive had provided him with a completely new and totally terrible direction. He could think of two ways to proceed. Tell Samantha what he'd learned. Or find a way to interview Schmidt. Either way he'd probably get shot.

This story was like a series of math equations with no right answers. He turned them over and over in his head all the way to Sheridan Square.

"Good lunch?"

Taylor jumped sideways. Samantha laughed from under a floppy hat.

"I said wait in the coffee shop."

"C'mon, we're not in the Ninth now."

"You know what I mean."

"Get anything good?"

"You're not going to think so."

21

————◆————

THEY WALKED IN silence to the subway. Taylor tried to think things through.

Who'm I kidding? There's no way this plays well.

He couldn't ignore what Slive had said. Samantha wasn't going to like it at all.

She didn't. On the 1 train uptown, he took her through the whole conversation.

"Dodd wasn't pumping me for anything." She stared at him like he was crazy. "That's pure bullshit."

"What about your father?"

"My father isn't corrupt. Period. Slive is sending you down some kind of rat hole. It's him you should worry about."

"Okay, so maybe your father's not—"

"Maybe? If I say he's not, he's not."

"Fine. Dodd still could have been working you. Did you two talk about your father?"

"I guess. We talked about all sorts of stuff until he went quiet. You spend a lot of hours in the car together."

"Slive said he was going to recruit Dodd into IA. We can't

simply disregard everything he said. What if there's something there?"

"Like what?"

"If your mother says she loves you, check it out."

"What the hell are you talking about?"

"It's an old Chicago editor's line. It means confirm whatever you're told or prove it wrong."

The train entered the 14th Street station with a *whump* as it left the tunnel for the open air of the platform. The brakes squealed. This station had lost only five or six percent of its passengers. Taylor remembered that from the piece he'd written in the morning.

He crossed the platform to catch the 2-3 express. Samantha didn't. Instead, she climbed the stairs to the token booths and the exit. Taylor quickly followed.

"Wait. We can figure this out."

He reached gently for her elbow.

She pulled away with a violent yank and turned on the stairs to face him. "You promised me the story wouldn't come first."

"We've got to know what's fact and what's fiction. Maybe Slive is sending me down some blind alley. Or maybe he was investigating your father," he held up his hands, "even if he's innocent. IA guys can do whatever the hell they want. Go wherever they want. You've learned that. What if he was using Dodd? What if Dodd was going into IA?"

"Bullshit." She kept going up the stairs. "Now you're just spinning bullshit. You just want the story. Nothing else." She clacked through the turnstiles.

He stopped on his side of the barrier. Why follow? He already knew Samantha well enough. If she wanted to get away from him, to be alone, there was little he could do. Would she calm down? See his side? No idea. She was ferociously independent. He wasn't going to change her mind now. He'd done the right thing. He'd told her everything Slive had said.

He slumped onto a plastic seat on the next express train,

miserable. The right thing sucked. The express stopped in the tunnel just short of Times Square for a good ten minutes, lights out. In the dark, he inventoried what he had. Jack shit. Samantha was gone. Slive had refused to confirm the story he thought he had and sent him off in a completely different direction.

Jersey Stein did say Slive was the guy who went in and cleaned out precincts. Was Taylor close to something on the Dodd killing that Slive didn't have yet? Or didn't want Taylor to have? It was possible. It was also possible Taylor had figured the shooting all wrong, and Slive really did want a story on Sergeant Mick Callahan reported.

What next?

The only thing he could think to do was confront Schmidt. He'd considered that an okay option when he had Samantha as backup. She'd been his partner in this dangerous story—a partner who could get him out of a jam.

No, Samantha wasn't just protection. With Samantha around the past few days, he'd thought less and less about Laura. And it hurt less and less to think about her. She'd taken away the loneliness. He missed her already, here in the dark of a New York subway tunnel.

At City News, he made a few calls until he collected enough quotes from worried homeowners to write up the power-lines-rotting-brains story on autopilot. As he finished typing, Novak burst out of his tiny office.

"WWRN, WWRN, WWRN."

"You a DJ now?" Taylor put the copy on Cramly's desk.

"I signed them. Station number five. An FM. I got our first FM, an easy listening FM."

"They have any *living* listeners?"

"Sure do." Novak followed Taylor back to his desk. "Can you do anything with that corruption story? The bonds? Anything? We need a big one."

"Don't really have it all yet." *Shit, is that an understatement.*

"C'mon, Taylor, give me something. The stations are looking for more. WWRN has adult listeners who love news with their Living Strings."

That was hardly a motivator. His stories squeezed between tracks of elevator music. This wasn't journalism. He was writing filler. How much does filler matter?

That's it. Filler doesn't matter. Doesn't matter at all. But it might flush out the real story.

He looked up at Novak as his revelation turned into a plan. "Think I can pull something together with what I've got. Not the whole story. Might be a big sketchy."

"That's my man. Knew you'd come through."

Taylor rolled another sheet into the Olivetti, flipped open his notebook and wrote the story he thought he had. Thought, but couldn't prove, not with sources on the record, not without ignoring Slive's warning that he was cold on some parts of it. He definitely wouldn't have been able to prove it to the satisfaction of any editor at the *Messenger-Telegram*, RIP.

He wrote it anyway, ripping through at breakneck speed. He'd been running the story through his head for days, changing it every time he learned something new. There was a cliché about stories writing themselves. This one did. That should have been his first warning.

He crammed everything into two pages. The stations demanded short stories. He didn't want anything cut from the red flag he was sending up into the night. Dodd was set up by corrupt cops at the Ninth Precinct, lured to his death by Mortelli, who was an unwitting victim in the murder plot with his own secret. That secret: $250,000 in municipal bonds. He shook his head as he typed the last lines. The story would certainly have been thrown back in his face at the *MT* for being more supposition than fact. He didn't care. This was filler, after all. He wasn't trying to *break* news with this one. He was trying to break the story open—flush out someone who would give him what he needed to report what really happened to Robert

Dodd. It was Taylor's way out of the dead end.

Desperate as he was, he knew there was one huge hole in the story left unfilled. If Mortelli was only the lure for Dodd, then a third assailant shot them both, probably using the missing gun on Dodd. Could be Schmidt. Could be someone else. That was not an accusation he could put out there yet. He knew *that* would be going too far, which wasn't saying much with this story.

Would Samantha see he'd kept his word? There was nothing about her or her father. He hoped so.

Cramly read the typescript. "The sourcing's really weak. I mean Christ, there isn't any."

Novak, just returned from buying sparkling wine to celebrate WWRN, grabbed the copy. "This *is* the right stuff. Scandal. A case full of bonds. Hero cop. Didn't want to tell you, Taylor, but I mentioned the briefcase to one of the station managers. He ate it right up."

Taylor, already feeling guilty for blind-sourcing a story to flush out the real facts, was compelled to explain in detail to Novak and Cramly where all the information had come from—the anonymous phone tip on the radio call, Rayban Lincoln providing the details on the cop beating Mortelli and shooting his dog. Novak nodded the whole time. He would have nodded at anything.

Not like the story's a fake. It all could *be accurate. Shit, now you're bullshitting yourself.*

Taylor's standards had dropped to the floor, along with the rest of his life. Samantha was gone. He was out of time. Instead of chasing sources, he was trying to get them to chase him.

"We needed this so bad," said Novak. "The contracts are all short term. We had to give them something big."

Novak put the story in the telecopier himself and stood by as the drum spun, sending the story to the first station on the list. The machine made a high whine, pathetic compared to the majestic thunder of a newspaper press running at full speed.

* * *

As far as Taylor was concerned, there was way too much of the suburbs in this story. But all his calls to Anthony Mortelli at the office had gone unreturned. Now it was after banker's hours, and the only way to catch him was at home. Strike that, at the Howard Johnson in Elmsford, where he'd been since his wife threw him out. Taylor could have easily gone back to City Island, let his trial balloon rise and wait to see what happened. That wasn't his way. He hated loose ends and unexplained details. There was guilt too. A lot of guilt. Having sent out a story that was as much smoke as fact, he was determined to do something so the next one was rock solid. He couldn't just wait. So here he sat on the New York Central, looking out at the broad Hudson River as the old diesel groaned north to Tarrytown. At least there was some scenery on this ride. Tarrytown was a busy commuter hub, with several waiting cabs. Expensive cabs. He almost choked on the nine dollar fair to Elmsford. He was living on a pay cut and knew Novak couldn't cover expenses.

He knocked on the orange door of room nine. Mortelli answered, his yellow polyester shirt unbuttoned near to his navel. The slicked-backed hair was sticking up.

With a look of almost happy surprise, he grabbed Taylor, pulled him into the room and slammed him into the wall. "Where are they?" Mortelli picked up a half-empty bottle of Canadian Club. The whiskey sloshed in the bottle. The ache from Taylor's bruised ribs blossomed into sharp pain. "My wife says you're asking about the bonds. Tell me where they are, or I'll crack your skull open like a Christmas nut."

"They're yours?"

"No more interviews. Tell me." He pulled the bottle back. His hand tightened on Taylor's jacket so the collar cut into the skin of Taylor's neck.

"You're not going to get much out of me. As far as I know, the cops have them. They were recovered from your son's building."

"Shit." Mortelli stumbled back onto the orange blanket of the double bed. He opened the bottle and took two big swallows.

"Then they disappeared," Taylor said.

"Disappeared? What's that mean?"

"I witnessed the cops taking them into their possession. I can't get anyone at the precinct to admit to anything."

"Not sure if that hurts me or helps me." More whiskey.

The news had taken the fight out of Mortelli. If he kept drinking like that, he wouldn't be able to get off the bed.

"Were they yours?"

He laughed and shook his head. "What's it matter if the cops fucking have them? My son took them from me."

"What was he going to do with them?"

"He wouldn't know what to do with them. He just knew they were important to me. I was supposed to let him stay in that shithole with those strays and sub-humans. I did that, he'd tell no one about the briefcase."

"John was twenty-four. What'd he have to worry about?"

"The last time he was at the house, I told him my brothers and I were going to grab him out of there and stick him in the psych ward. Guess he took me seriously. He stole them when he left that night."

"He used two hundred fifty thousand of your bonds to get you to leave him alone? Novel approach."

Mortelli drank the whiskey like water. "They weren't mine. Took them from the bank. Easiest thing."

Taylor remembered what Novak had told him about the audits. "Like the five million missing from the vaults."

"They didn't even get half of the story. It's far worse. I took the briefcase home in February. No one was paying attention. Figured I'd unload them over a few months. My timing completely sucked. Everything started falling apart a few weeks later when the Urban Development Corporation defaulted. Spooked everyone and put the whole market into a tailspin." Mortelli's shoulders slumped like he was folding in on himself. He stared into the opening of the Canadian Club bottle. "The market for city bonds went straight into the shitter. By summer, everyone was calling for better accounting, even *more* audits. They started going over *all* the records. I couldn't do anything with what I took, except maybe sneak them back in or destroy them. Before I could, John stole them."

"What do you know about your son's death?"

"Whaddya mean?" The anger returned. He leaned forward, but must have decided staying on the bed was the better idea. "I had nothing to do with that."

"He took the bonds. You're in real trouble if you can't get them back."

"Yeah, right. I kill him and somehow kill a cop—which is ludicrous by itself."

"Where were you that morning?"

"In my office. Surrounded by people."

"I'll be in touch."

On the train back, Taylor wondered if he could take Mortelli's story at face value. None of the other evidence pointed to him. He was going to go back to work on finding out where the bonds ended up. Now that he'd reported about them, he needed that question answered. Were the bonds related to the double killing? Probably not. The briefcase was a family affair. A weird one at that.

22

———— ◆ ————

THE NEXT MORNING, Taylor found Cramly standing in the door to the offices of the City News Bureau.

Cramly shook his head slowly. "It's really bad."

"What's going on?"

"Novak. The ambulance boys are working on him."

Taylor pushed past Cramly into the office. Whoever turned the place over wasn't looking for anything in particular. They were looking to destroy. Desks lay on their sides. Wooden drawers had been pulled out and smashed to kindling. Metal drawers were bent and twisted. The big Telecopier, the most expensive thing the City News Bureau owned, had received several mortal blows. The drum sat on the floor like a piece of pipe waiting for a plumbing project.

He stepped over the contacts from his two rolodexes, spread on the floor like a card trick gone wrong, and stood at the door of Novak's little office, looking down on the scene from behind the gurney blocking the way. The two ambulance men were getting ready to lift Novak. One eye was swollen shut and the other wandered aimlessly. Blood ran from his nose and mouth. Based on the slick smears on the floor, he'd lost a lot.

One ambulance driver counted to three, and the two gently picked up Novak's ragdoll body and lowered him to the narrow mattress. One arm was splinted. A quiet wheezing came out of his lungs, the air blowing little bubbles in the blood on his lower lip.

Taylor crouched down. "Henry, I'm so sorry." He touched the top of Novak's clammy hand. "Who did this?"

"Buddy, we've got to get him out of here. He's bad. Already in shock."

Taylor still leaned in. "Was it cops?"

"He can't tell you shit."

They wheeled the gurney through the door. Cramly looked down at Novak then up at Taylor.

"Who called it in?" Taylor asked.

"I did." Cramly pushed his hand through his sparse hair and squeezed the back of his thin neck. "I found him that way. When I left last night, he said he was going to work late."

"Fucking cops."

"How can you be sure?"

"You don't make this much noise without a call going in, even at night. Someone had to make sure that call got ignored."

"If you're right, we're in deep shit."

"We were in deep shit twelve hours ago when I wrote the story. I wanted to draw them out. Got my wish. Stupid, stupid move, trying to flush out killers with a story. I should have waited, waited until I had the real thing."

"Novak wanted it just as badly—maybe worse."

"Doesn't matter. I'm the one with the judgment. Been that way since we started at the paper. Now he's …. Go with him."

Cramly disappeared down the hallway, moving quickly for an old man.

Bet he can't decide which is more dangerous, being here or with Novak.

Taylor's guilt could easily have sat him down in the one working chair, kept him sitting and blaming himself until he figured the only thing to do was go down to the Blarney Rock at 43rd and Eighth and try and wash away the blackness claiming him. Somehow he mustered enough anger to shove back the guilt. The mixture had saved him before. Had got him going. It got him going this time.

On the wall of Novak's office remained the list of City News Bureau's four clients. No, five. Novak had penciled in WWRN last night before buying the bottle of sparkling wine. Bloody shards from the bottle were at Taylor's feet. One of the weapons used on Novak? Blood mixed with the blank sheets of newsprint they typed on, producing a sweet, pulpy, iron stink that drove Taylor from the smaller office. He put his shoulder to his own gray steel desk and with a loud groan, righted it. He picked up the Rolodex cards—seventeen years of collecting contacts—and put four messy piles on the desk. Those who ransacked the place weren't bright enough to know how much damage they could have done by taking or destroying those.

One of the phones on the floor still purred a dial tone.

"Thank Christ."

Taylor worked his way down the list of stations. Two didn't pick up, while a third was an engineer who "didn't know anything about news." On the fourth try, Taylor heard the deep tones of a DJ, Nicholas of the Night, who'd broadcast the overnight shift and was stuck doing fill-in for the morning guy.

"Do you read the headlines?"

"After midnight, yeah. There's a news guy before that."

"We sent over a story about the shooting of a cop yesterday evening."

"Corruption. Briefcase full of bonds. Good one. We read it a few times, before and after midnight, but had to stop."

"Why?"

"Got a call from a cop. An angry cop. Said the story was wrong. So I called my station manager. He's a bit of a chicken shit. Said to spike it."

"Cop say anything else? Give you a name?"

"Captain Callahan. Wanted to know where we got the piece from because it wasn't in any of the papers. Told him you guys. Figured if he had a beef, he should talk to you. Did he reach you?"

"Oh yeah, he reached us."

"He sure as hell was pissed. He was yelling right through 'Lyin' Eyes.' That's a four-minute song. Speaking of which. Gotta go. 'Feelings' only runs three and three quarters."

Nice touch with the name. Had to be Top Deck.

Taylor thought hard on what they might have learned from Novak that could be damaging. The phone tip about the radio call was anonymous. *Shit, Rayban.*

He tried to reach Samantha before he went downtown. Things were too dangerous. He needed her to know. He called her apartment. No answer. No surprise. She hadn't been back there in over a week. He now had more than one reason to talk to her father. The Sergeant picked up at his house.

"I'm already late for my shift." He was angry.

"Look, my boss was badly beaten, our offices wrecked because of this damn story. Please. Talk to me when you get off. Anywhere, anytime."

"Don't trust you. I'm not sure Samantha does either." *Not sure? That meant she couldn't have told her father everything. Yet.* "You helped her out, so we'll have a drink. Nelligan's on East 233rd, right across from Woodlawn Cemetery. Perfect place if you dick me around. Even better place if you're dicking my daughter around."

Terrific. A trip to the Bronx. What happened to crime stories that stayed in Manhattan?

He hung up. The wreckage of the office looked worse the more he stared at it. In less than a week, he'd managed to lose two jobs. One was careless, but two was just plain stupid—in this case, colossally stupid.

He called St. Clare's Hospital.

"Critical condition," said Cramly.

Taylor wondered how long Cramly would stay with Novak. Would he ever come back to the office?

THE SUBWAY RIDE downtown was fast, the cars nearly empty in the lull just after the morning rush. His car had two homeless men and an acoustic guitar player, but the musician had to leave when the bums started a fight over who would get to beg on that car. Make a nice little story if Taylor were in the market for nice little stories.

The anger driving him forward smashed into a wall of panic when he reached Rayban's regular corner on Avenue C. The boxes, blankets, and small collection of personal items were gone. A drunk clung to a light pole a quarter of the way up the block like the earth would flip over if he ever let go. The drunk nodded as if he understood when Taylor asked about Rayban. When the drunk spoke, slurred half words and drool came out, but nothing that made any sense.

Taylor went up both sides of the block. He pushed his way into the building where John Mortelli had had his squat, found the police padlock broken off and the apartment cleaned out. He walked one block west, where he found a well-dressed black man coming out of a building in decent shape. He said he was Joseph Walker, a social worker checking on clients. He knew of Rayban.

"I can't get those two into a shelter. Bad experience, I think, though they won't say. Something happened to Sally. Sometimes I'm not sure which is worse—the streets or the shelters."

"Have you seen him?"

"He over on C?"

"Gone from his usual patch."

"Rayban's got more than one. A circuit. Moves about every three weeks. Try the other side of the FDR, down by the river."

Taylor took Walker's phone number—always good to have

a contact who knew the neighborhood—and ran the length of 15th Street. At the FDR, he hopped the fence and dodged traffic across six lanes of cars, all of which would have hit him as soon as look at him if he hadn't been more nimble. About 200 feet north, both Rayban and Sally were lying on blankets set out in front of their boxes. The dog slept in Sally's.

"Reporter-man, welcome to our waterfront abode. With the sun at this angle, you'd almost believe the East River was a river. I'd stay here all year, but at some point the cops gotta move us along."

"You need to move now. Somewhere people don't know."

Rayban sat up. "What happened?"

"That information you gave me about Mortelli. Some corrupt cops may know it came from you."

"You said I'd stay out of it."

"Had to tell my boss. Somebody nearly beat him to death last night. I don't know what he told them."

"You've screwed us. Totally." Rayban stood up. "Where are we supposed to go? This is our neighborhood. You need to *know* your neighborhood to keep from getting killed."

"I'll help you find a place."

"Screw you. I've had enough of your help." He started stuffing the blanket into a beat-up black garbage bag. "C'mon Sally, we've got to get somewhere safe."

"Somewhere safe. Somewhere safe." Sally folded her blankets and towels and put them all in a big round hatbox. "The garage. The garage."

"We don't want to go back there." Rayban quickly folded his cardboard box into a neat square and used rough twine to tie it up. "You wanna know how messed up this is? Her family has a place on the Upper Eastside. Last March, when it got really bad, we snuck into the garage—they have a whole house with a goddamn garage. Her father found us. Cold, fishy little man. Just stared at her for ten seconds and called the cops.

She shook the whole time we waited. He told the cops we were burglars. Dumped in the system. That really messed her up. Sent her off to some other universe. She's only lately started coming back to earth."

"I can do it. I can do it."

Sally stood, picked up John-Boy's rope leash and handed Taylor a piece of paper folded into a tight triangle in the way kids did when they made paper footballs. Smeared ink and smudges of dirt covered it.

"I'm going to shut these cops down as fast as I can. Two, three days."

Rayban shook his head no, but Sally said, "Yes. Yes. Up in mountains. Up in the mountains."

Taylor looked at Rayban as if he were a translator.

"She still don't forget her family's schedule. Old fish eyes has a lodge upstate. He shoots at deer this time of year because there aren't enough steaks on his table."

"They're definitely away?"

"She's always right on that stuff."

"Back on Friday. Back on Friday."

"Then I have until Friday."

By now, Rayban's stuff was tied together to form a misshapen backpack, which he shouldered. "Don't take any longer. Sally's being brave now, 'cause she knows they're gone." He lowered his voice to a hissed whisper. "She gets put in the system again, she'll fall so far back into her skull I might never get her to come back out. Do it sooner. Because you well and truly screwed us. I don't want to be dead."

Rayban, Sally, and the dog started the walk along the Hudson River that would take them from one socioeconomic universe—Alphabet City—to an entirely different one—the Upper Eastside.

I'm losing track of the lives I've ruined.

He flipped the paper triangle once in the air, caught it and carefully unfolded it. The writing was a neat cursive.

Hello, whoever you are,

This is not a suicide note. I'm being SENT to my death. Least I think so. If you have it, I must be dead. I told Sally to give it to someone she trusts. Everyone thinks she's totally out of it. Even Rayban doesn't totally get her. He's overprotective. She knows who to trust. She learned the hard way.

I already told Rayban most everything about the cop, him shooting Moon. I didn't say anything about the business card. Rayban worries too much. He might do the wrong thing.

After the cop told me what I was supposed to do, he offered me five bucks for dog food. Said I didn't want anything from him. He smacked me again and threw the money on the floor. I picked up the singles when he left. Mixed in was the cop's business card. I'm not even putting that in this note. Too dangerous. I hope whatever happens to me, the dogs survive this. I know Rayban will help out there at least. I opened Perry Mason's collar, stashed the card in there and stitched it back up.

I've also written the serial numbers of the bonds on the back of this. If they haven't been found yet, the briefcase is in the shed where I keep the dog food. Dad thought I never listened. But I did. He said these numbers are gold. They are the one way to trace those things. I'm not sure if he's mixed up in this. He made threats. They're there just in case. I hope I was right about Sally and this note gets in good hands. Actually I really hope no one ever has to read this, but now I believe that's too much to hope for.

Peace,

Johnny Mort

Taylor turned over the sheet. Fifty seven-digit numbers

were neatly printed in two columns. This was a way to track the bonds. But that was nothing next to what was in Mason's collar. The dog was probably snoozing in the cabin of the houseboat. The business card in his collar would confirm who set up the murders.

23

———◆———

NELLIGAN'S PUB WAS like a trick box. From the outside, the place looked to be a nondescript Bronx storefront facing lines of marble tombstones across the street. When Taylor stepped inside, it was like he'd been transported from New York to a village pub in Ireland. The transition was so astonishing that he went outside to look at the front and walk back in again. This bit of reporter's observational instinct got him a good up and down from the gimlet-eyed bartender wiping nothing much with a clean white cloth. One old man sat on a barstool drinking a bottle of Guinness. Taylor had seen the dark Irish beer in a couple of spots in Queens—though neither of those came close to looking as Irish as Nelligan's. This place was posing for a postcard.

"What will ya be havin' now?" The bartender's accent had been imported with the Powers Whiskey mirrors, Irish road signs, framed black and whites of sheep, sea, and turf and the rest of the bric-a-brac.

"Rolling Rock, please."

"We've none of that trendy shite in here. If it's American you want, I'll sell you Schmidt or Pabst's. They're piss water too, if you want my opinion."

"Too right," said the Guinness drinker.

"A Schmidt, thanks."

The old man stared at him unapologetically. Taylor knew the look. You'd get it in any bar in his old neighborhood. In any neighborhood in New York. *What're you doing in my place? You're not from here.*

The old man, with a full beard and wool cap that looked like it came off the same postcard, offered up a test for Taylor. He slid over a blue and white Maxwell House can. Scotch taped on the side was a hand-lettered sign. "Give to Noraid. Help families in Ireland."

Noraid, the Irish Northern Aid Committee, funneled cash from the U.S. to the Irish Republican Army. Sticking a couple bucks in there would buy Taylor a little peace in here. It would also help buy guns over there.

He turned from the can to the bartender. "My mother always said charity begins at home. I'd like to buy this gentleman a round."

"What parish was she from?" asked the old man. "I'd imagine one over Arthur Avenue way. You look to come from that part of the world." He made it sound like Taylor sailed across the ocean to get there, rather than arriving from another Bronx neighborhood, an Italian one.

This will blow his mind then. "We're from Queens."

"Queens. Lousy with EYE-talians. Right Jimmy?" He spoke to the bartender like Taylor wasn't there. "Still take their money. A porter and a Jameson please."

"My mother was Greek Orthodox, actually." He toasted the bottle of Schmidt and sipped the beer. "Least I'm not Protestant, right?"

Jimmy the bartender was fast and strong. He grabbed one arm and lifted Taylor off the barstool and across the bar. Pain. Every time Taylor got yanked around, his bruised ribs started hurting again His bottle crashed on the shiny wood and splashed beer all over his pants and jacket.

"Hey, easy, fella."

"Don't easy me. The Troubles are something we *do not* joke about. I don't care if you're a Chinaman bowing down to his big fat Buddha. In fact, better that than your Greek church with its icons and false saints and other bloody heresies."

"Let him be." Mick Callahan stepped up to the bar. "The young man's not very bright. From what I hear, he's already had his head banged on a couple times too many."

Samantha's father, in faded work pants and a flannel lumberjack shirt, walked away from the bar to the jukebox, selected songs and sat down at a table to the right. Taylor wiped as much beer as he could off his pants and the front of the field jacket. Though his brother's old jacket had seen worse, Taylor hated the thought that he'd stink like a drunk—like his father.

"You buying another?" Jimmy smiled like his question was the day's best joke.

"Yeah, another. Didn't get to drink much of the first. Whatever Sergeant Callahan's having too."

Jimmy looked for Callahan to give the nod he'd accept a drink from the heathen, which he did, ordering a Pabst.

Taylor set both beers on the table. "Thought it would be Guinness."

"You have to be raised to that stuff. I was born here in America." The plain statement of fact sounded angry.

Taylor had to admit he was worried about confronting a cop about corruption. Still, that he'd done before. His problem was he wanted to have it both ways this time, to check a story he couldn't ignore *and* somehow hold onto Samantha. He didn't think that was going to be possible.

He touched the sharp corner of the small paper rectangle in his coat pocket. Mick Callahan's business card was the one dropped in John Mortelli's squat, because that's what Taylor had taken out of Mason's collar. He'd have laughed if it weren't such deadly information. It was the kind of secret clue he never encountered in his work. He was going to get shot for being a Hardy Boy.

Still, he needed Callahan to stay calm and listen. There was more to this than the card.

On the jukebox, Irish voices sung the one about the Wild Colonial Boy. Loudly.

Callahan leaned in. "Those two over there." He nodded at the bar. "They can spread a story faster than the *New York Times* and the *Irish Independent* put together. Everyone comes in here. That's why the music."

"Clancy Brothers, right?"

"Didn't know they had fans among the Eastern Rite."

"My father's half English, half Irish, full drinker."

"Catholic?"

"Atheist."

"To quote your poor joke, better than Protestant. But too much religion and The Troubles. It's my daughter I care about." The slight smile vanished. A strain came into Callahan's voice, worry and anger—with the edge going to worry. "Where is she?"

"Don't know. Haven't seen her since last night."

"I told her not to mess around with a reporter. She didn't listen. She never listens."

May as well go straight at him. Get this over with. "I talked to Detective Christian Slive yesterday. You know him?"

"Yeah. Is he after Sam?" Callahan's blue eyes looked intently at Taylor.

"He told me something your daughter didn't like, which is why I don't know where she is now."

"Well, if she didn't, doubt I'm going to either." Callahan finished off his Pabst and waved two fingers at Jimmy.

"No, I don't think you will either. Slive is anti-corruption—"

"Know what he does."

"He told me he was using Dodd to get information out of Samantha."

"Why, if he's not after Sam?"

"He's after you. Says you're running a drugs and extortion racket out of the One-Nine."

Jimmy arrived at the table with two more beers and Callahan took both of them. "Thanks. Open the backdoor to the alley for me, will ya?"

"I surely will." Jimmy smiled at Taylor. "A little Golden Gloves boxing tonight." He walked to the rear of Nelligan's.

Callahan toasted. "To the truth."

"What is?"

"Did you wonder why a shoofly on the Lower Eastside is working a corruption case in another precinct?"

Taking this awfully calmly.

"I did," Taylor said. "That's just one thing I need to check. He didn't tell me much. Just claimed what you're involved in is bigger than what's going on in the Ninth."

"Strong stuff. The kind of stuff that can get you shot in the face." Callahan said it without menace.

"That's not an original play, not after Serpico."

"Old habits die hard."

Taylor read people well. Thousands of interviews had taught him the skill. Yet right now, when the stakes really could be a bullet in his face, he couldn't tell where Callahan was going. Was he threatening Taylor? Slive? He wasn't exploding like an innocent man might. Something was off, and at the same time Taylor would bet his life—*was* betting his life—that Callahan wasn't the guy.

Which meant it was time to play his next card—the business card—and gauge Callahan's reaction. Because this was as much about Schmidt as it was about Callahan. With a minimum of fuss—Jimmy and the old man might still be watching—he put the card on the table. He told Callahan the whole story of John Mortelli.

Callahan shook his head. "Someone's going to an awful lot of trouble to put me in the picture."

"I agree. You see, there's a problem with the business card end of this. I'm certain it wasn't you in Mortelli's apartment."

Callahan set his beer down, looking surprised for the first time. "Go on."

"Whoever dropped the card, he didn't count on Mortelli giving the man's description to someone, a friend of Mortelli's in the neighborhood. The description doesn't match you, not in the least."

"You have the description?" *He actually sounds impressed.* Taylor flipped the notebook. While he did, Callahan signaled to Jimmy. "Two of the Jameson."

Taylor looked up. "Can't have a—"

"Better than a shot in the face." Callahan smiled, and again Taylor couldn't read his meaning.

He paraphrased Rayban's words. "The guy was tall, skinny, with a bullet-shaped head and medium-length black and gray hair."

"Always wished I was taller. But definitely not me."

"Description matches a cop named Schmidt who's running the gang in the Ninth. Samantha's sure it must be him."

Callahan knocked back the shot. "Samantha's not wrong much. I'll retire a sergeant in uniform. She'll make detective. If they ever let her."

"We need to figure out what's really going on for that to ever happen."

"You've got a dead man talking to your source. What good is it?"

"I don't work in a court of law. I work in the court of facts. In less than a week, I … Samantha and I have done some good reporting. I was stupid. I had some pieces but not enough to write a watertight story. I put out this half-assed version in the hopes that someone would talk. Instead, I got my boss nearly beat to death. This points to cops in the Ninth. Except when it doesn't. I need to fill in the holes. I need to get someone on the record about the Ninth. That Slive won't do. Instead he points at you."

Callahan stood up. "Drink your whiskey and come with me."

"What's going on?"

"You need to know when not to ask questions and when to just move."

Callahan strolled past the old man, patting him on the shoulder, and waved at Jimmy. "On my tab." Taylor downed the shot and followed, coughing.

"Off to the woodshed," Jimmy said. Laughter.

The door was propped open by a chunk of cinderblock. Callahan leaned back against the brick wall opposite. His hands were jammed in the pockets of his pants.

Taylor was confused. And worried. He'd thought he was making progress with Callahan. "Look, I already said it couldn't have been you in the apartment."

"It's not that. I don't want anyone else to even have a chance of hearing this. Loud music's not enough. Slive was closing in on the dirty cops in the Ninth. Must have been. Maybe he already had the screws into Schmidt. Maybe he needed Dodd to lock it down. Schmidt invents a bigger fish to get Slive off his ass. A guy like Slive loves cops turning on cops, so what would be juicier than getting Dodd to work Samantha to string up her own father? That's why Schmidt dropped a card with my name on it."

"Eventually Slive's got to figure out it was a distraction."

"Maybe after giving Schmidt enough time to get his business in order. Probably why Dodd was killed. This is all about the Ninth. They're using Slive's ambition—and he is a man of large ambition. They've got him chasing shadows." He took out a pack of Parliaments and lit up. "I just want to know Sam's safe. I've checked everywhere and everyone I can think of." He exhaled smoke. "I can't do anything until I know she's okay."

"What're you going to do?"

"Talk with Schmidt."

"Just talk?"

"We'll see. He came after me. Time I returned the favor."

"What about going to Slive?"

"Need to be careful there. If I screw with IA, I'm guilty—no questions asked. That much *has* changed in the department."

"That's a lot of power."

"It is ... too much when you're on the wrong end of it. I need to shut down Slive's source. I can't shut Schmidt down, not until Sam is safe. After that, we'll see."

"If I can confirm the details of what Top Deck is up to, the department will have to act."

"Good luck with that. Sounds like your half-story muddied up the waters pretty bad."

"Yes, it did." *Muddied up so many things.* "I need to convince someone to break ranks. A cop like Dodd was."

"No. You need someone Schmidt's taking money off of. Get them to talk. That's what Slive should be doing, rather than playing games with Dodd and Samantha and me. Find someone who's paying into Schmidt's pad."

"Will you let me know if you talk to her?"

Callahan dropped the cigarette, put it out with his toe and lit another. He eyed Taylor through gray smoke. "Not sure. I'd imagine she's pretty angry at you right now." He walked to the doorway.

"I'll let you know if I get anything."

"Do that." Smoke trailed Callahan as he entered the bar.

Taylor took the alley to the street and the street to the subway. It was now his job to find someone paying off Schmidt. To help Samantha and Mick Callahan—to keep the father from doing something crazy or worse. He owed Novak too. Rayban and Sally. Cramly even. Debts all over the place. He needed something on the record, a story that the stations would run and the papers would rush to pick up.

First, he'd make one stop along the way. He would visit First

National City Bank of New York before it closed for the day. John Mortelli's letter, with its list of serial numbers from the bonds, was in his pocket next to Callahan's business card. After, he'd spend all this time searching for Top Deck victims.

24

———◆———

CLIFFORD HARMON OF First National City was a small wrinkled man sitting behind a big oak desk. His hands stayed folded the entire time Taylor recounted the story of the briefcase. He remained in that position after Taylor finished talking, tapping his thumbs together in a slow steady beat. A huge picture behind Harmon depicted a clipper ship cutting through steep, foam-crested waves. Why had this prunified little man picked that painting? He didn't look like he did anything but sit behind the desk in the biggest office on the floor, lording over the bank's municipal bond department.

The thumbs stopped. "That's quite a fantastical story. Even in these fraught times for the city's finances."

"I *saw* the briefcase. The bonds."

"I *could* take your word for that. But I don't really take anyone's word for anything. I need documentation."

"I've got the serial numbers. Ask Mortelli about them?"

"I cannot. He no longer works for this bank."

Taylor stopped writing and looked up from his notebook. "Because of the bonds?"

"No, of course not. I told you that story was fantastical. Mr.

Mortelli's work wasn't up to this bank's very high standards."

"You're going to cover this up, aren't you?" Taylor pulled a copy of John Mortelli's note out of his pocket. "Here. On the back. He lists the serial numbers in the briefcase. Those are like fingerprints for a bond, right? What would happen if these numbers were made public?"

Taylor put the sheet on the desk. Harmon's thumbs started up again, beating a quicker time. He leaned over the sheet to look but didn't seem to want to touch the paper. Finally, as if worried about fingerprints, he picked the copy up by the corner and left the room. He was gone a long time. Taylor checked out all the nautical paintings hung on the dark, wood-paneled walls. Ships thundering cannon fire at each other. Ships wheeling into the sunlight. Ships racing to harbor ahead of a storm black as death. Maybe Harmon was some kind of Walter Mitty, sitting here, and at the same time standing on the decks of these vessels, ordering fire, turning hard from a giant wave, commanding the crew, instead of twiddling his thumbs while the city burned.

As the minutes ticked by, he slumped into Harmon's leather guest chair. He was anxious to get moving. The bonds were a loose end. And he hated leaving any story hanging loose. But he wanted to get on to his real mission—to follow Schmidt and hope he came up with something. He wished he knew where Samantha was, wished he could have her help. Two on a tail was better than one. That wasn't the only reason he missed her. Being a fuck-up was lonely work. He was desperate for company.

Face facts. Maybe, but only maybe, Schmidt collects from someone. Maybe, just maybe, that person will talk. Thin stuff.

He sure as hell wasn't going back to Slive until he had something solid, lest the IA man send him off on another wild goose chase.

Harmon didn't return to the office. Instead, a six-foot, 250-poundish guy, his blue blazer stretched across his chest and stomach to button once, lowered himself into Harmon's desk chair and unbuttoned that one button. Another man in a blazer, this one a little smaller but not much, came and stood behind Taylor's chair.

The one sitting put the list back on the desk. "We're pleased to report these bonds are accounted for in our vaults."

"Who are you?"

"Jordan. Director of Bank Security."

"How long have they been in your vaults?"

"They never left." His face was placid. "We would take any statement to the contrary as a direct threat to this financial institution."

"I don't care what you'd take. You're lying. Mortelli admitted—" Jordan nodded and the other blazer pulled Taylor out of his seat. He'd been thrown out of a lot of places before, but a bank was new. They had him outside in less than a minute.

Taylor stood on the sidewalk in front of the granite building with Jordan watching him.

To Taylor's surprise, Harmon came out on the sidewalk. "Jordan is a bit rough around the edges, but he is entirely loyal to the bank. Now you know the story. No one will say differently. Mr. Mortelli received a very nice severance package."

"I know what I saw. I've got the list."

"It would be your word against everyone else's. As I understand it—and don't let me tell you your business—a reporter isn't supposed to be his own source on a story. Not the only source, at least. How would anyone know you didn't make it up? Didn't you get in trouble for that before?"

The nine-year-old addict. Story's going to haunt me forever.

"The cops must have a record."

"The police can't have a record if the bonds were here all the time." He lowered his voice. "Do you have any idea what might happen if a story appeared, saying a substantial sum of city bonds wasn't where it was supposed to be?"

"I've heard this one before. Ford and all of Washington

would have proof New York can't be trusted."

"That's exactly right. I wonder. Do you have a greater responsibility than to one little story?"

Must be everyone's hymn now.

"Not a luxury a good reporter can afford. I'd never write anything." Taylor opened his mouth, closed it and thought a moment. "Mortelli's going to get away with it."

"If I might be a bit philosophical at this point—philosophical and off the record—there are many things that might be taken care of after a great catastrophe has been averted. This morning's *Times* reported the newest revenue projections. Did you read?" Taylor shook no. "The city has enough cash on hand to avoid default until a week from Friday. Eight business days until the guillotine. There is no time left. Washington must act. Good day, Mr. Taylor."

Harmon walked past the big security man, who stayed where he was. Taylor left angry, but already convinced there would be no follow-up story on the once-lost bonds. The rest of that tale would remain locked in First National City's vault until it would only interest historians.

Early the next morning, Taylor rented a Ford with money he didn't have at a place on West 36th. Having learned Schmidt was working the seven to three shift, he got to the precinct at 6:30 a.m. The sketchy part was watching the parked patrol cars and catching Schmidt getting into one. He didn't. He walked off on foot patrol, spinning his Billy club with zeal.

So much for smart planning.

Taylor left the Ford behind to collect tickets he also couldn't afford.

Two hours later, his feet burned, while Schmidt showed no sign of slowing down. He swung the stick, stopped, smiled, gave directions and asked quick questions at a couple of stores. Twice, Taylor thought handshakes covered cash being passed. Same smile, same swing of the stick, *and* maybe a flash of green. He wasn't absolutely sure and wasn't prepared to stop—losing Schmidt in the process—to try and work an interview.

The long walk gave Taylor time to think. Last night he'd stopped in at St. Clare's on the way home. Novak was unconscious and still in critical condition. He'd sat in the hospital waiting room for two hours. Family came and went. He felt too guilty to say anything to them.

He might have marinated in that guilt for Schmidt's entire shift, but his brain, probably as a defense mechanism, switched to considering the calls he'd made to sources late yesterday, before the hospital stop. He was trying to figure out something that didn't make sense. Top Deck was made up of uniformed cops, while protection for gambling and prostitution, at least in the days before 1970, was usually provided by corrupt undercover men. One source suggested the corruption in the Ninth Precinct appeared to be an unintended consequence of the anti-graft campaign. Internal Affairs had done such a good job cleaning out dirty plainclothesman and detectives that the whores and numbers runners were coming under increased pressure from the law. In the Ninth, they probably went to the uniformed officers not so much for protection from arrest but to get intelligence on what the plainclothes guys were up to. Another source also mentioned the cops were probably collecting on assorted violations from retailers—a typical source of graft for those in uniform. His next story wasn't going to miss a single detail. Even knowing that, the guilt was still there.

Taylor trailed Schmidt down Avenue B, staying on the other side of the street and 20 yards back. To avoid notice, he used shop windows on his side to watch Schmidt's reflection. Schmidt entered Rosen's Deli. An Asian man—maybe Chinese, maybe Korean—worked behind the counter. Schmidt and the Asian talked.

The conversation quickly became animated; the Asian started waving his hands wildly. The Billy club came up, and

Schmidt pushed the round end into the middle of the man's small chest. Schmidt must have been emphasizing points he was making. He poked that same spot as the man continued to gesticulate. Out of nowhere, a woman leapt up and wrapped her arms around Schmidt's neck. She didn't stay there long. With one hand, Schmidt whipped her to the ground and brought the club down once, twice. The Asian man put one knee up to come over the counter but found himself with a close-up view of Schmidt's revolver. The storeowner's head dropped. He went to the cash register, took out a handful of bills and gave them to Schmidt. The cop left the store swinging the club in neat figure eights.

Taylor crossed the avenue as soon as Schmidt was at the corner. In the store, the man kneeled next to the woman. Blood poured from her nose and a cut lip.

"Did you call an ambulance?"

"No, I … no."

Taylor went behind the counter, dialed 911, gave all the details, and came back around. "Put something under her feet in case of shock. Cover her."

The man shrugged out of his tattered red blazer and draped it over her. Next he took off his white dress shirt and folded it into a pillow for under her legs.

"What was the pay-off for?"

"Three months ago I was caught selling liquor without license. Three months. Still I have to pay one hundred dollar every week. There is no end. It breaks us." He stared at the woman. "She should have stayed out of it. Now look at her."

"Is it always Schmidt?"

The man came out of his daze and turned to Taylor suspiciously just as his wife moaned. "Who are you? Can't afford no more trouble."

"I'm a reporter. I'm doing a story on corrupt cops here in the Ninth."

He shook his hands in front of him. "I want none of that."

His wife opened her eyes, and he bent over her. She whispered in Chinese. The man answered. She spoke again, still whispering but angry. He sat back up. "My wife shames me. She asks me to have some courage."

In the ten minutes they waited for the ambulance, Mr. Hu told what he knew of the shakedown, moving onto other businesses. He wouldn't talk about gambling or prostitution.

"Mr. Harlan owns discount store in middle of next block. He didn't even do anything wrong. They told him he pay so he won't get robbed. He didn't. He got robbed. Cops offer to sell stuff back. He said no to that. They leave a pile of burnt broken things in front of store."

The ambulance arrived.

"What will you tell them?"

The revolving red lights made Hu's features dance. "Some robber came at her. We'll say same to police. You must keep our names out of this. This is as much courage as I can afford."

Harlan—short, bottle shaped, and dressed in a wrinkled seersucker suit that was wrong for the neighborhood and the season—invited Taylor into his office, a space cordoned off by boxes in a store that appeared to sell everything, with everything placed pretty much anywhere. He poured rye into two plastic tumblers and slid one to Taylor. "Mrs. Hu got herself beat up?"

"Pretty badly. They said you've had trouble too."

"That's too bad. I like them. I couldn't afford the local police tax. Insurance paid for the theft." Harman knocked back half the rye. "I don't have insurance for payoffs. They've left me alone since. Perhaps more profitable endeavors came along."

"Why don't you report them?" Taylor sipped his.

"You know, I like talking to reporters. I'm publisher of a weekly newspaper out in the Rockaways. Was my dad's business—business, that is, if you don't define a business as something that makes you any fucking money. I'm not talking with anyone who doesn't drink." Taylor finished half the cup.

It was raggedly rough and he liked it. Harman drank most of his and poured into both glasses. "But much as I like talking, reporting bad cops is another thing. It's one thing to dodge them. Don't even know how long that will last. I don't get the idea they're very organized. They take what comes. Different if you report them. You get every cop—straight, crooked, and undecided —crawling up your ass. I've got no violations, not doing anything illegal. They knocked me over once. I'm probably not worth bothering with after that. That's exactly how I want things to stay. How did you find out about the Hus?"

"I was following Schmidt to see if I could talk to his marks."

"Your lucky day then. Want to know where Schmidt is now? One stop on his rounds never changes. Two doors down is a walk-up, 3-D. Luce and Stacy. Whores, but nice enough ladies. They shop a lot here. Schmidt stops in, gets a little payment-in-kind along with his cash. Be up there now."

Taylor stood. "Thanks."

"This may be a broken-down neighborhood. There's still decent people here. We haven't gone completely into the shitter yet. Schmidt and his gang are going to push us there, the greedy fuckers. When you buzz, say Harlan said to ask for Luce." A disconcerting wink. "Schmidt likes Stacy, the poor thing."

Taylor took the stairs up to 3-D two at a time. He had his .32 out. He figured there was one way to handle this. He'd let Schmidt say whatever he wanted—if he wanted to say anything at all—but without the use of his gun or Billy club. After that, Taylor was going to get the hell out of there, tell Slive what he had and get the story transmitted in all its sad, bad, exact detail.

A chunky blonde with black roots opened the door. Taylor stepped into the apartment's living room, which had been furnished in a tawdry fantasy of a fancy sitting room. The couch and three chairs were plush and red, all with too many pillows. The gun held at his side, Taylor rushed down the hallway before Luce could yell, and hearing the expected noises, pushed open the door. He crossed the room and sat on a chair in the corner—which conveniently held all of Schmidt's gear. An ass rose and fell under the sheets to a wheezy sort of grunting that sounded anything but sexy.

"Officer Schmidt." The ass stopped like someone slamming on the brakes. The body rolled over. "We need to talk." Taylor rested the .32 on his knee as Schmidt pulled himself to a sitting position against the headboard. "Not the way I usually like to do an interview, but you're a special case."

25

———•———

"**M**AN, YOU ARE SHIT-DEEP IN A WORLD OF HURT."
Next to Schmidt, a more realistic blonde held
the bed sheet up to her nose. An odd sort of modesty for her
profession. Or did she think the sheet would stop bullets? Guilt
fluttered through Taylor. He wasn't even pointing the gun and
didn't like scaring her with it.

"You can leave, Stacy. My business is with Schmidt. Feel free
to call the police. Though I doubt he wants to take the chance
an honest cop might show."

"You're a fucking dead man. You're already inside your
coffin."

"And you're Johnny One Note." Taylor tried to keep his voice
even, but anger boiled up from deep inside. Stories weren't
supposed to do this. You couldn't care, not too much, because
when you sat down at the typewriter, you needed to look down
on the world you'd visited, perhaps uncovered, and describe
it with that disconnected objectivity the insurance executive
expected with his cornflakes. Dodd. Samantha. Rayban
and Sally. Moon. Novak. This whole neighborhood. Taylor
wouldn't mind seeing this bastard hurt some. Wasn't the job

though. "I'm not dead. I'm sitting here with the drop on Mr. Top Deck, who was in bed with a prostitute. What I am is a reporter with the City News Bureau."

"Never heard of it."

"You've got balls, I'll give you that. You almost killed my boss. Wrecked our office. This time, I've got the whole story on your racket. Just letting you respond to the charges against you. I'd hate a policeman of your standing to think you were treated unfairly. My service will send the story to its radio station customers. But I'm thinking this one is so good, I'm also going to give a copy to a friend at the *Daily News*. You and I can agree that lots of folks read the *Daily News*. Folks in the mayor's office read the *News*. The Chief of Department. Over in Internal Affairs, they read it too. So, now that you understand why we're here, is there anything you want to say about the bribes you and your fellow officers have been collecting from prostitutes, numbers rackets, and upstanding store owners?"

"Fuck you."

"I'll take that as a 'no comment.' Families to think of. What about murdering Officer Dodd to protect your operation? Same response?"

Schmidt tipped his slender head in the same way Mason did whenever Taylor tried to give the dog a command.

"You're dead anyway, but I'll tell you this. I had nothing to do with Dodd. If I were going to kill him, I'd have just done it. You'll find that out soon enough."

"I can quote you?"

"You won't get the chance."

Standing, Taylor picked up Schmidt's gear, eased his way to the bedroom door, stepped out and pulled it shut. The noise of a nude cop getting out of bed fast. Taylor sprinted for the front door.

Luce pulled it open, and as he passed, she whispered, "Please stop him."

He flew down the stairs and left Schmidt's stuff at the bottom.

At least that would slow him down. He hit the street and cut over to Avenue A with the intent of taking a zigzag path back to the precinct. He guessed—more like prayed—that was the last place Schmidt would look for him, considering that other Top Deck cops could be there.

He hoped like hell Slive was. The IA man would have to take seriously the information Taylor had on Schmidt.

My ass is on the line now. Five radio stations aren't enough to save it.

The *Daily News* wouldn't run the story without some sort of confirmation from Slive. They'd insist on checking everything Taylor had. All that would take time, which brought him right back to how his ass was really on the line now.

The rain started again and was driven into his face by a cold autumn wind as he reached the other side of Avenue A. He pulled the collar up on the field jacket, put on the wool hat, and hustled westward, checking behind for Schmidt. Nothing. At this point, any cop could be a threat.

Three soaked tickets stuck to the Ford's windshield. The cops of the Ninth liked easy pickings. He crossed to the front entrance of the precinct, was halfway up the cement steps when he spied Slive pulling out of the lot in an unmarked white Chevy. Taylor ran toward the car waving. Slive didn't see Taylor. But Taylor did see Slive's passenger: Samantha Callahan.

The car turned right, away from Taylor, on East Fifth.

"Shit, shit."

He sprinted back to the Ford, tore the tickets off, climbed in, and sped down the street. The light went red, stopping Taylor behind a car at the intersection as Slive's Chevy made the turn and headed south on Second Avenue. Taylor squeezed the steering wheel like he was wringing out a washcloth.

What was Samantha doing with Slive? Had she finally agreed to come in and talk? Maybe she'd decided that was the safest move. He hated not knowing what she was doing. He didn't want to think how angry she still was with him. He had to catch up with Slive before things got any messier.

Messier? There's a word. More like before I'm a mess on the sidewalk.

The light dropped to green and Taylor leaned on the horn. The big Buick in front of him crossed the intersection. Taylor made the turn. He took the middle lane of the avenue and was halfway through the intersection at East Fourth Street when he realized the Chevy had turned. The white car was already half a block east.

"Shit, shit."

He swung the wheel hard and hit the gas at the same time, trying to slip past a Checker Taxi turning from the far left lane—the lane you were supposed to turn from. The Ford wasn't quite fast enough. The cab smashed into the corner of the Ford's back bumper, sending the rear end of the car skidding. A yellow cab slammed into the Checker. Both cabbies were out of their cars at cabbie speed and coming straight at Taylor's car. One had a baseball bat.

"Sorry, guys. No time to work this one out."

He spun the wheel the other way and hit the gas.

Three tickets, a crushed bumper, a three-car accident. I'm not renting a car for twenty years.

He raced a block and a half and ran into traffic again, with the Chevy still a full city block in front of him. Taylor couldn't make up the distance. Each time the light went red, he was a street behind. Slive reached Avenue D, the western border of the giant Jacob Riis public housing project, which ran six blocks from East Sixth to East 13th along the East River. When Taylor got to that intersection, he couldn't find the Chevy up or down Avenue D.

"Shit, shit and shit again."

He banged the steering wheel.

Got to think.

Slive wouldn't come this way to get on the FDR Drive.

This wasn't the way to go north either. Avenue D petered out seven blocks up. For some reason—a reason Taylor couldn't fathom—Slive and Samantha must be somewhere in the Riis Houses. The complex, 20 buildings between six and 13 stories tall, had been built on a campus—a highfalutin word for a place plagued by crime and poverty—created by eliminating the Manhattan street grid. Only East Sixth and East 10th were left to cut through the project. Taylor, watched warily by several children and a woman with a shopping cart, rolled slowly along both streets to their ends. A wino on a bench wasn't wary. He smiled and waved.

By the time he got back to 10th and Avenue D, Taylor was second-guessing his gut instinct that they were in here somewhere. He took a right and drove north on D, passing several of the X-shaped, red-brick apartment towers. Just at the north end of the complex, D bent around toward the river. If this street had its own name, it wasn't posted. It dead-ended in front of one of the bigger Riis buildings. Slive's unoccupied car was parked in a spot next to a basketball court.

Taylor buzzed five, six apartments. Nothing. Maybe the system was broken. Maybe everything was broken. He pulled the door. It opened. The lock was so badly damaged that a piece of metal hung from the side of the doorframe.

The odor of trash mingled with pot. Down the hallway to the right, a black garbage bag stuffed on top of another had wedged open the trash chute door.

"Jeeeesus, what is this, Pig Day at the Riis?" A young black man came from the left hallway toward Taylor.

"I'm a reporter working a story."

"A story! Hell, I'm a story. You want to interview me?"

The man, with a beard and a medium-length, neatly trimmed Afro, stopped right in front of Taylor. The pot odor strengthened as if a cloud hovered around the guy.

Play the play you get.

Taylor took out his notebook. "Actually looking for a couple of police officers."

"Oh, so you *don't* want to interview me?"

"No, happy to. I'm a police reporter. I'm always interested in how the public thinks the police are—"

"Shitty, they're doing shitting. It makes me so goddamn angry." The man put his hands on Taylor shoulders, squeezed and looked into Taylor's eyes. He laughed. "I'm fucking with you, man." The laughter turned to heaving, like he was yelling out his mirth. "I saw your cops. That's why I said it was Pig Day. I'm Desmond. Follow me."

"Thanks. Taylor with the *Messenger*—with the City News Bureau."

"S'matter man, don't know where you work?" Desmond went through a metal door and up concrete stairs. "Elevators are out. Actually they aren't ever in."

After five flights, they stepped into the hallway. Desmond walked a few doors down and pushed open the door to apartment 5-H. Taylor stepped into the entryway. Samantha was handcuffed to the springs of a bedframe that had been propped into a corner of the living area. It looked like a torture device. She'd been stripped to her underwear.

Slive leaned against the counter of the efficiency's kitchen, which was cluttered with paint cans, tools, and glass jars. He smiled, looking welcoming, calm, and successful.

This is all wrong.

Taylor moved into the room toward Samantha. Without thinking.

"Welcome to the Playhouse," Slive said. "Take care of him."

Taylor dropped into a black hole, propelled there by a sharp, shuddering pain at the back of his head.

26

———— ♦ ————

HIS NAME REPEATED over and over again. Hearing almost hurt as much as thinking. His name made him think he was stupid for some reason—like he was the guy who'd walked into a trap.

Riiiiiight. Because I did.

"Taylor. C'mon, Taylor."

He cracked open his eyelids and the light dealt another hammer blow to the back of his head. He wanted to shut them tight but knew the pain would still be there even if he did.

"We're running out of time."

He opened his eyes all the way, and his stomach lurched. He kept from puking. His wrists were bound tight behind his back, his feet even tighter. Aside from the pain, the other sensation that managed to penetrate his scrambled brain was the hot prickly numbing of his feet going to sleep.

"Why?" It was the shortest thing he could say and hope to find out what was going on.

Samantha rose above him at an angle, still shackled to the mattress frame, still in her lacy white underwear. "Slive's coming back. They're going to kill us and film it."

"Film it?"

"A snuff film. He's going to make a snuff film. I'm supposed to be the star."

Now he had to close his eyes again. He'd been hit too hard. Those words didn't make any sense, and he didn't know how to force them into an order that would. Moving words around was what he used to do well.

"*Please* open your eyes."

"Sorry. Head's a mess. Thought you said Slive's making a snuff film."

"You heard right. He's running some kind of porn operation out of the Riis Houses."

"Jacob Riis?" Here was a fact that did make sense to his scrambled brain. He started mumbling. "Right, Jacob Riis. You know he was a journalist too. Reported on the awful conditions in New York's slums. *How the Other Half Lives.* That was his book. Collected his newspaper stories."

"What is *wrong* with you? We're going to die in a housing project and you're giving me its history?"

C'mon, think straight. "My head feels like it's been split in half." *Slive's running a porn operation? While working IA?* "Kristy Copper. Dodd's lead."

"I don't understand."

"Remember that missing person Dodd had you track down?" Taylor said.

"Yeah."

"She was a floater in the East River. Talked to her boyfriend. Said she worked in porn movies. He believed she was killed making a snuff film. Didn't get a chance to tell you. Or track down that lead. Story's always had too many damn leads."

"That's the connection then. Slive's making snuff films and Dodd was on to him. Slive set up the murders."

"Pretty good theory, given the situation we're in right now. How did he get you?"

"I called Priscotti after I left you Monday night. I wanted to grill him until I found out what was really happening. With Dodd. With my dad. With the corrupt cops. I met him at his place in Brooklyn. His mother was at bingo. Things went south fast. He told me *everyone* knew my dad was under investigation, then picked that moment to try and get romantic. Least what he thinks is romantic. I pushed him off. He got mad. Told me he was the one who put out the false radio call. He attacked me. I swung and connected. He hit harder. The next thing I know, Slive's standing over me."

"Priscotti's in this with Slive? What about Schmidt?"

"I don't know who's in with who anymore."

Taylor's neck ached from holding his head off the ground to look up while Samantha talked. It hurt less than his skull, but he didn't need any more pain. He lowered his head slowly to the yellow linoleum tile. From that sideways position, he noticed some things in the room he hadn't seen when he first rushed in. A blackboard on the wall. Two movie lights on metal stands. A hobbyhorse. Posters that looked like the kind schools used to teach the alphabet. He twisted at his tied wrists. The coarse rope burned, and nothing else happened. He knew the rope around his ankles was even more secure. The pins and needles in his feet told him so.

"I can't budge."

"Goddammit." Samantha rattled the handcuffs that secured her to the top of the bedspring. Belts lashed her legs to the bottom. "You're hogtied on the floor, and I'm shackled to this thing. They're going to come back and kill us. Me on camera."

Taylor shifted his legs against each other, a painful sort of rubbing where his ankles crossed. He had feeling above the ropes. *Was it possible?* He did it again.

"They didn't search me?"

"No. Tied you where you dropped. Probably thought you only carry notebooks. You don't .... Do have your gun?"

"In my ankle holster."

"What good's it going to do?"

"Not sure yet."

He struggled violently against the ropes around his ankles. Nothing. Breathing heavily, he closed his eyes to get his strength—just for a moment.

"Taylor!"

"Wha … was just resting."

"You probably have a concussion. Worst thing you can do is fall asleep." Samantha rattled the handcuffs again, this time more violently, and let out a yell. "I don't want to die here. I sure as hell don't want to die in Slive's porn."

Samantha was able to move her hands fairly well, even if they were shackled. An idea, a long shot idea, pierced the painful static in Taylor's brain. He wasn't sure how far it would get them, but doing something was better than the nothing of waiting for Slive to come back. He rolled onto his back.

The sledgehammer hit the back of his head again. "Goddamn that hurts!" Sharp pain stabbed through his crossed and tied wrists as the weight of his body bore down on them. His injured ribs chimed in too.

"What are you doing?"

He bit his lip. Couldn't even talk to explain the plan. He rotated his body and bumped on his back toward the bed frame rising at a 45-degree angle from floor. The pain was going to knock him out again if he didn't hurry.

"Taylor!"

Wrong, it did knock him out.

He started moving again. His put himself in a reverse sitting position, his butt against the wall and legs running up it. He'd need to stretch to reach her hand.

"This should be"—a grunt—"the easy part."

Wrong again.

Pushing with his arms and shoulders, he stretched to get his tied ankles close to Samantha's hand. "Get the gun out." He held the position for five seconds but Samantha was only able to use her fingertips to move his pants clear a few inches.

"You need to get closer."

Taylor slid back down the wall, huffing from the extreme exertion, but motivated to try again because his legs took the weight off his wrists once they were up on the wall. Of course that position only made his ribs hurt more. Again, he pushed himself into what must have looked like the worst ever attempt at a headstand. Just as Samantha reached and unsnapped the leather strap that held the pistol in place, Taylor fell over sideways.

"Damn. Almost had it."

Noise came from out in the hallway. Not noise, talking. "Shit."

The voices, a mumbling sort of patter followed by loud laughter, approached the door. And passed. A door opened, more laughter and a slam.

Taylor again shifted into position to crawl up the wall, feet first. If it didn't work this time, he might not have the strength to try again.

His ankle approached her hand. Because the leather strap was already off, the pistol started to slide out.

It was going to drop to the floor, out of reach.

Her hand shot forward and grabbed the gun by the barrel as it fell.

"Oh yeah, I got you." She shifted to hold the pistol by the grip.

Taylor collapsed onto his side.

"Think I can cover the door." She pointed the gun in her cuffed hand toward the entryway.

"How are you going to drop them all?"

"Qualified top five percent of my class on the range. Pretty good for a girl. What do you suggest?"

"Use it right now. Someone will come. Shots fired."

"This high up in the Riis Houses? You need more than that to get any attention." She sighted down the gun out the window. "We need to do something that will *definitely* get a response."

"Wouldn't recommend shooting someone."

"You can joke. Must be feeling better."

"Actually, no. Just trying to keep talking." It was then he remembered her cast. "What about your arm?"

"Hasn't bothered me in days. If there's pain, I'll have to play through it. Not much choice. Now, there must be something … the sector patrol. The car for this area should come down that street at least once every hour."

"Even better, you're going to shoot a police car."

"Near a police car."

"What if Slive comes back before then?"

"Back to plan A. I'll put bullets into the door, hopefully get Slive and scare whoever's with him."

"Not sure which idea is worse."

"You have a plan for what to do when you're tied up at the feet of a woman handcuffed to a bed in her underwear?"

"No."

"Special situations call for special approaches." Having a gun in her hand had taken some of the despair out of Samantha's voice. "Now keep talking so you don't drop off and die on me."

"Thought you were mad."

"You did come to rescue me—"

"I walked into a trap."

"You got here. Lots of points for that."

"I spoke to your father."

"Yet you live."

"He's really worried about you."

"This point, he should be. Wouldn't want to be Slive if he finds out about this."

"His story is Schmidt set him up to get Slive off the Oh-Nine cops."

"Do you believe him?" Samantha continued to watch out the window.

"I did. That was in a whole different universe. It's all about Slive now. We have no idea what his whole operation is. What anyone else's deal is."

"Top Deck's real enough."

"Plus a dirty Internal Affairs man in the precinct who makes snuff films. They working together?"

"Shit, Slive's car just pulled in. He's with the black guy who cold-cocked you. Plus two others."

Taylor rolled toward the apartment door, each revolution a belt in the head followed by wrenching pain in his wrists.

"What are you doing?"

"Blocking it. If they can't push the door open, you'll get off more shots—"

As if he'd given the command, she fired. His gun might be small, but it sent deafening concussive echoes bouncing around the one-room apartment. His head screamed in pain. He wretched and threw up.

"It's the sector car." Samantha pulled the trigger twice more. "Okay, that hurt. Three for a signal and saving three in case they don't get here in time."

He groaned.

"Got the front windshield of the Ford the Oh-Nine guys were driving past, then put one somewhere near the patrol car. Pretty good for a girl. Both officers are out. Positioned behind their car, waiting for backup."

"Slive?"

"He and his guys ducked when I fired. Now they're watching. No, they've figured out what happens next. They're in their car and out of here."

Taylor blacked out.

"Roll away from the door. Roll away from the door."

Odd chorus for a song.

No, a command.

He rolled.

When Taylor opened his eyes again, the legs of NYPD officers were all around him. They had guns drawn. None of the cops was looking down at Taylor. He could have been the rug. They stared at Samantha, all jaws dropped.

"Shit, Callahan. This is how you turn yourself in?"

"Stop gawking, and get me off this. You guys need to track down Slive. He just left."

"Why the hell would we do that?"

"Because he was going to kill us."

27

———◆———

CAPTAIN SEDGEMORE'S SMALL office—everything in the Ninth Precinct was cramped—had two metal chairs outside its pine door. Samantha was inside with the captain, dressed in street clothes she'd dug out of her locker. Taylor had had to argue furiously to keep from being taken to the hospital. Whatever had hit him—probably a sap—hadn't broken skin, so with no blood he was able to convince the cops he was fine. He wasn't, but he needed the captain more than a doctor.

The captain, on the other hand, had absolutely no interest in hearing from Taylor, who sat on one of the hard metal folding chairs, his head throbbing in nice even time with his pulse. A detective stopped by another office to talk to a lieutenant and gave Taylor a long look on the way out. He sat there half an hour. The story had changed. Actually, the story had been pulled out from under him.

Need something, anything official. If I can trade what I know ....

The door finally opened. Taylor rose to his feet. He had to use the wall to catch his balance as the room did a couple quick loop de loops. Samantha exited, head down and frowning, and walked straight past Taylor. He wanted to follow her, but needed this interview.

The office door was immediately filled with the blocky head and blue uniform of the precinct commander.

"We're not talking."

"I've got information you need."

"Just spoke to my officer. I know what I need. We don't air our dirty laundry in public."

"Samantha doesn't know the whole story." Sedgemore didn't respond to that. "What are you doing about Slive?"

"Ongoing investigation."

"This precinct has uniformed officers shaking down criminals."

Sedgemore yelled over Taylor's head. "Get the desk sergeant up here to throw this asshole out." The lieutenant picked up his phone.

On the first floor, Priscotti was at his desk doing paperwork. In the hallway leading to front door, Schmidt leaned against the wall. Two other uniforms stood with him.

Probably Top Deck.

Their eyes followed him as the sergeant escorted him out the front door into the late autumn afternoon. Rain was no longer in the air. A chill instead.

Samantha gave a small wave from the direction of Second Avenue. He went to her.

Concern pushed the frown off her face. "How's the head?"

"Only hurts when I think."

"You're safe then." She tried smiling, couldn't hold it.

"What did the captain say?"

"Let's go somewhere and sit. I hurt everywhere from that bed. You probably want to get off your feet too—even if you should really be in the hospital."

"All right. That place." Taylor pointed at a coffee shop across East Fifth.

"No! I want to get the hell away from the precinct. They

leered at me the whole way out. If the door weren't closed to me already, today did it. Hard enough without six of them seeing me in my underwear. I don't want to be around any of those bastards again."

"There's one bastard I do want to see," Taylor said, "Priscotti. When he scampers off to report to Slive."

"How do you know he will?"

"That's what rats do. So we wait and watch."

A short, middle-aged man with a Greek accent showed them to a table by the window. For Taylor, hearing him talk was like a welcome home. The odors from the grill right behind the counter were another story. Normally, they'd set his mouth watering. Instead, they set his stomach flipping. *Can't puke. She'll have me in the ER in a heartbeat.* He ordered a can of Canada Dry ginger ale and sipped from the tumbler. The light snap of ginger brought back a memory of being home sick from school, his mother handing him a glass after stirring away the bubbles. *Probably the last time I had it.*

"You need a doctor."

"Not going anywhere until I know we're both safe from Slive."

"Where's safe?"

"I don't know. What's the captain going to do?"

"Claims he's hamstrung, since Slive is IA and not under his command. Which is bullshit because next thing he says to me is my story sounds like a bunch of lies coming from someone who disappeared under suspicion. I'm indefinitely suspended. You know what they added to the list? Improperly discharging a weapon at Jacob Riis. 'Don't you worry, missy, everything will get looked into.' That was the last thing he said."

"How did we end up tied and handcuffed then?"

"Lot of theories on that going round."

"Did you tell him you were attacked on Halloween? Probably by some of his officers. You ran because you weren't safe."

"What's my proof?"

"I'm your proof."

"You're nothing. You're worse. You're trying to crap all over his precinct."

"He's an idiot."

"I don't know. I don't know anything anymore."

"What we don't know is what Slive's up to. Not all of it. Not how it ties together. He tells you he's going to put you in a snuff film. Kristy Copper may have been murdered making one—a crime Dodd seemed to be investigating. Is that Slive's main deal? Porn with murder? Is he connected to Top Deck? Protecting them? Christ, *why* isn't Sedgemore taking this seriously?"

"You said Slive has the great rep for cleaning up precincts. That's against what they believe I did. Abandon my partner. What I am. A woman wearing their uniform."

"Something needs to happen right away. We're real witnesses Slive has to get rid of fast."

Samantha sipped her Coke through a straw. "One thing I didn't get a chance to tell you. Slive's had his hair cut short since I went on the run. That crew cut. I realized it soon as I saw him."

"So?"

"Was medium length or a bit longer. He's got gray in there. Which means with the longer hair, his description—"

Taylor added it up. "Slive's tall. Bullet-shaped head. The cop who threatened Mortelli at the squat …. It could have been him, not Schmidt."

"Builds are similar. Hair *was* similar."

"That pretty much nails it. Dodd must have found out something about Slive's operation. Something that connected Slive to the killing of Kristy Copper."

"And this. Was too busy saving our asses to connect it. Dodd and I were the sector car that covered the Riis Houses for two months into the middle of October. If that's where Slive operates out of …."

"Do you remember anything?"

"No. But I had to take a course for four days during that time. He rode by himself." A pause. "The day after the class ended, that's when Dodd started acting all different."

"When was the class?"

"First full week of October."

"Kristy Copper was pulled out of the river on October Eighth."

"A week later, Dodd sent me looking for the missing person's report."

"Dodd sees something. Something involving Copper's death. Now he's a threat. Why didn't Dodd act? If he'd reported Slive, he might still be alive."

"This was an Internal Affairs officer. Maybe Dodd was trying to figure out who to go to and still have a career. Maybe it took him a while to put the evidence together. We don't know what he was doing during that period, except asking me to check one missing person. And talking to Slive several times. What he had to do was a lot harder than putting out a story and hoping you're half right."

"Ouch. Think that hurt more than my head."

"Should," she said. "This job is tougher than you think. *You* talk to a couple of people, write it up, and walk away to the next crime. We've got to live with what we do."

He couldn't take any more pain right now, emotional or physical. Didn't have the time, either. They could do a postmortem on the misery he'd caused after they were safe. *If* they were ever safe again.

"Need to make one quick call."

Jersey Stein at the DA's office picked up on the second ring. Taylor gave Stein everything he knew or guessed about Slive, Dodd, and Schmidt. He left out Mick Callahan. He knew why. Samantha.

Stein started asking questions just as Samantha started waving furiously at him. "No time. Either I'll be able to answer them or I'll be dead, and that'll be your answer."

"This isn't your job."

"No one else is doing it."

Taylor dropped money on the table and followed Samantha out the door. Priscotti was at the bottom of the precinct steps talking to another cop.

"How does he commute?" Taylor asked.

"Subway."

"Thank Christ. The Ford's still over at the Riis Houses."

"Without a windshield, don't forget."

"Ah shit, right. Your excellent marksmanship."

"What do we do if he leads us to Slive? We're unarmed."

"Step one, find Slive. Better we find him than he finds us. Step two, hope step three presents itself."

"Great plan."

Priscotti moved with strange little steps for a fat man. Taylor and Samantha kept him in sight while leaving a good distance, which turned out to be smart, since Priscotti was wary. He peered over his shoulder several times. The distance was dangerous too. They could lose him. They had no other choice.

Priscotti turned north onto Cooper Square and then left on East Eighth Street and appeared to be heading for the Astor Place subway stop, the starting place for the chase that ended Dodd's life. Half a block past the Cooper Union, Samantha pointed to where their patrol car had been parked when the mugging went down.

Priscotti didn't go underground at Astor Place; instead he walked to Broadway and the Eighth Street-NYU stop. Once he disappeared down the stairs, Taylor and Samantha jogged to keep from losing him. At the bottom, Taylor turned abruptly, caught Samantha by both arms and kissed her. Priscotti had stopped to buy tokens at the booth. A train was approaching.

"Let me know when he's got his tokens." Taylor leaned against the wall of the stairway holding Samantha so they looked like a couple saying goodbye. This pissed off the rush hour commuters streaming past them, all of whom had something nasty and specific to say. Samantha watched over his shoulder, and after fifteen seconds, nodded.

Priscotti clicked through the center turnstile and stepped through the nearest open doors to the R train.

Samantha used the far-left turnstile first. Taylor fumbled his token, and it dropped to the ground on the other side, rolling across the platform and off the edge. It was his last. No time to buy. He jumped the turnstile and joined Samantha a car ahead of Priscotti as the doors slammed shut.

"Hope he didn't see that scene of yours."

"You're not the only one."

Priscotti got off at Times Square. Taylor lost him almost immediately in the shifting crosscurrents of people moving between eight different subway lines. Ridership might be down, but the place was still a crowded maze during the evening rush.

"Damn. Where is he?"

"There." Samantha pointed at the broad back of a blue uniform going up the stairs to 42nd Street.

Taylor had a weird flash Priscotti was heading to the City News Bureau's offices. Who'd attacked Novak? Slive, Priscotti, or Schmidt? Or all of them?

Above ground, Priscotti strolled west on 42nd Street with its quarter mile of marquees offering porn of all types, colors, sizes, and flavors.

Even with the marquees, Times Square was a dim, grimy place. The famous flickering, flashing, dancing signs had been switched off due to the energy crisis. The only light came from plain old billboards and the porn marquees, and most of those made grim reading anyway. The lights were down and crime was up—way, way up. For that reason, most people stayed away at night, unless it was porn they wanted. Or they were the brave customers of the remaining legitimate Broadway houses. Many of the latter went door to door by cab.

A hooker in a skimpy plastic green dress leaned against the

wall under the sign of The Victory Theater, which had once been a legitimate house and then a grand movie palace but had sunk to pornography with most of the others on the long block. Why was she standing there? Catch them when they're horny?

Halfway down, Priscotti entered a porn shop that advertised a theater upstairs.

Samantha shook her head. "This is not good. No guns, no backup, no idea what's inside."

When they reached the store, Taylor cupped his hands to cut the nighttime reflections so he could see inside the shop. "Dildos, whips, eight millimeter films, looks like some of those new videotapes. A wall full of magazines. Sign says the movie upstairs is *Triple Timing Teacher Tallie Gets It Triple Times*. Now that's bad writing."

"What I meant was we have no idea *who's* inside. How many we're up against."

"We know Priscotti is, and unless he's a connoisseur of porn—"

"Oh he is that."

"If Slive's business is porn, he's probably in here too."

A beggar in a parka and pajama bottoms jostled Samantha, who pulled her fist back so fast the man yelled and ran toward Eighth.

Taylor cupped his hands again. "Here we go. Slive's on the stairs. Priscotti is coming up behind. They're carrying something. No, someone."

Samantha, who'd continued to stare at the bum, now turned to the window and peered in for the first time.

"Not *someone*. The Sergeant."

28

———◆———

Samantha grabbed the door. Taylor grabbed Samantha and pulled her back. "Whoa, you were just saying we don't know who else is in there."

"I know my father is. Changes everything."

"Fine, but don't just charge. Let them go where they're going upstairs. They see you, all hell breaks loose, and they've got your dad unconscious."

She stepped to the other side of the door. "Soon as they're upstairs, I'm in."

A payphone faced him at the curb. "One more quick call." Taylor dialed Stein. Of course he was away from his desk. Taylor left the address with another investigator and told him Stein should get there as soon as possible.

Samantha pulled the door open. "They're gone."

Cigarette smoke mixed with the sweetest sort of perfume. Taylor really didn't want to know what gave off that scent. Samantha walked straight to the counter.

The guy behind the register, with tangled hippy-length hair and the look of someone who could easily have fleas, appraised Samantha like she was a new piece of merchandise.

"Don't get couples shopping in here. Even the kinky ones send in the guy. How can I help ya out? Or in?" His chuckle was a wheeze.

"We're in need of something special." Samantha leaned in closer. "Something very special. I'm embarrassed to say it too loud."

"Ah well, you can tell old Cloudy."

He leaned in just as close. Samantha reached up, grabbed a big handful of dirty hair and slammed Cloudy's face into the counter. She didn't let go, smashing his face a second time. He slid across the counter and hung on its edge, leaving a trail of blood. Samantha leapt over, hip-checked Cloudy to the floor and pulled from below a sawed-off shotgun with electrical tape around the handle. She put it on a clean area of the counter. She rummaged around some more. Next came a big pistol—a .357.

"When did you dream up this approach?"

"The instant I saw Dad. One of the highest crime rates in the city. Good odds the counterman has something. Odds were even better, given Slive's working out of here. Added bonus. We don't need to worry about this scumbag for a while." She picked up the sawed-off. "Can you handle that?" The shotgun's barrel pointed to the .357.

"Not sure."

"You own a gun."

"Never really practice with it."

"More good news. Well, aim well and watch the recoil. Even without aiming, you get close enough, you'll hurt someone pretty bad with that cannon."

"Can *you* use a shotgun with your arm?" He pointed at the cast. "Lot more kick than my little pistol, and that hurt back at the Riis Houses."

"Yeah, probably going to sting some, but less than a bullet in the head."

Samantha jumped back over the counter and led the way to

the stairs. With the shotgun in one hand, she eased her way up to the red door at the top. She signaled to Taylor to get ready, so like some detective in a TV show, he held the gun with arms extended straight and rigid. Her eyebrows lifted. He kinked his elbows and loosened up a little. She nodded and opened the door. Groaning came out of the darkness. They both ducked and waited until simultaneously realizing the noise was the groaning of sex, not violence—and movie sex at that.

Taylor had to smile in spite of their situation. Samantha shook her head. She took a couple of steps into the darkness with Taylor right behind. The flickering light of the movie lit 10 or 12 rows of seats sloping down from where they stood. On the screen Tallie was definitely being triple timed. Cigarette smoke clouded the darkened theater.

Samantha crouched into a seat in the back row and Taylor slid in next to her.

From that vantage point, they could see four men watching the film, all of them sitting separately. No sign of Slive, Priscotti, or Samantha's father. The stairway running down along the rows of seats led to a door next to the screen. The word *exit* glowed above it. Aside from the door they'd come in, that was the only way out of the theater, barring someone crawling into the window of the projection booth four feet above them. Taylor pointed at the exit door with the barrel of the gun, a strange, heavy sensation. Like pointing death.

Samantha brought her lips to his ear. "Watch these guys as we go down."

"One's a lookout rather than a Teacher Tallie fan?"

"Who knows in this screwed-up game?"

They took the stairs slowly. The men continued to watch the screen. Flashes of the movie flickered off their eyes. One of the viewers, unaccountably, was crying. Taylor checked the projection booth. Only the beam from the projector and blackness behind. Maybe they'd gotten lucky and Cloudy also ran the machinery. If not, someone up there had to see them now.

On the other side of the door was a padlocked, alarmed exit to the street and steel stairs leading down to the basement.

Samantha took the first step down.

A small wedge of waxy yellow light from the exit sign illuminated the first half-dozen stairs. After that, they moved in near total darkness. Samantha would take a step, stop for Taylor to come down to the one she'd left, wait a couple of seconds and move to the next.

Murky light reappeared below them after twenty or so steps through that blackness. The bottom? Yes, and another door, just cracked open. With as much confidence as he had upstairs, Taylor went into his stance. Samantha slowly pushed the door open with her toe. They held for ten long seconds as their eyes readjusted to the light, Samantha slowly swinging the shotgun in an easy, level arc. Whatever her fellow cops thought, she knew her job.

They were at the entrance to a cluttered storeroom filled with sex toys and pornography. At least that was what was in Taylor's immediate vicinity. Shelves went back into the darkness. Again, there was no sign of the three men. Taylor went in first this time. To his right were several open boxes containing contraptions that looked better suited for torture than pleasure.

Samantha tapped his shoulder. "Go around left. I'll go right. We don't know how big this place is or where they've got Dad."

"And we don't know how long the sleazebag upstairs will be out."

She nodded. "Use that big gun if you have to."

She disappeared between two mannequins in leather and silk. The leather made Taylor think of punk rockers. He'd never considered the similarity to fetishism.

Need to get my skull checked when we get out of here.

He crept along the outside wall in the hope of linking up with Samantha wherever this basement ended. Battered metal shelves held unopened cardboard boxes. Stacks of porn mags were wrapped together in plastic. Three octagonal suitcases almost tripped him. Labeled with movie titles, they were the cases the film reels arrived in.

Light splashed between a break in the shelves ahead, and Taylor dropped low, creeping closer and closer to the back wall. There was another doorway. No sign of Samantha. Voices. He froze. Couldn't make out what was being said. He moved in as close as he dared. A man talking. It was Slive. The cool arrogance was easy to identify. A muffled response. Slive laughed like he was really enjoying himself.

Taylor lay flat and crawled forward, stifling a grunt as his injured ribs complained about the maneuver. He had to see what was happening on the other side of that doorway. Inching up, he peered around a stack of boxes. Slive stood in a small room lit by a bank of exposed yellow fluorescent lights. One tube flickered off and on with an insect-like clicking.

A card table in the middle of the room was covered with evenly stacked gold canisters, as in some strange poker game. Mick Callahan, now conscious, sat at a chair with his hands behind his back, presumably tied or handcuffed. No Priscotti.

If he's out here somewhere, we're in trouble.

Taylor prepared to slide back behind the boxes and listen out of sight, but Slive walked around the table and looked into the basement storeroom. Taylor froze.

"I'm going to kill you," said Callahan.

"You're going to do nothing." More of that pleased laugh. Slive picked up one of the little canisters. "Four minutes of eight millimeter film. Gold. Real gold. A very special clientele will pay hundreds, even thousands for one of these."

"Because you killed someone."

"An accident." Slive waved the hand holding the canister in dismissal. "Was supposed to be a bondage scene. Craig got carried away. Oh but what a fortunate accident. These films can make money we never dreamed of when we took over this business. This is the deal we were looking for. But you had to go and grow a conscience. Or did your balls shrink? We were already in the film business. Your idea in the first place. Why provide protection when we can own the whole business? A brilliant idea, Mick. Yours."

"Wasn't my idea to kill Dodd. You went too far when you pulled my daughter into this. She was never supposed to be near any of this. That's family, not business."

They're partners? Shit. What will Samantha do?

"Dodd was a big problem. You refused to see that. He saw our guys dumping the body."

"Didn't matter. Dodd couldn't connect you to it."

"Fuck that. He *did see* Priscotti because that fat idiot couldn't wait for a good time to deal with the body. Fucking idiot panicked. The only break was Dodd calling into me because a cop was involved, rather than trying to arrest all three of them that instant. Fucking Dudley Do-Right. I offered up Schmidt. Said he was running the porn operation with Priscotti and I needed more time to bring them all down. But Dodd wouldn't drop it. Couldn't be bought. And *you* couldn't make up your mind what to do about him. Doesn't matter now. Tonight I'm going to take care of you with the gun that killed Dodd. The one Mortelli is supposed to have used." He held up an automatic. "One of my rules. Never dump a dirty gun. They always come in handy. Buried guns. Guns tossed in the water. They get found every time. What do you think the detectives will make of it? Oh wait. I'm the detective on this case. Everything's covered, nice and neat. Schmidt never knew he was working for me. You didn't even know he was. Let's face it: our partnership started falling apart long ago." Slive laughed. "Schmidt thinks Priscotti's his boss. Imagine, that fat oaf. Why would the IA guy be running the game? I collected and protected and no one knew. Now I own something even bigger."

"Not if you leave bodies everywhere. They'll get you."

Slive bent to the floor to pick something up, rose to his feet holding a black bra of fishnet and frills. He attached the straps to Callahan's ears so the cups stood on top his head. Slive's other hand held a stack magazines. These he spilled on the table in front of Callahan and in his lap.

"They're going to have *some* questions when they find you. A big thick file on everything you've been up to in the One-Nine will hit the right desk tomorrow morning. You're more than a distraction. Sergeant Mick Callahan. How did we miss him the first time? Look what the hell he's been doing. Now this, on the other hand …." He held the film canister up toward the light like it was some sort of religious relic. "The clientele for these … I've only just tapped into. I'll take in one hundred, two hundred thou a film. I'm going someplace where the occasional disappearance is no big deal. Maybe down by the border. Turn these out just fast enough so the sickos will be desperate for the next one."

"You're the fucking sicko."

Slive hurled the canister at Callahan, hitting him square in the face. The canister popped open. Black spirals of film fell down Callahan's chest. Blood ran from his nose to his mouth and chin. "There's your last bit of the business, me boyo."

On the other side of the doorway, Samantha crawled toward the light from the small room. Her face was set and serious, as it had been when she split from Taylor.

She hasn't seen or heard anything yet.

Taylor held up his hand to tell her to stay where she was. He pointed to the doorway and held up two fingers.

From around the corner behind her, Priscotti appeared. His gun was out and touching the back of Samantha's head before Taylor could do anything.

29

———◆———

SAMANTHA FROZE. PRISCOTTI, staring intently down at her, didn't see Taylor where he lay in the shadow of the boxes on the other side of the wash of light from the door. Not yet, at least. He couldn't move. Just had to hope.

"Slive, we've got a family affair."

Priscotti prodded Samantha to stand up and move into the doorway.

"Why, the brave policewoman. How did you find us?" Again Slive laughed like this was the best game he'd ever played.

Mick Callahan's reaction was the opposite. For the first time he sounded panicked. "Sam, what are you doing here?"

"I was trying to get Slive before he got me. Followed his lapdog."

Priscotti slammed an elbow into Samantha's back. "You're going to end up in that movie anyway. Maybe I'll get to play a part."

"How long were you there?" said Mick Callahan. "What … how much did you hear?"

"Ah, yes." Slive took a lock of Samantha's auburn hair in his fingers and rolled it back and forth. "Mick's little girl. A stalwart in uniform. You have no idea what Daddy's been up to. How about I brief you?" He took her by the arm and forced her into another chair at the table. Priscotti handed Slive his cuffs, which Slive clicked on. "Let me tell you about The Sergeant, my partner all these years—"

Callahan was up with a roar. Bent over with the chair handcuffed behind him, he charged Slive. The barrel of Priscotti's gun flashed. Callahan fell backwards, hit the wall and slid down onto his side. Taylor rose from his crouch. Blood darkened the left shoulder of Callahan's flannel shirt.

Slive slapped Priscotti hard with an open hand.

"What's that for?"

"He's handcuffed to the goddamned chair. I'd have knocked him down. Now we've got a mess to deal with."

"You said we were going to make a mess tonight."

"Not *here*, you complete idiot."

"Dad! Dad, say something."

Now what do I do? That office is a death box.

Priscotti and Slive were both armed. Samantha was cuffed to a chair behind Slive, and her father at the back, now wounded, lay on the floor, attached to his chair. Taylor was outnumbered and outgunned. He had to get one of them out of the office. Divide and conquer. Or at least divide and not get shot.

Taylor stuffed the .357 in one of the outside pockets of his field jacket, fell back three rows, and slipped between the shelves. He brushed a box. A cloud of dust swirled up. He had to sneeze, but somehow did it silently. The act of holding it in made the wound at the back of his head explode with pain. Bent low, he moved toward the center aisle that divided the rows of shelves in the basement. Something glinted in a plastic tub. Handcuffs. No, not handcuffs. These were for cuffing someone's hands and feet, with a chain that connected both sets of bracelets.

Could come in handy.

In a tub next to them were whips and cat o' nine tails.

Also helpful. Time for a disturbance.

He grabbed one of the four-way manacles and a cat o' nine tales, drove his shoulder into the shelf on his right, and raced across the center aisle. By the time he was pressed up against the opposite wall, the first shelf had toppled into the next with a crash and then sent over another with an even louder noise. The dominos tumbled to the back of the basement where the office was. Half the room's shelves were down.

"What the fuck?" That was Priscotti.

Taylor shoved the cuffs and cat into his other jacket pocket and pulled out the collapsible Polaroid.

"Who'd you come with, Sammie?" That was Slive.

"Who *would* come with me is the question."

The crack of flesh on flesh. Samantha cried out. Taylor moved to the center aisle and peered around the shelf. Slive stood over her. He didn't look like he was enjoying himself now. "That goddamn pest of a reporter?"

"Don't trust him."

"Then why did he rescue you?" He turned to Priscotti. "Find him and shoot him in the fucking face."

Priscotti slowly walked down the center aisle. The cop swung his gun left over the tumbled shelves then right as he reached each new intact row. Taylor stood with his back to a shelf. Priscotti stepped into full view, pointed the gun at the fallen shelves and started swinging back toward Taylor. As he did, Taylor stepped out and put the Polaroid in the fat cop's eyes and tripped the shutter. The flash went off and Priscotti's gun roared, ripping the head off a mannequin.

Lightning.

Thunder.

Stay focused.

He dropped the camera and yanked out the cat o' nine tails. With all his strength, he swung at Priscotti's face. Priscotti screamed as lashes appeared and filled with blood. Taylor hit him again, harder.

Priscotti dropped to his knees, his hands on his face. Taylor hauled him behind the row of shelves to get out of Slive's direct line of fire, put a knee on his back, and snapped a handcuff on his right wrist, then his left. Priscotti's head cleared enough to know this was trouble and started bucking like a steer in the rodeo. Taylor got kicked in the face as he cuffed the right leg. A thunderous roar. A box above exploded. Feathers floated down. Slive was shooting through the shelves. Two arms and a leg would have to do. He scrambled back to the wall as Slive fired again.

Priscotti screamed in pain. "Stop! You shot me."

"Your fault for letting him jump you. Where is he?"

"Oh God, I'm shot. Help me."

"Where the fuck is he?"

"I don't know."

"Well, get back here."

"Can't." His voice was a pained whine. "He cuffed my arms and a leg. I'm going to bleed to death chained here."

"Is that you, Taylor? Because you turned out to be a complete pain in my ass. No matter. I'm going to kill you and these two. I'm going to solve all my problems in one night."

Taylor didn't answer. He slipped along the wall up toward the small room, stopping at each row of shelves to check for Slive in the doorway, or even a shadow that would tell him something. He was only going to get one shot, and he was far from being a good shot. Everything depended on skill he didn't have using a gun that hefted like a bazooka.

Priscotti moaned. "Slive, please come help me. I need help. I'm shot." His voice rose. "What kind of partner are you?" He started screeching. "Help, help. I need—"

Slive's gun cracked once from the doorway. Priscotti went silent. "Guess this is the night to tie up all my loose ends." A scraping noise. Slive pushed Samantha's chair into the doorway. He crouched down behind, using her as a shield, and sighted his gun on her shoulder.

"Get out of here," yelled Samantha. "Lock the basement door and get backup. He can't do anything. He's trapped with enough evidence to bury him forever."

Slive hit Samantha hard above the right ear with the gun. A half scream and her head lolled to the side. It was all Taylor could do not to call out her name. He moved to the last row of shelves and aimed between boxes at the doorway. The only shot he had was of Samantha.

"She's wrong, you know. They'll all be dead and I'll still get away. Surrender in three, or I shoot her."

"One." The muzzle turned toward the side of Samantha's head. "Two."

Give in. Talk us out of this.

Before he could step in the open, a shadow rose behind Slive. Mick Callahan, somehow back on his feet, blood covering his chest, screamed something that wasn't words and ran head down at Slive like a wounded rhino.

For Taylor, time didn't so much slow down as jump and stutter like in a silent movie.

Callahan drove Slive into the right wall of the office. Slive yelled, spit, and struck at Callahan. With both feet, Slive kicked Callahan away and then shot him three more times. The .357 was at Taylor's side, then up and aimed at Slive. Taylor fired. The kick threw the gun high. Taylor pulled it back down and closed the distance to the doorway.

Slive fell back with a leg wound. He brought his gun up to fire. Taylor shot again, catching Slive in the arm. He spun once, twice, spraying blood on the wall, then tumbled onto the table, tipping it over and crashing onto the floor. Gold canisters dropped all over him, opening to spill more black strips of film everywhere.

Taylor kneeled in front of Samantha, who had blood trickling down the side of her head into her ear. "Hey, you with me?"

She groaned and her eyes fluttered. "What happened?"

"The short answer is Slive hit you. The long answer will have to wait until your head hurts a lot less."

"That could take a really long time. What about my dad?"

Taylor picked up the handcuff keys from the floor and unlocked her. "It's not good."

"God, no."

"You need to keep it together a little longer." Her eyes were filling with tears. "Watch Slive while I run upstairs and call for help. Can you?"

She rose with a groan and leaned against the door jam, taking the gun from Taylor.

"You sure you can?"

"I'll shoot him if he ever moves again."

Keeping the gun aimed at Slive, she walked on shaky legs to crouch next to her father.

Taylor ran through the basement past Priscotti's still handcuffed body. He took the stairs two at a time to the theater, where the same four guys had sat through everything that had happened in the basement.

In the store, he found Jersey Stein browsing the shelves like your average shopper. Cloudy was on his feet holding a handkerchief to his face. "That's him." The counterman pointed at Taylor. "He was with her. She hit me and they took my guns."

Stein peered over a shelf at Taylor. "What's going on?"

"You need to get four wagons down here. Three people shot in the basement and an officer hurt. And get more guys from your office. Make the calls, then come down. Cuff that bastard too." Too late. Cloudy was out the door and running west on 42nd Street. "Never mind. He's the least of our worries."

Stein went out to his car to use the radio. Taylor went back even faster then he'd come. Samantha had unlocked Mick's handcuffs and had her father's head on her lap, the gun half trained on Slive.

She was sobbing. Her father was dead.

Taylor wondered if it would have killed The Sergeant anyway

to explain himself to his daughter. Then he wondered if he'd ever be able to do it. The facts had always been everything to him. These would stab like knives.

30

———◆———

ON NOVEMBER 21, Taylor walked into CBGB to celebrate. Sort of. He'd spent most of the past nine days getting grilled by investigators. This morning, Jersey Stein had told him off the record he wouldn't face charges for shooting Slive, who had lived, in part, because of Taylor's crappy marksmanship. Slive would be charged with the murders of Dodd and Mortelli—he'd used Dodd's gun to kill the punk—another count for Kristy Copper and various charges related to his corruption and porn activities. It appeared Slive used cleaning out precincts as a cover for his own criminal operations. He'd moved into IA from one of the more corrupt stations right as the Knapp Commission was beginning work. Call it reading the writing on the wall. Call it a business decision. After that, the more cops he put away, the more control he had.

Stein had worked it out so Taylor would only have to pay for the damages to the rental car and the tickets. The DA's investigator had thrown around "life and death situation" a few times. No one in the Ninth was in a position to argue.

There ended the good news in Taylor's life.

He'd tried to get Samantha to join him, just to get out of her apartment. She wouldn't. She'd repeated what she'd said before. She didn't blame him. She had to make some decisions. Taylor knew she wouldn't go back to the cops. He still hoped she'd come back to him.

Frederick the Dutch slid a beer across the bar. "On the house, my friend."

"Free beer at CBGB? World ending?"

"Everyone knows. You figured out who killed Johnny Mort. Cleared his name. The whole neighborhood talks."

Must be word of mouth. They didn't get it from any story *he'd* written. He'd typed up the whole thing in the shortest form he could and hand-delivered it to the City News Bureau's five radio stations. Broadcast news abhorred complexity. The stations boiled it down to shootings with a mention of pornography. After that, he'd called Tom Sabatini at the *Daily News* and given him everything. Over the past few days, when investigators weren't interviewing him, Sabatini and his editors were. The story ran a week after the shootings across pages six and seven under Sabatini's byline. Taylor didn't get a mention.

There was one other bit of good news this evening. The Ramones were starting a three-night gig. He needed "Blitzkrieg Bop" to make any kind of celebration of this.

Six days later, the City News Bureau re-opened for full-time operation. The office had been re-equipped as a result of several anonymous donations—Taylor guessed from news organizations around town. They never liked attacks on their own, even if their own was an unknown newswire two weeks old.

Taylor stopped in at an office down the hall first. Lew Raymond & Associates, Investigators. Samantha sat at a desk in the front office, looking at once both odd and lovely in a skirt and blouse. A deep voice boomed from the backroom.

"Your boss does have some pipes."

"Yeah, was in radio."

"A deejay?"

"No, before that. He played a detective in the old radio days."

"No, don't tell me—"

"Lew Raymond, Consulting Detective."

"And he does it for real now?'

"Has for years. His given name was Marion Sarnoff. Seems to know his stuff, least when it comes to cheating husbands and sticky-fingered shop clerks."

"I'm sorry. I know this isn't what you—"

"No apologies. Thank you for putting in the good word. Who knows? He might even end up respecting my work. Says a woman is perfect for staking out stores and love nests. People are less suspecting. Already treats me better than all the boys down at the Oh-Nine. I was never going to make detective on the force. After what my dad did …." Her head dropped during a long pause. She looked back up at him with those blue eyes. "You never know. Maybe some really interesting cases will come along."

"Some interesting cases come along, then we'll both have something."

"That we will."

"Lunch?"

"Yes. But *not* Howard Johnson."

Novak was in the office, his right arm in a sling, and already talking about how he was going to expand the business. He'd somehow convinced Cramly to come back, and Terry Simpleton—an ex-*Messenger-Telegram* reporter who drank more than he wrote—had signed on because he had nowhere else to go.

Just like me.

Novak came over and sat on the edge of Taylor's desk a few minutes after he'd settled in. "I've got an idea."

"Uh-oh."

"I'm trying to sign some of the suburban papers. After all

that stuff you were chasing, how about a feature on what's really going on in Times Square?"

"You want a story on the porn business?"

"Atmospheric, just, you know, without mentioning the porn itself. Out in the suburbs they love to hate the city. Look at these I had done." He put down several grainy black and whites. A porn shop. Several theaters. Women dressed to sell. Tawdry Times Square at its lowest best. Except any offending film titles and store names had somehow been blurred out.

Taylor had to laugh. "I get it. Cake and eat it too. See what I can do."

He went back to reading the *New York Times'* banner story. The night before, President Ford had abandoned his opposition to helping the city and proposed $2.3 billion in federal loans to save New York from default. Legislation was expected to race through Congress for the President's signature. New York City would not, after all, drop dead. Not even a President could let that happen.

Photo by Domenica Comfort

RICH ZAHRADNIK HAS been a journalist for 30-plus years, working as a reporter and editor in all major news media, including online, newspaper, broadcast, magazine, and wire services.

Zahradnik held editorial positions at CNN, *Bloomberg News*, Fox Business Network, AOL, and *The Hollywood Reporter*, often writing news stories and analysis about the journalism business, broadcasting, film production, publishing, and the online industry. In January 2012, he was one of 20 writers selected for the inaugural class of the Crime Fiction Academy, a first-of-its-kind program run by New York's Center for Fiction.

A media entrepreneur throughout his career, he was founding executive producer of CNNfn.com, a leading financial news website and a Webby winner; managing editor of Netscape. com, and a partner in the soccer-news website company, Goal Networks. Zahradnik also co-founded the weekly newspaper, *The Peekskill Herald*, at the age of 25, leading it to seven state press association awards in its first three years.

Zahradnik was born in Poughkeepsie, New York, and received his B.A. in journalism and political science from George Washington University. He lives with his wife Sheri and son Patrick in Pelham, New York, where he teaches elementary school kids how to publish online and print newspapers.

Drop Dead Punk is the second book in the Coleridge Taylor Mystery series, which began with *Last Words*.

For more information, go to www.richzahradnik.com.